LOUISE M. GOUGE

Cowgirl Under the Mistletoe

D0378149

HARLEQUIN® LOVE INSPIRED® HISTORICAL

LOVE INSPIRED BOOKS

Recycling programs for this product may not exist in your area.

ISBN-13: 978-0-373-28387-3

Cowgirl Under the Mistletoe

Chapter One

October 1884
Esperanza, Colorado

The Denver & Rio Grande train pulled out of the Esperanza station, sending last night's dusting of early snow into small flurries. They rose up to meet the white smoke streaming from the engine and leaving behind the smell of burning coal. As Deputy Grace Eberly watched the departure, she swiped away an unexpected tear and then glanced around. It wouldn't do to have folks see their deputy sheriff crying like some silly girl. Fortunately, the only person left on the platform was good ol' Reverend Thomas, who really wasn't all that old, just friendly. He smiled and touched the wide brim of his well-worn black Stetson.

"You're going to miss your sister, aren't you?"

She stepped over to him and gave him her best deputy scowl. "You'd better not tell anybody you saw me cry." Tall as she was, she could stare down

on most men but stood eye to eye with the reverend when she wore her boots.

"You? Cry?" He grinned in that annoying way of his that showed he wasn't in the least bit intimidated by her badge, her gun *or* her height. "Not at all. I assumed you had some grit in your eyes."

She chuckled. He could always be counted on to cover for folks, especially her. Of all the people in town who might want to condemn her for being a trouser-wearing female peace officer, this man of God would seem the most likely. Instead, he appeared to understand her abiding need to hold outlaws accountable for their evil activities. When her next-younger sister, Beryl, had been shot by that no-account Dathan Hardison and his slimy partner, Deke Smith, the minister had been a great source of comfort to the family. Never once did he condemn Grace for crippling Deke with a well-aimed bullet. She could almost allow that his prayers above all others had kept Beryl from dying.

Thoughts of her closest sister brought another annoying swell of emotion. Beryl had survived the shooting, went off to boarding school for a spell and then came home only to fall in love with an English dandy who'd come to town for a holiday. Now she and Percy lived in England, and the family would probably never see them again.

To make matters worse, Grace's next-to-youngest sister, Laurie, now rode on the train speeding eastward along the tracks. Once it crossed La Veta Pass through the Sangre de Cristo Mountains, it would head north, taking her back to music school in Den-

ver. Her short visit home had ended far too soon. Grace would miss her something terrible.

With Maisie, the oldest of the five sisters, busy with her doctor husband and their new baby boy, Grace considered looking to their youngest sister for companionship. But Georgia walked around with her head in the clouds reading books all the time. Grace didn't care much for books. Besides, at fifteen, Georgia was a bit young to depend on for a close, womanly friendship. With Beryl and Laurie gone, Grace had never felt so alone in all of her twenty-three years.

Sure as shooting, none of the other unattached younger women in the area wanted to pal around with her. And, like Maisie, her married friends had husbands and children to tend to. But, also sure as shooting, Grace never expected to marry. What man wanted a wife who stood half a head taller than he did and could likely outride and outshoot him?

Grace had watched the dainty behavior of her friends Susanna and Marybeth, who'd married the two oldest Northam brothers and lived at the next ranch over. She'd admired the gals' fancy manners and pretty speech. Even Grace's younger sisters had begun to copy those female ways, although they still worked the family ranch like men, as all of them had since childhood. But Grace couldn't bring herself to act all silly and helpless around men. The cowhands on their family ranch would laugh themselves blue in the face if a giant of a woman like her ever put on such airs.

Being tall and broad-shouldered did give her some advantages on her days off when she did her share of helping her folks keep the ranch going. She could

buck hay bales all day long and had never seen a mustang she couldn't wrangle, another reason men steered clear of her. What did she care? Weren't a single one she cared to take up with.

"Grace." The minister still stood by the yellow clapboard train station. He'd been mighty nice to join the family in seeing Laurie off, but for some reason he'd hung around. Maybe waiting for a telegram. She could hear the clickety-click of Charlie Williams's telegraph just inside the open window.

"Yeah? You need something, Rev?"

"Indeed, I do." His waved a hand toward Main Street. "Mrs. Winsted's daughter-in-law opened that new ice cream parlor last week. Have you been there?"

"Nope, sure haven't. Seems sort of disloyal to Miss Pam." Never mind that Grace loved ice cream. She'd keep taking her noon meals at Williams's Café.

"Not at all." His Southern drawl rolled out pleasantly on his baritone voice, just like when he preached his heartwarming sermons every Sunday. "In fact, Miss Pam can't say enough nice things about Nelly Winsted's desserts."

"That a fact?" She pondered the idea for a moment. "You don't think it's too cold for ice cream?" The October wind hadn't picked up for the day, but there was still a bite in the air.

"It's never too cold for ice cream." He chuckled in that kindly way of his, and her heart felt an odd little kick. Oh, no. She would *not* let herself grow feelings for the unmarried preacher. Every unattached girl for miles around wanted to lasso this handsome man and drag him to the altar. She would not line up and make a fool of herself like the rest of them did.

Nothing would ruin her reputation as a competent, dependable, levelheaded deputy faster than her acting like a moon-eyed heifer.

"Would you like to give it a try?" From the way he asked the question, Grace guessed the minister was looking for companionship, too, if only for this morning. Safe companionship, with no worries she'd try to hogtie him. She'd proved that to him ever since that time several years ago when he'd bought her box dinner during the church fund-raiser, disappointing a whole passel of girls who'd hoped he'd choose theirs.

While they'd eaten, the two of them had discussed Bible verses she'd been wondering about, a safe subject for any two folks, and she'd learned a whole heap of important stuff about the Good Book, the only book she considered worth reading. Since then, they'd had several more chin-wags about the scriptures, and they'd grown comfortable around each other. That day at the fund-raiser, she'd figured he'd bid on her box to keep her from being left out. He was kind that way, and she admired him for it. Admired, nothing more. She wouldn't ruin a good friendship by thinking on useless feelings.

"Come on, Grace. Let's try out Nelly's place."

Right about now, a big dish of ice cream sounded like the perfect way to console herself over Laurie's departure. Food could comfort a body that way, especially sweet food. "If you insist."

"I do." He offered his arm.

She stared at it like it was a long-tailed jackrabbit.

"Um…" More of those foolish feelings wound around her heart, so she stepped back. "Don't mean to be rude, Rev, but as deputy sheriff, I'm gonna de-

cline your gentlemanly offer, if it's all the same to you." She offered a crooked smile. "Appearances, y'know."

"Ah, yes." His eyes revealed no offense at her refusal. "I understand."

Good thing he did, because she didn't. She didn't like this brand-new giddy response to an old friend. Must be all the weddings that had happened in recent months. But she'd locked away her hopes of marriage as securely as most girls locked up their hope chests. No sense at all in dreaming about things that would never be. She'd leave that to her dreamy-eyed youngest sister, Georgia.

Micah Thomas liked keeping company with Grace Eberly. Unlike most other unmarried girls in his congregation, she never behaved in that giddy, flirtatious manner that made him uncomfortable. She had a level head and an honest way of looking people straight in the eye. Her friendship was the perfect antidote to this strange depression he'd felt lately. Until last Friday, when he'd joined two more local couples in holy wedlock, he'd been able to conduct weddings without a single thought of marriage for himself. Like the Apostle Paul, he'd always felt called to remain single so he could do the Lord's work without the encumbrance and expense of a wife and children.

But even before last week's ceremony, he'd begun to sense that something was missing in his life. It didn't help that Genesis 2:18 kept coming to mind. If the verse was true—and he believed every verse in the Holy Bible was God-breathed truth—that "it is not good that the man should be alone," then the Lord

would have to bring him a "helpmeet" from some-place, because he certainly had no plans to court any of the young ladies in the congregation. That would stir up all sorts of hornets' nests, namely among certain mothers, each of whom thought her daughter would make a perfect preacher's wife.

Micah knew better. It took a special woman to marry a minister, one with her eyes wide open, knowing her husband's congregation would hold her to a higher standard than anyone else, higher even than the preacher. Such a woman would have to be especially strong both spiritually and emotionally, and more than a little sure of herself as a person. Some ministers' wives he knew of had faded into sad little shadows under such demanding scrutiny. He would have to make sure it never happened to the woman he married.

If he married. He still had a hard time reconciling marriage and his God-given ministry, which took all of his waking time and then some. Then there was the matter of the small salary he earned as the minister of a small-town church. Folks gave what they could, but it wasn't enough to support a wife. If the Lord wanted him to marry, He'd have to bless a particular enterprise Micah had undertaken a while back, one that no one in the congregation knew about, or needed to know about, even though it was perfectly honest and aboveboard. But the chances were slim it would be successful.

"What's your favorite ice cream flavor?" Grace shot him a glance without missing a step, her stride as long as his, yet as graceful as that of a mountain lioness.

"Back home we had blackberries growing wild on our land, so I'm partial to blackberry syrup over vanilla." He pictured his family's Virginia home, tragically broken by the war. Because of his uncle's stand against slavery and Micah's agreement with his uncle, only one friend had ever kept contact with Micah's branch of the family after the war. Recently that friend, Joel Sutton, had written to say some folks were coming around to mend fences and renew old friendships. Micah would have to think about asking him to send him a bride, just as Rand Northam's family had done for him. After three years of marriage, Rand and Marybeth were still as happy a couple as Micah had ever seen.

The more he thought about it, the more the idea appealed to him. After all, in the Bible, Abraham had sent a trusted servant to choose a wife for his son Isaac, and Isaac had loved Rebecca from the moment he laid eyes on her. Not every couple had to know each other for a long while before they fell in love and married. Arranged marriages could turn out just as well. If Micah decided to go on a quest for a wife, he might do well to seek Joel's help.

"Maybe," Grace said, "we ought to get a group together and go up to Raspberry Gulch next summer so you can get your fill of berries." Her blue eyes, no longer tear-filled, sparkled in the midmorning sunshine, as though she were ready for the excursion today.

"Sounds like a fine idea." Anything to keep her spirits up. Micah had noticed her drooping shoulders at church yesterday, the way she used to carry herself before she earned everyone's respect for stopping an

attempted bank robbery. On Sunday, he'd figured she was missing her younger sister even before Laurie left. Today he could see how right he'd been.

Grace really was a pretty girl, despite her tomboy ways, with a sweet face and ready smile. She and her sisters all had the same fiery red hair. But where the others had masses of fuzzy curls, Grace's thick waist-length hair was straight, except where the ends curled up in a thick cluster. She usually wore it tucked up under the wide-brimmed cowboy hat that now hung down her back on its leather strings. For some reason, today she'd let her hair blow in the autumn breeze. He liked the look on her. He'd tell her that, but she didn't receive compliments too well.

They arrived at Nelly's Ice Cream Parlor, and Grace opened the door to usher Micah in. He wouldn't chide her for it. It was just her way, as when she refused to take his arm. Many other girls in town would have grabbed onto him as though he were a prized bull to be shown off.

"Thank you." He stepped over the threshold into the warm, bright room and removed his hat. Right away, the aromas of cinnamon, coffee and sugar filled his nostrils and whetted his appetite for something sweet.

Several customers waved or called out a greeting as they sat at small round tables dotting the room. The backs of the white wrought iron chairs were shaped like hearts, and more than one person seemed to be eyeing his or her companion with a hint of romance. Micah could see he would be conducting more weddings in the near future. Once again, that odd melancholy crept into his chest, this time even

stronger. Yes, he needed to look for a wife. It truly was not good for a man to be alone.

"Welcome, Reverend Thomas, Deputy Eberly." Nelly Winsted came out from behind the serving counter, drying her hands on a white towel with red stripes. "Have a seat wherever you like." When the Rev responded to her greeting in his usual friendly way, she gave him a sugary smile that reminded Grace the woman was an unattached widow.

An odd protectiveness sprang up in her chest. The last thing the Rev needed was another female chasing after him. Best to charge right in and head her off in a different direction. "Howdy, Nelly. How's business?" Silly question. The room was near to full of customers, so anybody could see she was doing well.

Nelly turned a dimmer smile her way. "Why, just fine, Deputy, thank you. My mother-in-law was right when she invited me out here to open my store. Everybody likes ice cream, don't they? Now, what may I bring you?" Her gaze returned to the Rev, and her smile lit up again.

Honestly, the woman was thirty-six if she was a day, way too old for the Rev, who was just shy of thirty. She had a thirteen-year-old son and an eight-year-old daughter, to boot. Maybe that explained her flirty ways. She wanted a pa for her children and figured the handsome preacher would be the best influence on them. Grace couldn't fault her for that.

"Let's sit over here." The Rev waved a hand toward a table by the window, which did Grace's heart good. He wasn't ashamed to sit where every passing citizen of the town could see them together. That

was a long sight different from some other unmarried men in town who only spoke to her when they had a crime to report. Not that she saw the Rev's actions as favoritism. He treated everybody in his flock with the same kindly regard. Weren't nary a person in these parts he wouldn't chat with till the cows came home, if that person had a spiritual need or just a listening ear.

As they took their seats, he said, "Miss Nelly, I'll have some vanilla ice cream, if you please. Would you happen to have any blackberry syrup to go on top?"

"Why, yes, I do. I'll bring it right out. And you, Deputy Eberly?"

"Same. No syrup."

The little woman bustled away like she was on important business. Grace supposed she was, especially with supporting two children all by herself. When she brought their glass bowls of ice cream, she'd added a touch of whipped cream and some pecans to the Rev's two large blackberry-topped scoops. Grace's bowl held one small plain scoop. She could barely hold in a laugh at the widow's obvious ploy.

"Will there be anything else?"

The Rev ordered coffee, and Grace gave a nod that she'd have some, too.

After Nelly brought their coffee, she focused on Grace. "By the by, Deputy, did my mother-in-law happen to tell you about her stolen items?"

Grace sat up straight. "No, ma'am, she didn't." She hated to leave her ice cream unfinished, but such was the nature of her job. "I'll check into it right away." She shoved back from the table.

"No need to hurry, Deputy." The Rev set a hand on hers, sending a bothersome tingle up her arm. She quickly dismissed it. "If the matter were urgent, Mrs. Winsted would have contacted you right away."

Grace didn't want anybody to think she shirked her duty, but what he said made sense. She glanced at Nelly, who seemed less than pleased by the Rev's words. "Did Mrs. Winsted report the thefts to Sheriff Lawson?"

"Could be."

"I sure would regret letting this fine ice cream of yours go to waste, Nelly." She gave her a crooked grin. "Mind if I finish it before I check into those thefts?"

Nelly blinked and sputtered, offering a strange combination of smile for the compliment and a huff of annoyance, probably because Grace wanted to stick around. "Of course not."

Grace scooted her chair back up to the table and dug in, taking small bites like her dainty friend Rosamond would instead of filling her spoon and shoveling it all into her mouth like she wanted to do. "Mmm-mmm. Mighty good."

The Rev also took small bites like he wasn't in any hurry to finish either. "Now, Deputy, which Bible passage shall we discuss today?"

"What—?" Grace blinked just as she caught the hint in the Rev's eyes. "Oh. Um. Well. I, uh, I've been troubled by Romans 8:28—"

"Excuse me." Nelly bustled away again. She was the only skinny female Grace had ever seen who could bustle when she walked.

His eyes twinkling, the Rev concentrated on his

ice cream for a moment before asking, "What in particular troubles you about the verse?"

Now she was on the spot, but he was the rascal
who put her there. "I suppose 'all things work together for the good' means '*all* things.'" She released
a sigh, thinking of her sisters who no longer lived
here, especially Beryl. This man had a gift for seeing
right through a person, so she might as well open up,
at least partways. "I understand why Laurie wanted
to go to music school, 'cause she sings and plays
piano so pretty. She may even decide to come back
and teach here in the Valley. That'd be a blessing for
sure. But I just wish Beryl and Percy had decided to
buy some land here instead of going back to England
to settle down."

Understanding filled his remarkable gray eyes,
fringed all the way around as they were with dark
lashes. My, they gave him a particularly appealing
look. "You were especially close to Beryl, weren't
you?"

Grace nodded. "Growing up we looked almost
like twins." She coughed out a dismal laugh. "Until
I grew taller than our older sister when I was twelve
and she was thirteen." Shrugging away the memory
of those awkward times, when all the boys on the
schoolyard began to taunt her, she sighed. "Beryl
and I still did everything together until…" An unexpected lump clogged her throat.

"Until the bank robbery?"

The kindness in those fine eyes threatened to undo
her, and she could only nod.

"Beryl never blamed you for her injury. She believed you did the right thing to stop that robbery.

And remember, you saved Marybeth from the out-laws. Everyone admired your courage, especially Beryl."

"I know. Last year, after she and Rosamond opened their high school, we got close again, and she made sure I knew she didn't hold a grudge against me." She chuckled softly. "I even helped her straighten out a couple of boys in her science class."

"Good for you. I know she appreciated it." His gentle smile didn't waver, while most men would have scowled at her ability to tame unruly scamps both young and full grown.

Grace scooped the creamy remains from her bowl into her mouth and savored the rich vanilla flavor. "Gotta say this for Nelly, she sure can whip up a fine batch of ice cream." She shoved back from the table, stood and adjusted her gun belt around her hips. "Guess I'd better head over to the mercantile and see what Mrs. Winsted has to say about those robberies."

The Rev took his last bite and stood, too. "I'll go with you. I need to purchase a few supplies for the parsonage." He placed a dime on the table to pay for the ice cream.

"Thanks. I'll pay next time." Grace wouldn't make a scene, but she also wouldn't let him pay for all of their fellowship times. Her job and her share of the family ranch provided more than enough to give her a comfortable life and far more than his measly salary as the church's pastor. Maybe she should sneak an extra fifty cents or more into the plate each Sunday to help with his support. That'd buy him some good cooking at the Williams's Café or maybe a new Sunday shirt.

"I just might take you up on that, Grace." He put on his hat and made it to the door before her and opened it. "Anytime you want to talk about your sister, I'll be happy to listen. Or Romans 8:28."

"I just might take you up on that, Rev." She echoed his words in a singsong way to show him she was all right now. He rewarded her with one of those teasing smiles. They had an odd sort of understanding in their friendship, it seemed, and she liked it a whole heap that it was two-sided.

Their boots thumped in rhythm on the boardwalk as they approached Mrs. Winsted's mercantile, marking a companionable cadence. A quick look revealed that Dub Gleason and his gang, a bunch of worthless bums, weren't sitting in front of the store. Maybe it was too cold for them. She'd attended school with them, and they still liked to torment her with insults when they thought nobody else was looking.

Grace couldn't guess why the Rev wanted to stay in her company today, but she wouldn't complain. It did her heart good to know she had a friend to confide in. Or just to spend time with. 'Course, it wouldn't last for long because one of these days, he'd give in and marry one of those pretty little gals who clamored for his attention, and propriety would cut short their friendship. It would be hard to take a step back and regard him only as her pastor. In fact, the thought soured the ice cream in her belly.

Although he didn't need to refill his pantry quite yet, Micah silently thanked the Lord for giving him an excuse to stay in Grace's company. At the train

depot, he'd felt the Lord's nudging to stick around and see how he could help her. He was pleased to see she seemed to have perked up a little over the past hour. Still, despite her cheerful words, her eyes exuded a lingering sadness, and he couldn't guess how to help her overcome her loss. He'd have to make it a matter of more concerted prayer because Grace Eberly was an important asset to this town and the surrounding community. Both she and everyone else needed to recognize that.

Welcoming them both to the mercantile, Mrs. Winsted first turned her attention to Micah. "What can I do for you today, Reverend Thomas?"

Micah thought she should assist Grace first, but if he said something to that effect, both ladies might end up being embarrassed. "Thank you, ma'am. I'll need some flour, cornmeal, beans, rice, bacon—"

"A bit early for your usual monthly order, isn't it?"

Micah gave her a bland smile. "I'm honored that you remember my schedule."

"We aim to please." She glanced over her shoulder. "Homer!" Her clerk emerged from the back room. "Reverend Thomas's regular monthly order."

Micah gave her a slight bow and approached the counter where Homer Bean had begun to assemble his purchases. Behind him, he could hear Grace ask Mrs. Winsted about the thefts.

"Why, I've already told Sheriff Lawson everything I know. Such odd things to be stolen and odd that I didn't notice them being carried out. A coffeepot, a bag of coffee, some tins of food, a box of expensive linen stationery." The sensible shopkeeper's voice held an uncharacteristic note of worry. "I gave the

sheriff a complete list, and he said he'd look into the matter."

"Yes, ma'am, he and I both will." Grace's soft response held a calming quality, almost like a mother soothing her frightened child. "You can count on us to make sure your shop is protected."

Micah's heart warmed. Grace certainly had a comforting way about her. He couldn't imagine why some cowboy hadn't come along and married her. Maybe while he was searching for his bride, he could search for a husband for his good friend. She deserved a fine Christian husband to show her how remarkable she was. Of course, it would take an equally remarkable man to be her partner in marriage.

"Can I help you carry these groceries, Rev?" Grace came to the counter and started to lift the wooden box Homer had filled.

"Thanks, but I can manage." Micah took the box from her. No Southern lady he'd known would ever offer to carry such a load or even be able to, but these cowgirls were a different breed.

"I almost forgot your mail." Mrs. Winsted, also the town's postmistress, retrieved some letters from her little cage at the back of the store and tucked them into Micah's box.

"Thank you, ma'am." Two letters. More than he usually received in a month. An odd little kick smote him in his chest. Would he already have an answer from New York? No time now to check the fronts of the envelopes. With his hands too full to doff his hat to Mrs. Winsted, he gave her a friendly nod. "I'll settle my bill soon." And if that letter was the one he'd been looking for, maybe he wouldn't always have to

keep a tab. Though he mustn't get his hopes up too high in that regard.

She shook her head. "I'm not worried about you paying your bill, Reverend. Not like I worry about some in this town."

Micah paused briefly. This wasn't the moment to inquire about her concern, so he'd save it for another day. "Thank you."

"Well," Grace said as they left the store, "I'd best head over to the office and see what Sheriff Lawson has to say about those thefts." She touched the brim of her hat, a manly gesture he wished she wouldn't do. "Thanks for the ice cream."

"You're more than welcome." With the heavy box in his hands, Micah couldn't return the courtesy of doffing his hat, but she was already headed down the street anyway. He lifted a silent prayer that someday a fine man would come along and treat Grace like the lady she was, the way she deserved to be treated.

Micah sighed. Dear Grace. If the Lord wanted him to help her, He'd have to show him how. One thing he'd learned in his seven years of ministering to this congregation was that a wise pastor never tried to change a person. His job was to love and accept his flock as they were and let the Lord make the changes. One thing did occur to him. Finding the thief might take her mind off of her sister's departure. Maybe he could even help her investigation. He would enjoy having more time in her company.

By the time he'd walked the two blocks to the parsonage, his heavy load was wearing on his arms. He managed to balance the box against one hip as he opened the door, which he never locked. Other than

storekeepers, no one in these parts locked up, but if thieves were at work, he might have to reconsider that practice and warn others to do the same.

After putting away his groceries, he took the letters from the box. The first was from Joel Sutton. Micah had been thinking of Joel not an hour ago. Maybe the Lord was nudging him to write that letter to his friend and ask for help finding a mail-order bride. It all depended on what the second letter said.

Sure enough, it was from New York. His pulse racing, Micah tore it open. A bank note fell to the floor. He snatched it up. Two hundred dollars! Gulping so loudly he could hear himself, he slumped into a chair to read the missive.

Dear Mr. Thomas,

We are delighted to inform you that your novel has been accepted for publication by Wyatt, Leader, and Davis Enterprises. Please find enclosed an advance on the sales we fully expect your exciting story to garner. In addition, we hope you will consider Wyatt, Leader, and Davis Enterprises when seeking to publish your next story. Our readers eagerly await every such book about the Wild West. With the added element of Christian morality infusing your story, we expect to greatly broaden our readership. Although our authors generally prefer to use their own names in an effort to find fame, your chosen nom de plume, A Cowboy Storyteller, seems most fitting in this case.

Unless we hear from you to the contrary, we will rush the publication of this delightful novel

so it will be in the hands of numerous booksellers by early December, just in time for Christmas. With its seasonal theme, we can expect sales to set records, thereby generating significant royalties for you.

Please sign and return the enclosed contract. We urge you to send another story as soon as possible. Yours sincerely...

Micah laughed out loud. If this wasn't the Lord's leading, he didn't know what was. Now he could get married. Whatever Joel said in his letter, Micah would answer right away. To his shock, Joel's letter announced that he and his sister would arrive in Esperanza the first week in December. Displeased with the failure of Reconstruction, they were leaving the South in hopes of finding a more peaceful life in Colorado. Joel also said his sister, Miss Electra Sutton, had recently graduated from finishing school, and she hoped to find an upstanding Christian husband who held on to none of the bitterness many felt over the war.

Micah laughed again. "Lord, You never cease to amaze me. You put the thoughts in my mind even as You were laying out Your plan. Are You bringing a bride right to my doorstep?"

As a finishing school graduate, Miss Sutton would be a great asset to his ministry. Further, with the sale of his book, he would be able to support her without asking the church for a raise in salary, something he knew they couldn't afford to give him. Micah recalled that the newly married Rosamond Northam Wakefield, also a finishing school graduate, always wore

the latest fashions. Miss Sutton would no doubt be fashionable, as well, and he would have to support her wardrobe choices.

What would she think of him? Of his far from fashionable and somewhat threadbare clothes? Only one solution came to mind. He would take some of his earnings from the sale of the book and change his entire wardrobe, beginning with his old broad-brimmed Stetson. One of those handsome new bowler hats would be more fitting for a minister.

He'd go over to the haberdasher's right now and make that purchase. After that, he would visit the tailor next door. Joel and Miss Sutton would be here in December. That should give him enough time to have new clothes made.

He laughed aloud again. In a few short hours, the Lord had certainly shaken the very foundations of his simple bachelor life. And Micah couldn't be happier about it.

After leaving the Rev, Grace headed back to the sheriff's office just north of the bank. She found Sheriff Lawson seated at his desk shuffling through wanted posters. He looked up at her with a scowl.

"Bad news, Grace. Those varmints who tried to rob the bank in '81 have escaped from Cañon City State Penitentiary with the help of their old gang."

Her blood turned cold, and her heart seemed to stop. She drew in a slow breath to calm herself and hide her alarm. "That a fact?"

"Just got a letter from the prison warden. Hardison's gang helped him and Smith break away from a work crew bustin' up rocks in a quarry near the

prison." He snorted in disgust. "Turns out I put three of his gang in a Kansas prison five years ago." He shuffled the posters again. "I'm looking through these to see if I can find pictures of Hardison and Smith. Not counting the newcomers in the past three years, I'm probably the only person around here who doesn't know what they look like."

Even though the crime had taken place over two years before Lawson came to town, he knew all about their robbery attempt and how Grace, two of her sisters and two of the Northam brothers had kept them from succeeding.

"Word from other inmates is that they vowed revenge on the people who stopped them." The sheriff held up a poster briefly before continuing his search. "Said they'd 'finish the job,' just like their gang said to me when they were sentenced."

Grace snorted, doing her best to sound unconcerned. "Just let them try." Brave words, but bravado wouldn't keep her friends from harm.

All things work together for the good of those who love God, to those who are the called according to His purpose.

The verse she and the Rev had briefly discussed came to mind. Right now it didn't seem to her that these "things" were working together for good. But at least Beryl and Laurie would be safe from the two varmints, as would Tolley Northam, who'd gone to law school in Boston just over a year ago. If Hardison's gang was set on revenge, the folks who'd especially need to be on the lookout were Rand and Marybeth Northam. And Grace, of course.

On her way home this afternoon, she would make

it her business to inform the whole Northam family about the breakout. And her own ma and pa would also need to keep their eyes peeled and their guns handy. Grace's family never went anyplace without weapons because of snakes and coyotes in these parts, but now they'd have to be even more careful of the two-legged kind of danger. At least Georgia hadn't been involved in stopping the robbery, so the outlaws wouldn't be after her. Unless they decided to—

She shook off her forebodings. In spite of the threats, she had other matters to attend to.

"Mrs. Winsted tells me she had some things stolen from her mercantile." Grace wouldn't wait for Lawson to get around to telling her about the thefts. Sometimes he forgot to mention important stuff and yet expected her to know it. Maybe it was because his wife anticipated all of his thoughts. Grace never made any claim to being a mind reader. If she ever married, which she wouldn't, she'd let her man know from the start that he needed to speak out.

"Yep." The sheriff combed a hand through his thick, graying hair. "I figure it's some local boys just getting into mischief."

"If we catch 'em and put 'em behind bars for a few days, that'll give 'em a scare they won't soon forget." Grace checked the coffeepot sitting on the potbellied stove. A slow fire kept the brew simmering, and even this early in the day, it had already turned to sludge. She settled for a drink of water from the cold crock Mrs. Lawson kept on the side cabinet.

"Maybe get them into Sunday school classes." The sheriff accepted the tin cup Grace offered him. "Nate

and Rand Northam have turned around several boys with their good teaching."

Grace nodded, although she still thought a few days in jail would be a good place for wayward boys to start. "Just have to find the troublemakers."

They tossed around several ideas, not the least of which was asking other merchants in town whether they'd noticed small items missing from their stores. They'd also need to inform folks about the outlaws.

"I'll go over to the hotel." Grace adjusted the hang of her gun belt on her hips. "The shops over there might be easy targets with all the comings and goings of unfamiliar folks."

"Yep. You do that." Lawson continued to pore over the posters like he was digging for gold. "I'll check the other end of town."

"Yessir." Grace ambled out of the office and strode down Main Street toward the Esperanza Arms. She'd never understand why Rosamond and her new dandy husband, Garrick, had chosen that name. Maybe Garrick's uncle, the Earl of something or other, had planted that English-sounding name on the hotel. Maybe they'd named it for the wing currently being added to the north end of the building and the wing they planned to build to the west. Grace reckoned they couldn't exactly call it the Esperanza Wings. She laughed out loud at the thought.

"What's funny?" The Rev fell into step with Grace as she continued down the dusty street.

"You following me, Rev?" She kept on laughing, even as her heart did a stupid little hop.

"Not on purpose." He chuckled. "We just always seem to be going in the same direction."

A bothersome shiver, not at all unpleasant, swept down Grace's spine. She had to stop these involuntary reactions to him. No man had ever affected her this way. The Rev himself hadn't ever. It was downright nonsense. But when did feelings ever have anything to do with *good* sense? She mentally put her foot down, ordering those feelings to vamoose.

"So, what were you laughing about all by yourself?" He seemed in a jolly mood himself.

She dared to cut him a glance, knowing he'd be wearing that teasing grin. She was right, so she returned a smirk. "I was just wondering why they named the hotel what they did."

They stepped up on the boardwalk outside the building at the same moment Rosamond and Garrick Wakefield emerged through the fancy etched glass doors.

"Well, what do you know?" The Rev waved a hand toward the couple, who'd shared a double wedding with Beryl and Percy last year. "Here are the folks to ask."

"Ask what?" Rosamond's eyes shone with pure joy, just as they had on her wedding day. They'd recently returned from their honeymoon and now were teaching at the high school as well as running the hotel.

Grace tamped down a mild case of envy, both for their happiness and for their getting to see Beryl last summer.

The Rev shook hands with the Englishman. "Good morning, Garrick. How's business?"

"Excellent, Reverend." Garrick's brown-eyed gaze

lit on his pretty wife, and he smiled. "Couldn't be better."

Grace wondered what it would feel like to have a man she loved look at her like that.

Rosamond sidled over to her and touched her arm. "What was your question?"

Grace traded a look with the Rev, and they both laughed.

"I was just wondering why you called the hotel the Esperanza Arms when it's wings you're adding, not arms. Why not call it the Esperanza Wings?"

While the Rev and Rosamond laughed heartily, Garrick tilted his head and blinked. Then he chuckled. "And you came all the way over here together to ask that?"

Grace hiked up her gun belt. "I don't know why the Rev came, but I'm here on official business."

Everyone sobered right up.

"What is it, Grace?" Rosamond lifted her hand and came just short of putting her arm around Grace's waist, as she might any other female friend.

Grace stepped back an inch or two before that could happen so she could maintain a look of authority. "Two things. There's been some items stolen from Mrs. Winsted's mercantile. I need to check with the shopkeepers here at the hotel—" she waved a hand toward the row of six shops that lined the south side of the hotel along Main Street "—to see if they've had the same trouble. Anybody said anything to you?" She directed her question toward Garrick.

"Not to me." He looked at Rosamond. "Sweetheart?"

"Not at all. Surely they would tell us. Don't you

think it's a good sign they haven't reported a robbery?"

"Pretty good." Grace nodded. "I'll just tell 'em to be on the lookout. Sheriff Lawson thinks it might be boys out for mischief."

"What's the other thing?" Rosamond moved back over to Garrick, and he placed a protective arm around her. She nestled under it, and they both stared at her like they were expecting bad news.

Grace wondered what it would feel like to have a tall, strong man put his arm around her that way instead of her always having to be the strong one. She cleared her throat crossly to dismiss the foolish idea.

"Dathan Hardison and Deke Smith broke out of Cañon City State Penitentiary with the help of their gang. They're vowing revenge on the folks who put them there."

Rosamond gasped. "Rand and Marybeth." Naturally her first concern would be for her brother and his wife, who had helped to stop the bank robbery and put the outlaws in prison.

Grace considered her own sisters' participation in stopping the robbery. "Good thing Laurie and Beryl aren't here." Once again, she'd allow that Romans 8:28 applied in this case.

"You're in danger, too, Grace." The Rev grunted in his gentlemanly way. "But I don't think anyone will be safe as long as those men are free. We'll have to pray those lost souls will see their need for salvation before they cause any more harm."

Grace clenched her jaw. She *had* been praying, and look what it got. The varmints broke out of the strongest prison in Colorado, and now the decent

folks of Esperanza would be living in fear until they were caught. For the hundredth time in nearly three years, Grace wished she'd shot Dathan Hardison and his crazy-as-a-loon partner dead.

"Well, I've got business to tend to. 'Scuse me." She touched the brim of her hat like a man would do and strode away, her heels thumping on the boardwalk. The Rev caught up with her, only this time the cadences of their footfalls didn't quite match, as they had earlier.

They arrived at Cappello's Haberdashery at the north end of the building and stepped inside the open door.

"Welcome, welcome." The sprightly little Italian man grinned broadly, causing his wide black mustache to wiggle oddly. "What can I do for you fine folks?"

Grace asked about possible thefts, and he reported that no such thing had happened in his establishment.

"But I shall be on guard." Mr. Cappello waved an index finger in the air like Caesar vowing to defend Rome. "And you, Reverend Thomas. What is your pleasure today?"

The Rev was already trying on hats in front of a mirror on the glass countertop. "I'm thinking of changing my style." He looked at Grace. "What do you think?" He indicated the bowler he sported, so different from his Stetson. Although both were black, the bowler changed his look from that of a man who belonged in the West to a citified dandy.

Grace coughed out a little laugh, unable to subdue a slightly derisive edge to her tone. "You goin' courtin' or something, Rev?"

He turned his attention back to the mirror. "I've been thinking about it." He spoke absently, as if talking to himself.

Grace's heart plummeted to her stomach. Now she'd lose his friendship for sure. Then what would she do? One thing was certain. She wanted the best for her friend, so maybe she should help him look for a young lady who was worthy of him. That idea didn't sit too well with her, though she couldn't imagine why.

As Grace and the Rev checked with the other five businesses, all reporting they'd had no thefts, she felt like she was in the company of a different person. That hat truly did the Rev no justice, not out here in Colorado. He looked more like some city slicker, a dandy, a tenderfoot, like the ones who came through town from time to time and either toughened up or fled back East.

They neared the street where they'd go their separate ways, and he stopped and touched her arm. "Grace, I've been thinking."

"You're gonna take that silly-looking hat back to Mr. Cappello." She could only hope.

He chuckled and shook his head. "No. This is a bit more serious than our differing opinions about my attire." He glanced up and down the street. Although a whole lot of people walked about tending their business, none were close by. "I want to help you and the sheriff investigate the thefts at the mercantile." His gaze was steady, like when he was making an important point during one of his sermons. "And I want to help you put Hardison and Smith back in prison. Hardison may have thought very little about

our few short private chats, but I learned more about him than he realized."

"That a fact?" She considered the idea. With Sheriff Lawson getting a bit absentminded these days, she knew she'd need help to solve both crime problems. She had in mind her married friends, the Northam brothers, but maybe the preacher, being single, would prove a better partner. He did have a whole heap of insight into human nature. "Yeah, that sounds good." She laughed. "Who would suspect that a preacher, especially one wearing a bowler hat, might be trying to catch outlaws?"

He blinked like he was surprised, and she feared for a second or two that she'd overdone her teasing. Then he laughed with his usual good humor. "So it's a deal?" He held out his hand.

She gave it a hearty shake. "It's a deal."

Chapter Two

Micah prepared his notes for the Wednesday night prayer meeting with special care. He must say just the right thing about the outlaws and the local robberies. The people of Esperanza were hardy, stouthearted folk. Otherwise they wouldn't be living here in this harsh land. But no one ever benefited from their town leaders stirring up alarm. Of course most folks probably already knew about both threats.

Most of the time, only a third of the congregation came to prayer meeting. Some folks lived too far out of town to make a midweek trip. Others only came on Sunday to put on a show. The more involved members of the church knew the importance of praying together, so they made every effort to attend on Wednesday evenings.

After one more prayer for guidance for tonight, Micah made his way from the parsonage to the church, entered by the back door and set his notes on the lectern.

At the same time, Nate and Rand Northam came through the front door, early as always, to set out

hymnbooks. Micah walked up the aisle to shake their hands and then glanced over Rand's shoulder. "Any other Northams coming tonight?"

"No, they all stayed home," Nate said. "Grace told us about Hardison and his crazy crony, so we moved our wives and children up to the big house so our folks could look out for them."

"If only I hadn't killed Hardison's cousin." Rand's drawn expression revealed both worry and sorrow. "He never would have come to Esperanza for revenge in the first place. He never would have noticed our small town." He shook his head. "Never would have tried to rob the bank."

Rand had shot the outlaw's cousin, a wanted murderer, for cheating in a card game in Del Norte over six years ago. Three years ago, Hardison had showed up and tried to charm the community, all the while threatening Rand in private. He'd even come forward in church one Sunday pretending a conversion experience. But his eyes lacked the look of a man whose repentance was genuine, so Micah hadn't trusted him from the start. In their few subsequent chats, Micah further discerned the falseness of his supposed conversion.

"You've been forgiven, Rand." Micah set a hand on his younger friend's shoulder. Here was a prime example of true repentance. "You need to forgive yourself once and for all. Besides, as you well know, men like those two don't need an excuse to do evil."

Rand's expression cleared. "Thanks. I have to keep reminding myself that the Lord's truly and completely forgiven me. Times like this make it harder."

"Just look at it this way, brother." Nate poked an

elbow into Rand's ribs. "Mother can't ever get enough of her grandchildren, so this is her opportunity to spoil them." He chuckled. "Poor Dad. He won't have a moment of peace with the three of them climbing all over him."

"Soon to be four, come December." Rand's remorseful expression cleared, and paternal pride took its place. "I'm glad for an excuse to make Marybeth stay with Mother. She always tries to manage things on her own, but Randy's getting to be a handful, and in her condition..." He stopped and offered a self-conscious grin, as if embarrassed for discussing such a private matter with them. "She needs Mother's help."

At the reminder of Rand's impending expansion of his family, Micah had an odd moment of longing, a yearning even, he'd never felt in all his twenty-nine years. How rewarding it must be to have a wife and children to care for. He'd love to have a sweet little daughter or an energetic little son to rear. Maybe when Miss Sutton arrived, he'd be well on his way to having that family. Only two months until he found out if it was even a possibility.

Forcing such thoughts to the back of his mind, he recalled his discussion with Grace about all things working together for good. Here was another positive thing about Hardison's escape from prison. Marybeth had to let go of her independent streak and depend upon her kindhearted in-laws for protection.

Micah probably wouldn't be able to convince Grace that anything good could come from the outlaws' escape. He hadn't seen her since Monday, but he did know she hadn't liked the new bowler hat he'd bought to improve his wardrobe before Miss Sutton's

arrival. Somehow the thought bothered him. Maybe he shouldn't have bought it, but Mr. Cappello didn't carry wide-brimmed hats such as cowboys wore, and he needed the business. Micah couldn't please everyone. Besides, he liked his new look, including the suits he'd ordered from the tailor. Maybe he'd make a few more changes before Miss Sutton arrived. If Grace didn't like them, he'd have to tease her out of her disapproval.

Other folks began to fill the small church, all moving forward to the front pews to keep the prayer meeting cozy. While the Northam brothers handed out hymnbooks, Micah greeted each person with pastoral affection. These were his children, even the old ones. If he never had a wife or offspring of his own, he would always thank the Lord for giving him this responsibility and joy.

George and Mabel Eberly, Grace's parents, arrived along with their youngest daughter, Georgia. Grace soon joined them in the second row. She sat sideways on the pew, probably so she could keep an eye on who came into the sanctuary. That protectiveness always impressed Micah. She made a good deputy. A good friend.

Would she still be his friend if she found out his next book was about her? He'd better keep that a secret, just as he'd decided not to let anyone know about his writing. Folks might be offended if they knew he'd created some characters based on them. Worse still, they might no longer trust him as their pastor. Not that he'd ever think of using situations shared with him confidentially. No success was worth betraying a friend.

Rand led the congregation in an opening hymn, and then Micah took his place behind the lectern. As he surveyed his flock, he noticed that every man wore a gun and every woman carried a reticule that drooped as though containing a heavy object. At the same time, every congregant's expression bespoke peaceful determination. Micah chuckled to himself. He needn't be concerned about these good folks. They'd look out for one another. In fact, after the prayer meeting, he'd go home tonight and clean his own guns. The men with whom he'd attended seminary in Massachusetts would be shocked, but out here in the American West, Micah wouldn't be the only preacher who carried a sidearm.

After the final prayer, Grace's parents, Georgia and the rest of the congregation filed out of the pews to the stirring tones of "Onward, Christian Soldiers," a song well suited to the battle that threatened Esperanza. Grace stayed in her seat in the second row because she never tired of hearing Mrs. Foster play the church organ. The kindly old lady's face always took on a sweet glow while she played, as though the words to the songs came straight from her heart.

Tonight it wasn't the music that kept Grace seated, but a bittersweet pang. Due to Mrs. Foster's fine teaching, Laurie had thrived as a piano student well enough to be accepted at the Denver Music Conservatory. After she completed her studies, she might find a teaching position—or a husband, either of which would probably take her away from home forever.

Grace already felt bereft. With Beryl gone for good and Laurie's return not certain, nothing would

be the same around here. Of course Grace wouldn't want Laurie to pass up an opportunity to teach music someplace else, but she hoped her sister would come home in a year or so and take dear old Mrs. Foster's place as the town's music teacher. In spite of her enthusiastic playing, the older lady was growing feeble and often needed help to get her chores done. Just yesterday, Grace had moved into her boardinghouse to be closer to work. Even though she needed to do that, it took her away from her family. Her days seemed to be getting lonelier and lonelier with everyone she cared about moving away or occupied with their own lives.

"You're deep in thought." The Rev walked over and sat beside Grace, resting one arm on the back of the pew. "Anything you want to talk about?"

"Nope." Grace emphasized the word with a shake of her head. Here was another person she cared about who would likely be leaving her. Not going away, but leaving the closeness of their friendship as soon as he found some young lady to court. "Just listening." She nodded toward Mrs. Foster.

"She certainly has a gift, doesn't she?" The Rev smiled as the last chord died away.

Mrs. Foster gathered her music, stepped down from the organ platform and followed Grace's family up the aisle. These days she was still trying to persuade Georgia to work harder at her piano playing, but Georgia never seemed to remember to practice.

Grace stood and settled her gun belt on her hips. "Time to go."

The Rev stood, too, even though he'd had a long day of ministering to folks in the area before conduct-

ing the prayer meeting. Always the gentleman, even around Grace. She appreciated his courtesy since he was the only man in town who treated her that way. Well, except the Northam menfolk, but they didn't count because they were like brothers to her and her sisters.

"It's mighty good of you to move in with Mrs. Foster." The Rev followed Grace up the aisle toward the double front doors. "I'm sure she appreciates the company."

"You know it's not just for company. When Hardison tried to court Marybeth, Mrs. Foster did all she could to stop him. The sheriff and I want to be sure she stays safe."

"As I said—" The Rev gave her that look of his, the one she liked and disliked at the same time, chiding her for not receiving compliments well. "It's mighty good of you."

"Uh-huh." She didn't know why she hated to be praised. She just did.

They'd reached the front doors and stepped outside into the cool evening. The Rev's house was closer to the church's back door, so he hadn't needed to escort her out.

"There you go following me again." She pulled her hat up on its strings and plopped it on her head.

He chuckled, a warm, comforting sound that always made her feel good.

"Actually, I've been trying to think of a way to ask you something."

Her heart stumbled oddly, so she posted her hands at her waist and cocked her head. "Yeah?"

"You know I'm a fair shot with a rifle, but I've

never learned to fast draw my revolver. Would you teach me?"

She gave him a sidelong look. "You funning me, Rev?"

He laughed out loud. "I'm entirely serious. You never know when it will come in handy, especially with notorious outlaws making threats against our community."

Grace faced him and crossed her arms. "I'm a little confused. You're a man of peace. A minister of the Gospel. But you want to learn how to outdraw an outlaw."

"Outdraw an outlaw. That has a poetic ring to it, however disconcerting the idea behind it may be." His jolly expression faded. "To tell the truth, I've wrestled with the notion and prayed about it for some time. The Lord reminded me that He sent David to defeat Goliath and Joshua to bring down the walls of Jericho, to name only two biblical warriors. I wouldn't like to take a man's life, but I do believe it's no sin to protect good people from danger."

A sense of wonderment filled Grace's mind and heart. There was no end to the depth of this man. "Rev, I'd be pleased and proud to teach you all I know about how to draw fast. If it doesn't snow, let's start tomorrow morning before the winds get bad."

"Would Friday work as well for you? I have some folks to visit tomorrow."

"Friday it is."

A pleasant sensation warmed her heart at the thought of spending more time with the Rev before he found his bride. As she strode up the dark street toward the boardinghouse, hurrying to catch up with

Mrs. Foster, she decided to help the older lady prepare his supper for tomorrow evening. The married ladies in town took turns sending meals to the minister, but they'd deemed it unseemly for the single ladies to participate lest it become a contest to win him through their cooking. Of course, the Rev didn't know anything about that. Nor did anyone need to know if Grace put some of her own cooking into Mrs. Foster's basket. She'd have to think real hard to decide which of her special recipes to prepare.

On Friday, after Grace completed her morning rounds of Esperanza and the surrounding area, she rode out to the vacated ranch northwest of town. A thin layer of powdery snow covered the house, which was little more than a ramshackle cabin, and the grounds, which included the barn and two or three other outbuildings. In a nearby field, straggly cornstalks and a rusted plow bespoke broken dreams of a pioneer family who'd come out here about the time Grace's father and Colonel Northam had staked their claims and succeeded in building vast cattle ranches.

The Rev waited for her by the corral, so she rode that way. From time to time, she wondered what people thought about her spending time alone with him. Young women of good character always took along a chaperone when they were in the company of a man, even when a couple began to court. Yet no one had ever mentioned such a thing to Grace, as if they weren't concerned about her reputation. Or didn't consider her a lady. While it made her deputy job easier, something always nagged at the back of her mind about it, not to mention causing a dull, foolish

ache in her chest. But since the Rev had reminded her that the Bible said all things worked together for good for God's people, He must have planned for her to be tall, plain and gawky so she'd make a good deputy.

Before leaving home this morning, Grace had made up her mind to enjoy his company for as long as she could before he found himself a wife. So as she rode into the barnyard, she summoned up a happy disposition more like her sister Maisie's than her own.

"Mornin', Rev." She pasted on a big smile as she dismounted from Mack, her black gelding, and ambled over to him. The Rev wore his black Stetson, looking more appropriate for today's task than he would in that ridiculous bowler.

"Good morning, Grace. It's a great day for shooting." The Rev held a small burlap sack that clattered like it was full of tin cans. "Let's see how many of these we can knock off the fence." He nodded toward the corral.

"Good idea." Grace helped him line up the cans on the top rail. "You know, Rev, these cans won't be shooting back. Are you sure you can face a man who's trying to gun you down?"

He grunted. "Not at all sure. As you well know, it would be a real test of mettle." His eyes lit up with a look she took for admiration, just not the kind she'd begun to wish for. "A test you passed quite admirably three years ago, young lady."

A silly streak of gladness jolted through her at his calling her a lady, especially considering her earlier thoughts. She stared down at her boots and kicked at a rock. "Didn't exactly have a choice back then, did I? It was them or us." And they'd nearly killed Beryl,

a tragedy Grace had never been able to shake off, even after Beryl recovered and went on with her life.

"Yes, it was. And we all need to be ready to protect one another just as you did the first time Hardison and Smith came to town, especially since they might be bringing their gang with them."

"Then let's get to it. The wind will be kicking up pretty soon." Grace had a feeling these lessons weren't really necessary, but at least it gave her more time with the Rev. She would take all she could of that.

Micah wished he could convince Grace that nobody faulted her for the shoot-out at the bank. She'd saved lives that day, not to mention every depositor's bank account. But like Rand, when the memories came back, she let them get to her. As her pastor and friend, he would continue to seek the Lord's guidance in encouraging her. So often she shrugged off his compliments.

What would it take to give her more confidence? Was there any way he could help, or should he leave that up to their female friends? Once he was married, he wouldn't have to worry about such things; all the more reason to marry soon. If Joel's sister turned out to be the Lord's choice for him, Micah would soon be able to set aside such concerns when counseling young ladies. His wife would always be nearby to ensure propriety.

"First of all," Grace interrupted his thoughts, "you need to lower your gun belt." She demonstrated by adjusting her own to a comfortable drawing level.

Micah did as she said and then tucked his frock coat behind his holster. "Like that?"

"Yep. Now show me how you draw."

Suddenly self-conscious, Micah had an unexpected memory flash before his eyes. His older brother had always dared him to do this or that and then taunted him for not performing perfectly the first time. He dismissed the memory. Grace might tease him, but she wouldn't criticize. He gripped the handle of his gun and quickly slid it from the holster, then fanned the hammer with his left hand, firing off three rapid shots. Each time his hand hit the weapon, it threw off his aim, and not one shot struck an empty tin.

"Uh-huh." Grace's tone held no condemnation. "Mind if I ask where you learned that?"

He cleared his throat, and his face warmed. "Last July Fourth at the fastest draw contest."

"Uh-huh," she repeated. "Sometimes cowboys like to show off with that style because they think it looks fancy. But if you ask 'em, they'll admit it's a little hard on the gun's action. Plus their six-shooters need fixin' real often. Anyway, it's not even the fastest draw."

"Ah." Micah returned his Colt Peacemaker to its holster. "And I fell for it. All right, you show me the right way."

She gave him a brief nod and stepped away several paces from him. "Thumbing is the best way. You grip the handle and at the same time place the tip of your thumb on the hammer." She demonstrated as she spoke. "As you begin to draw, let your thumb roll off the inside of the hammer. At the same time you're drawing, get a full grip on the handle, aim and

squeeze the trigger." Her Colt .45 fired three times before Micah could blink, and three tin cans flew off of the fence.

He whistled in admiration. "I see what you mean." He slowly went through the smooth motions, returned his gun to his holster and then drew quickly but without firing. The roll of his thumb seemed the key because it had to bring the hammer back and yet not hold it there. The pull of his trigger finger felt instinctive. On his third draw, he fired, knocking a can from its perch.

"Good job, Rev." Grace seemed about to slap his shoulder, but turned the gesture into a strange little wave. "Most folks can get the hang of it with one lesson. You have the advantage of being real good with your rifle. I didn't have to remind you to keep your eye on the target."

"Thank you, ma'am." Warmth spread through his chest. Her approval meant a great deal to him. Maybe she wouldn't mind if he confided in her about his plans for courting. After a few more fast draws, a reload and a few more cans scattered across the corral, he holstered his gun. "I think we're done here, but I'll keep practicing. May I buy you some ice cream as a thank-you?"

An odd, almost vulnerable look crossed her pretty face. "I'd rather have some of Miss Pam's pie."

"If we're going there, we'll just have dinner. What do you say?"

She shrugged in her endearing "aw-shucks" way. "Sounds good."

While Micah retrieved the battered cans from the corral, he spotted fresh hoofprints in the smattering

of snow. "Say, Grace, I didn't think anyone was living here."

She strode over to him and eyed the ground and then knelt down to trace the wider-than-normal horseshoe print with a slight indention on one side. "Hmm. Could be our man Hardison. Could be a drifter taking shelter last night."

She stood and walked toward the half-open barn door. Micah followed her inside, and they both looked around. The unusual hoofprint wasn't repeated, and nothing caught their attention as being disturbed.

Outside again, Grace tilted her head toward the run-down cabin and spoke a little louder than necessary. "Well, let's get back to town." She drew her gun and walked toward the wood frame abode.

"Good idea." Micah also spoke loudly, while the hair on the back of his neck stood on end. Had they been watched the whole time they were shooting?

Grace again tilted her head, this time toward the side of the cabin. Micah nodded and ambled around the corner to peer in through a shattered window. The room held broken-down furniture, but nothing seemed out of the ordinary.

From the other side of the room came the screech of a rusty-hinged door opening, and soon Grace appeared in the room. She caught his gaze and shook her head. "The snow on the porch didn't have any prints, and the dust hasn't been disturbed in any of the rooms, so I reckon nobody's been in here."

Micah nodded his agreement. Every afternoon, the wind blew a new coat of dust over the entire San Luis Valley, so those fresh hoofprints could only be a few hours old.

He met Grace by their horses. "Why would anyone want to ride into a corral like that if they weren't going to take shelter in the barn or the cabin?"

"Maybe some drifter stopped to see if there was any hay in the barn."

"Could be." Micah heaved out a quiet sigh of relief. The idea that they might have been watched had unnerved him, and yet Grace had remained as cool as an autumn day. Most girls he'd ever known were skittish as colts about such things. What a woman Grace was! He felt privileged to be her pastor and her friend.

The Rev didn't seem to be in any hurry to get back to town, so Grace kept Mack's pace to a moderate walk. After a few hundred yards, the Rev seemed inclined to talk, so she gave him an inviting smile.

"Something on your mind?"

He chuckled in that way of his that always put her at ease. "I could use your advice." He tilted his Stetson back on his head a ways. Once again, she felt pleased that he hadn't worn his dandified bowler hat. That thing sure did annoy her, though she couldn't say why she concerned herself so much with his appearance.

"About shooting?"

"No. I think we covered that this morning." He gazed east across the San Luis Valley toward Mount Blanca, which was nearly snow-covered despite it only being October. "I have guests coming to visit from Virginia around the first of December. Joel Sutton's a childhood friend. After the war, he and his folks were the only people who remained friendly.

The rest treated my family badly because my uncle fought for the North." He gave her a rueful smile. "Some in the South continue to fight the war even though it's been over for almost twenty years. Even my decision to attend seminary in Massachusetts angered many people, and they didn't want any part of me after I graduated. Couldn't get hired in a church, no matter how many I applied to."

Grace shook her head in disgust. The war wasn't his fault. In fact, he was truly a man of peace. Those people didn't know what they were missing to reject him that way. "Their loss is Esperanza's gain. Now tell me about this Joel Sutton."

The Rev leaned down to pat his horse on the neck, a gesture Grace found endearing. He took care of his horse just like he took care of the folks in his congregation and anybody else who needed a kind touch, including her. "Joel and I have been corresponding for a few years, and now he wants to come out here, he and his sister."

Grace didn't need for the Rev to tell her the rest. This sister was probably a gracious Southern belle like Susanna Northam, all pretty and petite and just what the Rev needed in a preacher's wife. But if all things worked together for good, then Grace should assist him all she could. Maybe she'd even play matchmaker and help him get the job done.

"So, are these folks going to stay at the hotel, or should I see if Mrs. Foster wants to take in a couple of new boarders?" Grace liked that plan. She could get the measure of the woman and decide if she was good enough for the Rev.

"No, I think they should stay at the parsonage. I

have those two extra bedrooms, and they're rarely put to use."

Grace held her breath and counted to ten while she considered how to answer. "Will you be comfortable with a single lady staying in your home?"

"I'm not sure. That's why I wanted your advice. Do you think anyone will be offended, considering that Joel will be there, too?"

For some odd reason, Grace wanted more than anything to say yes, the whole town would be offended. That by all means, Joel and his sister should stay someplace else. Anyplace else. But she couldn't lie. Nor could she explain her reservations about the plan. After several seconds of listening to the clop of their horses' hooves and an occasional bird calling out from the thickets along the road, she sighed to herself.

"Well, Rev, we don't have a whole heap of gossips around here, and most folks don't pay them any mind when they do speak out of turn." She had to force a smile as she finished her thought. "I think you should have your friends stay at your house so they don't have to pay rent. Maybe that sister can feed you some fine Southern cooking and put some meat on your bones."

Why had she said that?

He sent a worried frown her way. "You think I'm too thin?"

Oh, my, no. Not thin at all, and certainly not the opposite. He appeared as strong as any hardworking cowboy, although she had no idea how a preacher who read books and visited the sick all day could be so well put together. She also had no idea why she'd

made such a foolish remark about putting meat on his bones. The local ladies kept him well fed with their best cooking. Now, how could she turn this into teasing?

"Naw, not *too* thin." She grinned. "Just on the edge."

He laughed. "Don't say that to Mrs. Foster. She already sends over enough food for a small army."

"I've noticed that." Grace chuckled. After some serious thought last evening, she'd decided to put four pieces of her special fried chicken into Mrs. Foster's basket. Of course he had no idea, and Mrs. Foster had promised not to tell. Not that Grace meant anything by it. She was just trying to be helpful. That was all. Yet it pleased her that he hadn't complained about last night's supper.

"She did something special with that fried chicken last night." Micah could still taste the mouthwatering fare. "Best I've ever eaten."

Grace looked away quickly, and Micah followed her gaze westward toward the San Juan Mountains, seeing nothing of significance.

"Something grab your attention?"

"Nope. Just checking the landscape." She gave her familiar dismissive shrug, but when she faced toward town again, she seemed to be fighting a smile.

Maybe she was embarrassed about her comments regarding his health. Ladies and gentlemen didn't usually discuss such matters. And yet Grace always spoke the truth, painful or not, so Micah had a feeling she might be right about his condition. He'd always vowed not to become a flabby, indolent preacher, like

some he'd met. However, being too thin wasn't any healthier. So far he'd managed to stay fit, but maybe he needed more exercise.

Very few people knew that, weather permitting, he rose early six days a week before anyone else was out and about so he could run around the outskirts of Esperanza. After that, he lifted the barbells Bert, the blacksmith, had made for him, which he kept hidden in one of his extra bedrooms. He'd have to find a new place for them before Joel and Miss Sutton arrived. Would have to find another place to do the lifting. Maybe when he ran, he needed to add another lap around town.

Other than Bert and the sheriff, no one seemed to know about his exercising, which was just as he preferred it. Like his writing, he kept his exercise private, a part of his life that belonged to him alone. Once he married, he'd tell his wife, of course. But for now, he did what he had to do to keep up with the hardy folks in his congregation. No one needed to know how he managed it. In fact, telling others about it might seem boastful. And surely his cowboy friends would laugh at him for having to go out of his way to stay strong and healthy while their normal work kept them in fine fettle. Not that he minded teasing. Their good-humored remarks made him feel even more a part of the community. But he would still keep his exercise a private matter.

"I hope Miss Pam still has some of her beef stew left," Grace said as they dismounted in front of Williams's Café. "I didn't realize how late it was." She nodded toward the brand-new clock tower above the bank. "One thirty. The pickings will surely be slim."

Before Micah could voice his agreement, Mrs. Winsted barged out of her store two doors down from the café.

"Grace, where have you been? I couldn't find the sheriff, either."

All business now, Grace hitched up her gun belt and strode over to Mrs. Winsted. "What happened?"

Stifling his surprising disappointment that their time together would be cut short, Micah followed her onto the boardwalk and focused his attention on Mrs. Winsted.

Hands fisted at her waist, the older woman glared at Grace as though her troubles were the deputy's fault. "Why, I've been robbed again, and this time it's even worse."

Chapter Three

Grace eyed Dub Gleason and his friends, who sat outside the store and watched with smirking grins. She didn't suspect them of the thefts. To a man, the four of them were the laziest polecats she'd ever seen. The most energetic thing they did was make fun of her when no one else was around.

"Let's go inside." She nodded toward the open door of the mercantile. No use broadcasting the details of the robbery. As stupid as Dub and his friends were, they'd blab anything they heard all over the place. The guilty party might hear them and figure out a way to hamper the investigation.

Mrs. Winsted turned in a huff and stormed back into her store. Grace didn't fault her for being upset, but it seemed this usually levelheaded lady was becoming more like her daughter-in-law every day.

Behind her, Grace could hear the Rev's footfalls. She turned and gave him a quizzing look.

He returned that bothersome attractive smile of his. "As I said the other day, I want to help."

"Right." She shrugged. "Come on, then."

Inside the store, Homer Bean, the clerk, was straightening merchandise behind the counter.

"Hey, quit that." Grace tried not to bark the order, but Homer jumped nonetheless. "Don't be moving stuff around. I need to look for clues, and you might cover them up."

"That's just the thing." Mrs. Winsted pressed trembling hands against her temples. "Nothing seems out of place. If I didn't know my inventory like the freckles on my granddaughter's nose, I'd say nothing had been stolen. Whoever took the items cleverly shuffled the other merchandise to fill the empty spaces."

When Grace reached back to retrieve the pencil and pad of paper she kept in her hip pocket, her elbow met something solid. She glanced to the side and saw it was the Rev's arm. A pleasant shiver slid up to her neck, but he seemed unmindful of the contact. Instead, he was staring around the large room, frowning thoughtfully like he was the deputy doing the investigation. Grateful for his help, she poised her pencil over the paper. "Now, ma'am, what was stolen?"

"Well…" Mrs. Winsted huffed a bit and stared off as though gathering her wits. "Several woolen blankets, a tan Stetson, a pearl-handled Colt .45, a Remington rifle and ammunition for both guns." She gazed around the room. "That's what we've figured out so far." She tilted her head toward Homer to indicate he was the other part of *we*. "Last time it was a coffeepot, a bag of coffee, some tins of food and other such items a person might steal if he was needy.

This time it's much more serious, with guns being stolen and all."

"Yes, ma'am." Grace listed the items on her pad. "Show me where they were displayed." Even though she knew the store pretty well, she hoped to calm Mrs. Winsted down by keeping her occupied.

The locked gun case appeared just as the woman had said. Seven handguns were displayed in an orderly fashion with no obvious empty spaces.

The Rev bent down to study the lock on the front of the case. "It doesn't look as though it's been tampered with." He straightened and looked to Mrs. Winsted. "Where do you keep the key?"

Grace felt a pinch of annoyance that he asked the question before she had a chance. She'd have to talk to him later about letting her lead the investigation. "Is it nearby?"

"No." Mrs. Winsted walked toward the door to the back room. "I'll fetch it."

"Wait. I have an idea." The Rev gave Grace an apologetic grin. "If you don't mind?"

Grace answered with a scowl, but he'd already turned his attention back to Mrs. Winsted.

"I know this may sound odd," he said. "However, it may help us to find the thief."

Mrs. Winsted glanced doubtfully between the Rev and Grace. "Deputy?"

Grace hid her annoyance with a smile and a shrug. Oh, she truly must speak to the Rev about this. He was damaging her image of authority. "Go on, Rev. Anything you can do to help."

"Very well." His gray eyes twinkled with excitement, which considerably diminished her irritation.

Not only was he way too handsome when he smiled, he seemed to be enjoying himself in a mighty big way. She couldn't scold him for either one of those.

"I recently read Mark Twain's *Life on the Mississippi*, which is a collection of his short stories. In one story, a murderer was caught because his bloody thumbprint was left on a piece of paper, and he was later identified through that mark. Recent research has shown that no two people have identical finger marks. Maybe we could find the thief's prints on the key or this case." He indicated the glass display. "Of course, we'd have to be sure no one else touches either one while we figure out how to capture the image. Then we can try to find the person whose prints match it."

Grace stared at him with new respect shaded with just a smidgen of skepticism. If what he said was true, it would help law enforcement immensely.

"Oh, dear." Mrs. Winsted frowned in dismay. "I'm afraid we already dusted and wiped down everything this morning. It's the first thing Homer does every day. Isn't it, Homer?"

"Yes, ma'am." The young, sandy-haired clerk had joined them by the gun display as soon as the Rev started talking about the Twain story. "And I've already handled the keys this morning when I showed Mrs. Bellows some items in the jewelry case."

"Hmm." Grace wrote brief notes so she'd remember to tell the sheriff about the whole conversation. She wondered whether he'd heard about finger marks. "Let's have a look at the other places."

Mrs. Winsted pointed to a plaster hat stand molded in the shape of a man's head. "They stole the tan Stet-

son that should be here and put this porkpie hat in its place." She leaned against the display case, and her usually friendly face drooped into a weary expression.

Grace patted the woman's forearm. "Don't worry, Mrs. Winsted. We'll get to the bottom of this. Now, who were your last few customers just before you closed up yesterday?" She glanced at Homer to include him in the question.

They both offered names, and Grace wrote them on her pad, flipping to a second page to list them all.

"The last person out the door was Adam Starling," Homer said. "He bought some flour for his mother and asked to put it on their tab." He cleared his throat. "Not that this means anything…"

"Go on." Grace kept her eyes on her notes. She'd had some concerns about sixteen-year-old Adam but would keep that to herself for now.

"Well…" Homer shuffled his feet. "The last thing Adam looked at was the pearl-handled Colt .45 that's missing now. Said he sure would like to have one like it someday. I, uh, I took it out of the case and let him hold it. I don't like to make judgments about folks, but if a man could look hungry at a gun, then I'd say that was how Adam looked at that revolver."

A sick feeling rose up inside of Grace. She snapped her notepad closed and stuck it back into her pocket. "All right. I'll report this to the sheriff. If either of you think of anything else, let one of us know."

She strode toward the front door only vaguely aware that the Rev was on her heels. Outside on the boardwalk, he touched her arm to stop her. She did

stop, but only because Dub and his friends had wandered down the street.

"Grace, I can see what you're thinking, but you're wrong about Adam."

She shifted her gun belt and gave him her best deputy glare. "That so?"

"Yes." He wasn't in the least bit intimidated by her tough posture, which pleased her in the oddest way. "Why would such a hardworking boy risk everything— his family, his reputation, his jobs—for a gun? Or for any of those other missing items?"

"I'll admit he's always seemed like a straight-up fella." She wouldn't speak about the way Adam avoided her. Lots of men in town avoided her because they didn't know how to behave around a female peacekeeper. She preferred that to Dub Gleason and his pals. "But you gotta admit a poor family like the Starlings don't have much in the way of necessities. Maybe he needed the rifle to kill jackrabbits for their supper."

The Starling family had been in town for about a year and a half. Adam's father had yet to recover from injuries sustained when outlaws beat him and stole the payroll he was delivering for the railroad. Adam was still in high school, and he worked hard at three jobs to support the family. Mrs. Starling took in sewing and laundry, but the family still needed help from the church from time to time. Grace didn't mind their receiving charity. Christians were supposed to take care of needy folks. But the way Adam had been avoiding her recently, refusing to look her in the eye at church or ducking around corners if he

saw her during the week, caused her some concern even before the robberies. What could he be hiding?

"I'm sure the Starlings already have a gun of some sort for small game hunting."

Grace eyed the Rev. "I suppose. But from what Homer said, seems like Adam wants something finer than whatever they have."

"That doesn't mean he'd steal to get it." The Rev exhaled a sigh that almost sounded cross, not his usual calm reaction to troubles. "Adam comes from a decent Christian family. His father held a position of trust for the railroad, and Adam has always been a fine young man. Everyone in town knows how hard he works."

"Maybe he's tired of working so hard." Grace crossed her arms over her chest. "I know he had to spend a lot of his savings to get that special medicine for his little sister last winter."

"Now, Grace—"

"Now, Rev." She held up a hand to silence him. "You don't want to suspect him because you always see the best in everyone."

"Is that a fault?" An uncharacteristic hint of defensiveness colored his tone.

My, he was getting peevish. Grace ignored the question. "You also preach that nobody's righteous, that we've all sinned and come short of the glory of God. The Bible tells us how God's judgment came on evildoers in a mighty way. Think about Jericho or Sodom and Gomorrah. Or the Babylonian captivity."

His jaw dropped slightly, and he stared at her for a moment and then shook his head. "We certainly can't discount those Old Testament stories, but through

Jesus Christ, God extends mercy." He took on his concerned preacher look, tilting his head slightly and stared into her eyes. "You know this, Grace. You've accepted Jesus as your Savior."

"I have." His gaze bored into her, and she stared off in time to see the sheriff enter his office down the block. "But even if a man's trusted the Lord, he can still go wrong if he's tempted bad enough. Adam may just be taking a wrong path. If he is, it's my job to make sure he doesn't get away with it."

"Make sure he doesn't get away with it, or restore him to the right path?"

"Same thing." She wouldn't enter a war of words with him because she'd be sure to lose.

The Rev blew out another long breath. "Admiring a fine gun doesn't make him guilty of theft." He again tilted his head in an appealing way. "Neither does being the last customer of the day."

Grace started to mention how Adam had been avoiding her of late but changed her mind. The Rev would only find a way to turn her suspicions around. "Well, I just saw the sheriff go into the office, so I need to go over and report the robberies to him." She stepped down from the boardwalk onto the dusty street.

The Rev chuckled and called after her. "Does that mean you won't be having dinner with me?"

She glanced over her shoulder. "Aren't you sick of my company by now?" It was a dumb thing to say. Even as rough-mannered as she was, she knew better than to say such a thing to a friend.

"Not at all, Grace." Was that a trace of sadness in his eyes? "But I have a feeling you're tired of my

preaching. Thanks for the shooting lesson." He tipped his hat and gave her a little bow. He was one of the few men in town who offered her such courtesies. "Good day, my friend."

Her heart aching over their disagreement, Grace watched him walk away. This was best, of course. In a couple of months, the Rev's guests would arrive, and that Miss Sutton wouldn't want a plain, too-tall, gawky female deputy hanging around her future husband.

One thing was sure. Grace would get to know the lady to be sure she was good enough for the Rev. If she turned out to be a snob, Grace would... Well, she'd figure something out to discourage him from marrying the wrong woman both for the Rev's sake and the sakes of all the good folks in the congregation. She chuckled to herself. If the lady truly was the uppity sort, Grace and her sisters, Georgia and Maisie, would teach her a thing or two about living in the West.

Feeling the loss of his friend's company after a mostly pleasant morning, Micah stopped into Williams's Café and purchased some sandwiches to eat at home. Odd how he'd only recently begun to understand what it meant to feel true loneliness. All the more reason to get married. Joel and his sister couldn't get here soon enough to suit him so he could find out whether the Lord had chosen Miss Sutton to be his wife.

Seated at his kitchen table, he laughed to himself over the way Grace had irritated him earlier as they discussed Adam Starling. Micah rarely got ir-

ritated, so he'd been surprised by his own reaction to Grace's unbending attitude about punishing the thief. This had been their first real disagreement, and he'd found himself bothered by her Old Testament legalism, which was clearly at odds with her name. He supposed her occupation affected her view of wrongdoers. Or perhaps she'd chosen her occupation because of her views. In any event, a series of sermons about how God's grace and mercy were more powerful than vengeance might open her eyes and her heart. Besides, if Adam was the thief, he needed help, not punishment.

Micah briefly considered consulting Garrick Wakefield, who'd helped the Starlings when they came to town last year and now employed Adam at the hotel. Yet he didn't want to cast doubt on the boy. It was probably best for him to speak to Adam himself to see if he could discern any guilt in his demeanor. For now, he would do some of his own investigating to find out whether Mark Twain's assertions about finger marks were true. Further, the next time he was in Mrs. Winsted's store, he'd advise her and Homer not to disturb that sort of evidence if the robbers struck again. Other than that, he would search for other clues about the thefts.

He finished the first roast beef sandwich and eyed the second one. "Miss Pam," he murmured to himself, "your cooking is just too delicious. This should be my supper, but I can't resist eating it now." His appetite always increased in colder weather.

As he ate, he considered what had been stolen. No jewelry was missing, although the glass display held several valuable gold rings, watches, bracelets, watch

fobs and assorted brooches and tie pins. If the thief needed money, he could sell such items in another town and word would probably never come back to Esperanza. The only missing merchandise appeared to be survival necessities. Micah couldn't imagine the Starlings needing woolen blankets because the church had supplied them with quilts. Further, Mrs. Starling was an excellent seamstress and could make more if they needed them. As for the guns, no one in Esperanza would take such weapons because all of their neighbors would recognize them as stolen. When the time was right, Micah would tell Grace about his thoughts.

His dinner finished, Micah went to work organizing the bedroom he'd used as an office for the past seven years. Yesterday he'd purchased a single bed, bedding and a chest of drawers to accommodate Joel. His large oak desk took up too much space, so to give Joel some privacy, he'd need to move it to the small room behind the church sanctuary. After school let out, he'd find Adam and ask him to help arrange the furniture. He'd also use the opportunity to try to detect any signs of guilt in the boy.

Although Micah had appreciated Grace's advice about hosting the Suttons, he decided to ask Mrs. Foster, as well. He walked the two blocks to the elderly lady's boardinghouse, where he found her in the kitchen, as usual. She motioned for him to take a seat at the table, where she placed a piece of lemon cake before him.

After enjoying a few delicious bites, he explained his situation and asked her advice.

"Why, it sounds fine to me." She poured Micah a

cup of coffee and handed it to him. "Just be sure Mr. Sutton is always in the house with you and his sister, and propriety will be satisfied."

"That should be easy enough." Micah spent more time away from the parsonage than in it. "Now, what do you advise for furnishing her room?"

Mrs. Foster thought for a moment. "I have a spare bedroom suite in storage left by a tenant who moved back East. You may have that."

Micah sat back and grinned. Once again the Lord had provided before he asked. "That would be wonderful. Thank you, dear lady. You've solved two problems for me."

He would need help to move the furniture. Since Adam would be in school until almost four o'clock, Micah returned home to review his sermon notes for Sunday. Satisfied with what he'd written, he retrieved his most recent manuscript from the top drawer of his desk.

He liked this story even better than the one he'd already sold, but he needed to work on his main character a bit more. He jotted down a few notes about his conversation with Grace regarding the thefts because the incident perfectly suited his fictional female sheriff. Following Charles Dickens's custom of naming characters after their personality traits, he'd tentatively called his heroine Willa Ketchum, but today the name sounded a little silly. He tapped the end of his pen against his cheek and stared out the window beside him.

"Charity." He said the name aloud, but it didn't sound right. "Mercy? Grace?" He laughed. "That

would give me away for certain." The new name would have to wait.

He sat back and stared at the half-filled page. Closing his eyes, he tried to imagine the next scene for his story. In his mind's eye, he saw Grace wearing that determined look on her fair face as she insisted Adam was the thief. Micah had intended for his heroine always to be clever at solving crimes, always successful at catching outlaws.

"Well, *Miss Ketchum*, maybe it's time you made a mistake."

Chapter Four

December 1884

"Finally. Hardison and Smith." Sheriff Lawson pulled two wanted posters from a newly arrived stack. "You wouldn't think it'd take two months to get these sent out after a prison escape." Studying the photographs printed on the papers, he grunted. "Hardison looks like a snake oil salesman, and Smith looks like forty miles of bad road."

Grace peered over the sheriff's shoulder. "Yep. That's them all right." A mixture of disgust and sorrow filled her. "Hardison wasn't bad to look at, and he dressed and spoke well, so he had a lot of people fooled." She hadn't paid all that much attention to the man when he first came to Esperanza because she hadn't been a deputy at the time. Her stopping these two slimy varmints in the midst of their evil deeds had motivated folks to offer her the job. "As for Smith, he didn't show his ugly face in these parts until the day they attempted to rob the bank." She

shook her head, as if that would get rid of the bad memory.

"It's interesting the way these sorts always find each other." The sheriff scratched his jaw as he always did when he was cogitating. "Like Jud Purvis and the rest of their gang I put in the Kansas penitentiary, they all seem to have a magnet inside that draws evil to evil."

"I wouldn't argue with that." Grace was glad to see the keen look in his eyes as he studied the posters. He'd been hired for his reputation as a no-nonsense lawman who always got his man. With Esperanza being such a peaceful town and community, he'd had very little to do over the past year and a half. Since news of the outlaws' escape arrived in October, though, he'd stood straighter and walked with a more purposeful stride. Grace supposed a man needed to feel useful, but she would just as soon no criminals ever reared their ugly heads to threaten her loved ones and friends. Reminding folks to obey the law and keeping the peace were her reasons for wearing a badge.

"Good afternoon." The Rev poked his head in through the door, bringing with him an icy blast of early December air. "How are you folks doing?"

Grace's heart did an annoying little hop inside of her chest, as it had for the past two months, much to her continuing annoyance. My, he looked fine today, mainly because he was wearing his Stetson and a heavy woolen overcoat instead of that silly bowler hat and his black dandy suit he bought two months back. To cover her bothersome reaction, she shrugged with feigned indifference. "Fair to middlin'."

"I'll be a lot better if you step inside and close that door." Sheriff Lawson scowled at the Rev. "Hasn't anybody told you it's winter?"

"Of course." With his usual good humor, the Rev chuckled as he minded what the sheriff said. Then he got serious. "Mrs. Winsted asked me to tell you she's had a few more items stolen. She's a bit distraught, of course, and doesn't want to leave the store, so I said I'd let you know."

"Was it just more survival supplies?" Grace pulled out her notepad. She'd been keeping a growing list of the items. Other than the guns and ammunition stolen at the first, over the past two months only food and a few articles of clothing had disappeared from the mercantile. A man's coat, some gloves, woolen trousers. She had to admit she hadn't seen Adam Starling wearing the stolen goods. Maybe he sold them to somebody out of town. She found it frustrating never to catch him in the act of stealing, no matter how closely she watched him every time he entered the store.

"That's right. Coffee, cornmeal, a large ham and some bacon."

"A big ham?" The sheriff gave the Rev a long look. "Either the thief has a big appetite or he has a lot of people to feed."

"Good point." The Rev chuckled again and placed a hand over his belly. "That reminds me. I haven't eaten dinner yet. Will both of you join me at Williams's Café?"

"You two go ahead." With one eyebrow lifted, the sheriff shot Grace a glance and grinned for the first time that day, although she couldn't imagine why.

"My wife would have a fit I didn't wait for her to bring me my dinner."

"All right. I guess I'm hungry enough for dinner." Against her better judgment, Grace would go. She'd tried to avoid being alone with the Rev ever since he mentioned his friend and his sister were coming to town. What she couldn't avoid was sitting in church every Sunday and listening to his fine sermons or bumping into him unexpectedly around town. No use denying that she was developing feelings for him, which would only lead to her heart being broken. Even if he returned her affections, she'd never make him a good wife. A minister needed to marry a proper lady, and Grace wouldn't begin to know how to be one. If she tried, everyone would see right through her. Would even laugh her to shame. Besides, she didn't care in the least for phonies, and she refused to be one herself.

Grabbing her woolen jacket and hat from the coat rack, she put them on, then allowed the Rev to hold the door for her. Outside, the cold, brisk wind blew into their faces and made it hard to speak. Even though the sun beamed brightly over the San Luis Valley, it offered no heat. By the time they reached the café just a half block down and across the street, Grace felt chilled from head to toe. Once inside, they ordered Miss Pam's special chili and cornbread, along with plenty of hot coffee to thaw themselves out.

"What brought you out today, Rev?" Grace was determined to keep the conversation light. "You just like to freeze?" She held her coffee cup in both hands to warm them.

He chuckled in that way of his, a deep, warm

sound that made her think of thick molasses being poured on fresh hotcakes. "I went to the mercantile to pick up my mail. A good thing, too, because my friend Joel wrote to give me the date of his arrival. And his sister's, of course." Taking a bite of his chili, he closed his eyes as if savoring the spicy flavor. "Mmm-mmm."

"Is it soon?" Grace would be glad to meet the lady, glad to see whether she suited the Rev, glad to be done with her own foolish feelings.

"This Wednesday." He buttered his corn bread and took a mannerly bite. "That is, if a snowstorm doesn't come along in the next two days and close La Veta Pass. Then they'd be stranded in Walsenburg for the winter."

Grace could only hope. Wait. That was wrong on two counts. She would never wish that any good folks got stranded in a strange town for who knew how long. And hadn't she just been thinking about how much she wanted this ordeal to be over?

"I know you'll be glad to see them." There. She'd said something nice—and entirely true.

"I will."

They continued to eat in silence for several minutes. Once the Rev finished his chili, he gave Grace a speculative look.

"Say, do you like to work with children?"

"Who? Me?"

He laughed, and this time it sounded jolly, even musical, if one could say that about a man's laugh. "Yes, you."

She gave him a guarded look. "Don't you dare ask me to teach Sunday school." She had no idea

how to work with little ones, and the older children, mostly from sixth grade on up, still made jokes about her just as their older brothers who were her age had done when she was in school with them. She would never again subject herself to such torment. "I mean, I like young'uns all right, but—" Mostly her nephew Johnny and the Northam brothers' children. She wouldn't mind having a few of her own, but that would never happen.

He blinked those penetrating gray eyes and gave her a mystified look. "All right. I wasn't planning to ask you about Sunday school, but that answers the next question I was going to ask."

"Which was?"

He shrugged. "You know that Marybeth has been organizing the children's Christmas pageant for the past two years."

Grace could anticipate his next thought. "And in her condition, she can't do it this year."

"Um. Yes." A faint bit of color appeared beneath the tan of the Rev's cheeks. Like the true gentleman that he was, he wouldn't speak about Marybeth being with child.

Raised on a ranch where all sorts of births took place, not to mention helping with her sister Maisie's lying-in, Grace didn't understand such reservations, but she did respect him for his manners.

He seemed in a hurry to move on. "Everyone enjoys seeing their children put on the pageant, so I don't want to cancel it." He blinked again, this time like he'd found a solution. "Maybe Rosamond Wakefield would like to do it." Tapping his fingers on the table, he gazed out the window. "Or better still, per-

haps Miss Sutton." He gave a decisive nod. "That's it. I'll wait until she arrives and ask her. There will still be several weeks to plan and practice. Mrs. Starling always helps with the costumes, and Nate Northam likes to build the scenery..."

As he continued to name the usual volunteers for the annual event, Grace stopped listening. The way things were going for her, Miss Sutton would take over the pageant for sure. All the more proof that she would make a perfect wife for the Rev.

In spite of all her good intentions to move back from her friendship with the Rev—for his own good, of course, Grace had a feeling she'd just missed an important opportunity to impress him in a big way. She should have overcome her reservations and said she'd work with the children. If it wouldn't look ridiculous, she would smack herself in the forehead for her foolishness. Instead, she'd just order some chocolate pie and try to eat herself out of her misery.

With little going on in the community this past October and November, Micah had had plenty of time to work on his novel. Although he still had a few elements to work out, it was nearing completion. A good thing, too, because a letter had arrived today from his editor imploring him to complete and send it as soon as possible. In addition, the man said his first book should be in stores back East within the week, and if snow didn't stop the shipment, even people in Esperanza would be able to purchase the book before Christmas.

Micah tried to subdue the giddy feelings of delight that filled him, but some days it was harder than others

to keep from sharing his joy with somebody, anybody. In truth, he also struggled with pride when he thought about becoming a published author. Imagine, he'd be standing in the ranks of people like Nathaniel Hawthorne and Mark Twain, although he never expected to attain the same degree of fame.

"It's a privilege, a gift from the Lord," he kept reminding himself. "Not something to brag about."

Perhaps his struggle with pride was the reason for those elusive story elements. Still, he felt confident that, given time, the Lord would show him just the right way to pull the action and characters all together. One thing he found interesting and even amusing was the affection he'd developed for his heroine. While he still wasn't pleased with the name Willa Ketchum, he figured time and prayer would bring the right name to mind.

As the day of the Suttons' arrival approached, he found himself growing more nervous than he'd been that day seven years ago when he'd delivered his first sermon to the good people of Esperanza Community Church. Although he could barely remember what he said back then, he must have impressed the congregation, for they had welcomed him with open arms and hearty handshakes. Would Miss Sutton think well of him, too?

He'd done everything possible to make sure she would. His new black suit had been pressed to perfection at Chen's Laundry, as had his white shirt and gray waistcoat. He'd bought a gray cravat at the haberdasher's and new patent leather shoes to replace his boots. His carefully brushed black bowler hat topped his ensemble. He'd even scandalized Mrs.

Winsted—in a humorous way, of course—by purchasing a manly scented bergamot cologne. The storekeeper informed him that Napoleon Bonaparte had been partial to bergamot, but Micah wasn't sure that was the best recommendation for the product. Nonetheless, he dabbed a tiny drop of the fragrant liquid behind one ear in hopes that it would improve his appeal, or at least not drive Miss Sutton away.

And what of his own feelings for the young lady? Would he be like the biblical patriarch Isaac, who loved Rebecca the moment he saw her? To calm himself, Micah rationalized that perhaps Joel might not be playing matchmaker after all. Even though he'd mentioned wanting to find a husband for his sister, perhaps this trip was merely exploratory as they considered whether to move to Colorado permanently. Micah supposed Joel would need a trade, but where did his interests lie? A position was now open for a science teacher at the high school, and Joel had always been a bit of an inventor. Would he qualify to teach?

As much as Micah tried to occupy his mind with such questions, only one thing dominated his thoughts, overshadowing even his joy at seeing his old friend after more than ten years: Was Miss Sutton the woman God had chosen for him?

He left the parsonage and strode toward the train depot, arriving just as the great black locomotive chugged into sight, white smoke flowing from its smokestack. To his surprise, Grace and her older sister, Maisie, stood on the platform.

"Good morning, ladies." Micah doffed his hat, noticing the smirk that passed between the sisters.

Ah, yes. Grace didn't like the bowler. Perhaps he should have asked her advice about his attire. "Are you meeting someone today?" He nodded toward the approaching train.

"Yep." Maisie cradled her infant son in her arms. Little Johnny was bundled up in bunting against the cold but sunny day. "We want to meet your friends."

"That's right." Grace gave him a smile that held a bit of wiliness. "My, my, Rev, you sure do smell good. Just like a city dandy." She laughed, and Micah's heart did an odd little turn. What was she up to?

"As I was about to say, everybody ought to have a welcome party when they arrive in Esperanza." She tilted her head toward the yellow-and-brown train station, from which several friends emerged: Maisie's husband, Doc Henshaw, Rand and Nate Northam, along with their wives and children, and Georgia Eberly, all chatting and smiling as if this were a grand party.

Laughing at his own foolishness, Micah relaxed. "Thank you all for coming. I'm sure the Suttons will be delighted to meet everyone."

The train slowly chugged into the station and came to a stop with a screech of brakes and mighty puffs of steam blasting from the undercarriage. A half dozen workers jumped into action, unloading luggage and freight while passengers emerged from the Pullman cars and set about claiming their possessions.

"Micah! Here we are." A brown-haired man disembarked from the second passenger car, waved and then turned to assist a young woman as she stepped down.

She was stylishly dressed in a brown traveling suit with black trim and a matching wide-brimmed hat

sat elegantly on her upswept dark brown hair. Knowing he should go to meet them, Micah found himself unable to move because of the crowd. He could only stand and stare as Joel and his sister made their way toward him.

Miss Sutton's ivory complexion appeared flawless except for a faint blush on her cheeks. A cameo brooch on her high lace color enhanced her attire. The smile she aimed at her brother might be described by a poet as glorious, revealing even white teeth. Her blue eyes sparkled with good humor, as though she were on a grand adventure and couldn't wait for the next episode. The young lady looked as if she'd just stepped out of a painting by one of the old masters. At least that was the way Micah would describe her if she were a character in one of his novels.

All around him, his friends exclaimed over her beauty in hushed tones and a couple of low whistles. Except for Grace. Micah heard her sigh, though he couldn't imagine why. As for himself, he continued to stare and stare, waiting for his heart to respond. Instead, it sat in his chest like a cold lump of coal, feeling nothing.

He forced his feet to move forward and shook hands with Joel. They slapped each other on the shoulder and laughed heartily.

"You haven't changed a bit." Joel shook his head as if in disbelief. "Not even a hint of gray in that dark hair of yours. You using bootblack to color it?"

"Not hardly." Micah laughed again. They'd always insulted each other in fun, so it would be like old times. Still, he refrained from returning a similar jest because Joel did bear a few signs of aging. Although

he hadn't yet passed his thirtieth birthday, strands of gray frosted his light brown hair, and worry lines had settled around his eyes. Even his posture seemed a bit stooped over. Were those changes a result of his difficulties back home in Virginia? Still, Micah must return a friendly insult, or the moment would turn awkward.

Still holding Joel's hand, he said, "You call that a handshake? When you meet the cowboys out here, you'd better tighten your grip or they'll think you're a dandy."

Sorrow flickered across Joel's lightly tanned face. Had Micah unwittingly hit a nerve?

"I'll be sure to remember that." Joel gave him another bright smile and then stepped back to draw his sister to his side.

She moved forward with elegance that should have impressed Micah, but again, he felt not the slightest attraction.

"Electra." Pride and fraternal affection shone in Joel's eyes. "May I present the Reverend Micah Thomas, who caused me no end of grief when we were boys?"

"How do you do, Reverend Thomas." Her smile was the picture of graciousness.

"Miss Sutton." Micah took her offered hand and bent to kiss it. "It is a pleasure. Welcome to Esperanza. Welcome to the Wild West." He added a soft chuckle to his last words, trying to force some feeling into this encounter.

"Ahem." Nate Northam's artificial clearing of his throat reminded Micah of the welcoming party behind him.

Before he could begin introductions, Nate's wife, Susanna, hurried forward and introduced herself and her small family in her soft Southern accent. "Miss Sutton, I know we're a bit more formal in the South, but out here, most people use first names. Do you mind if we call you Electra?" She grasped the lady's hands and placed a kiss on her cheek.

Miss Sutton drew back, her eyes briefly widening. She seemed to catch herself, but the smile she offered didn't quite reach her eyes. "By all means, we must follow local customs, mustn't we, Joel."

"Of course." Joel offered a tired laugh that wasn't entirely jovial as he shook hands with Nate.

The others moved up to meet the two newcomers, and Micah stepped to the side. Clearly Miss Sutton preferred the old customs. He couldn't fault her for that, but he would address her accordingly. Besides, she had just traveled across the country and needed time to rest before she could be expected to adjust to Western ways. Still, he wished he felt more than compassion for her. Did this mean the Lord hadn't sent her to be his bride? Or did it mean the Lord *had* sent her, and Micah would grow to love her? Or wasn't he meant to have a marriage like Isaac and Rebecca's? For the first time in his life, he experienced confusion and disappointment over the direction the Lord seemed to be leading him.

Grace stepped over and nudged him with her elbow. "Electra? What kind of name is that?"

Her slightly derisive tone should have raised his defenses on behalf of the newcomer. Instead, he had to stifle a laugh. "According to Joel, it's an old family name."

"You don't say. That's truly sad." Grace snorted out a laugh that had the entire group turning their way. She stepped over to Electra and stuck out her hand. Electra looked at it as if she had no idea what to do with it. Grace, being Grace, grabbed Electra's hand and shook it up and down as though she were pumping water.

"Pleased to meet you, Miss Sutton. I'm Deputy Eberly, but you can call me Grace."

Obviously shocked, Miss Sutton questioned Joel with a glare. He shrugged. Miss Sutton turned back, offering a lifted chin instead of a smile and stared down her nose at Grace the way Micah's mother used to do when required to meet someone she'd rather not know. "How do you do, Deputy Eberly."

And with that, Micah felt a door close in his heart. But if Miss Sutton was not the Lord's choice for him, who was? And how on earth would he figure it out?

In spite of his quandary, he offered another smile to the young lady and followed Joel to help him make arrangements for their luggage. The welcoming party dispersed, everyone somewhat subdued after Miss Sutton's cool response to their warm reception. Micah did notice that Susanna Northam remained behind to speak quietly with the newcomer. Perhaps with her sweet Southern manners, she could help Miss Sutton overcome her icy reserve.

Chapter Five

The moment Miss Sutton lifted that flawless, sculpted chin and stared down that aristocratic nose—a little difficult because she wasn't all that tall—Grace knew she wasn't right for the Rev. A quick glance at his smiling face revised her opinion. Maybe he wanted a snobby ice queen. Even as Grace chuckled to herself over that title, she felt her heart sink. Not only would the congregation suffer under such a pastor's wife, but Grace herself, well, she would lose her friendship with the Rev for good. But then, that's what she'd expected to happen anyway.

She hiked up her gun belt and touched the brim of her hat as a parting gesture to all and then headed down the street toward the sheriff's office. Maisie fell in beside her and looped an arm around Grace's. Her mother and sisters were the only people Grace allowed such familiarity. Wouldn't do any good to refuse them because they'd grab her anyway.

"So much for our neighborly reception." Maisie glanced behind them and waved at her baby boy,

Johnny, who snuggled in the arms of his proud pa, Doc Henshaw. After he'd delivered countless babies to the women in and around Esperanza for five years, he and Maisie finally had their own child. "It takes all kinds, doesn't it?"

Grace laughed at Maisie's remarks, despite the hollow feeling in her chest. "I suppose."

"Any success in finding the thieves?" Maisie nodded toward Mrs. Winsted's mercantile as they walked past it.

Glad to talk about something besides the ice queen, Grace shook her head. "She's had a steady stream of things stolen, little by little, mostly inexpensive survival items. But a theft is still a theft whether it's penny candy or a fancy Remington rifle." Now that the Rev would be busy with his company, Grace would be on her own in solving the crime, especially since Sheriff Lawson had become more absentminded. Working on her own might prove to be the best, because she still had her sights on Adam Starling, while the Rev insisted the boy was innocent. Those thoughts restored her deputy focus. No use thinking about losing the Rev's friendship when she had the responsibility to protect the community.

They stopped at the street where Maisie and her family would turn toward their two-story home. "Will we see you at prayer meeting tonight?" Her sister gave Grace's waist a squeeze before releasing her to loop that same arm around her husband's.

"Wouldn't miss it." Grace hiked up her gun belt. She expected Maisie's, or at least Doc's, expressions to show disapproval of the way she lifted the heavy leather belt to make it sit more comfortably on her

hips. Although the Rev never said anything, he didn't seem aware of the shadow that crossed his face when she did it. Instead, Maisie's and Doc's faces beamed with their usual acceptance, not only of her behavior but of everything about her. Oh, how Grace loved her family. What would she do without them?

She placed a kiss on baby Johnny's chubby cheek—he and her horse, Mack, and Ma, of course, were the only creatures she ever kissed—and said her good-byes before heading over to the sheriff's office. Inside, she found her boss poring over a new stack of wanted posters.

"These just came in the mail this morning." He shook his head in disgust and glanced behind him at the pictures of Hardison and Smith hanging on the wall. "Maybe I'm just getting old, but it seems the world's getting worse by the day."

"Yep." Grace poured herself some coffee from the new blue pot simmering on the roaring potbelly stove. Five matching pots had arrived at Mrs. Winsted's store in early October. The sheriff's wife had purchased one for her husband's office and one for her home, and two still sat on the shelf at the mercantile. The fifth had been one of the first items stolen from the store. Grace should probably make a visit to the Starling home to see if they had it. She could just hear the Rev chiding her for her suspicions, but she considered being suspicious an important part of her job.

"By the by, here's a letter for you, Grace." Not even looking up from his wanted posters, the sheriff held out an ivory linen envelope.

"Thanks." Grace felt a rush of excitement over

this rare arrival of a letter addressed directly to her, not to the whole family. Had Laurie written from music school? Had she splurged on the expensive-looking paper at some fancy Denver store to let them know she'd visit home again over Christmas? Or was it from her sister Beryl, all the way from England?

The instant Grace took the letter in hand, dread swept away all pleasant feelings. The stationery looked exactly like the type Mrs. Winsted sold, a box of which had been stolen from the mercantile in the first robbery. Further, the clumsy writing of Grace's name on the envelope was far different from Laurie's or Beryl's elegant penmanship.

"It's not even stamped." Grace plopped down into a chair beside the sheriff's battered oak desk. "This can't be good."

"Huh?" He looked up from his stack of papers.

She grabbed his carved wooden letter opener and carefully slit the envelope open. Hating the way her hands shook, she pulled out the letter, unfolded it and read the chicken scratch writing.

Be warned. You will pay for what you did.

Grace's heart felt like it had dropped to her stomach. She'd been threatened before, mostly by cowboys who'd imbibed too much at the Independence Day celebrations and didn't like her confiscating their weapons. To a man, every one of them had apologized profusely once they sobered up.

This was different. This connected the thefts from the mercantile with Hardison and Smith. After all, the two outlaws had vowed to take revenge on every-

one who'd had a hand in putting them in the Cañon City State Penitentiary. Grace, being the one who'd led the group that captured them, would be their prime target.

"What is it?" Sheriff Lawson's voice held a stern tone, and his eyes took on a steely glint. "You're as pale as that paper."

She held out the letter, which he took and read.

"Cowards." He thrust it back at her, his expression grim. "This scare you?"

She shrugged. "More like sets me on edge. It's not like we didn't know they were coming. It was just a matter of when. Now we know they're here, so we can figure out how to apprehend them without anyone getting hurt." Brave words she didn't entirely believe.

"Good girl." He grinned, even as his sharp gaze searched her face.

Like Miss Sutton had at the train station, Grace sniffed and lifted her chin to show her disdain or, more truthfully in her case, to hide her alarm, her fear over the direct threat the outlaws had sent to her.

An odd thought interrupted her musings. Maybe fear of new surroundings had caused the ice queen to act so stuck-up. Maybe Grace should give the woman a second chance. After all, if she was going to marry the Rev—

For the second time in about two minutes, Grace felt her heart drop to her stomach. Right now she didn't know which bothered her more, the threatening letter or the idea of the Rev marrying anybody, especially an elegant beauty like Miss Sutton.

On the positive side, Grace was pleased at the recent change in Sheriff Lawson. For all of his com-

plaints about the increase in lawlessness, this old lawman just needed to feel useful. She laughed to herself. The Rev would say "all things work together for good." Maybe in this case, he was right.

"Reverend Thomas, your parsonage is absolutely charming." Miss Sutton stood in the center of the parlor pulling off her kid gloves as she gazed around the room.

After a leisurely dinner in the Esperanza Arms dining room, Micah had brought his guests to his home, which he'd done his best to clean and arrange into a welcoming if temporary abode for them. Miss Sutton's praise, like her comments on just about everything she'd seen so far in Esperanza, seemed to come from the heights of aristocratic judgment, polite enough and yet with an edge of hauteur that hinted at the obvious inferiority of the object under discussion. Even the wealthiest inhabitants of this community never spoke that way to anyone, *about* anyone. To Micah himself, however, Miss Sutton was the soul of warmth and friendliness.

"Of course it could use a woman's touch." She ran a finger over the small table beside his brown plaid settee, which suddenly looked a mite shabby to Micah. She looked at her finger, apparently searching for dust, and gave him a nod of approval at not finding any. "Would you mind if I do a bit of rearranging and decorating while Joel and I visit you? It will keep me occupied while you men catch up on old times."

While the young lady's rich Southern accent reminded Micah of the best parts of his home life in Virginia, her proprietary attitude sent a thread of

unease skittering down his back. Had his old friend come with a serious expectation that Micah would marry his sister without their even learning whether they were compatible? Which, at this point, Micah was fairly certain they were not.

"Elly, what a thing to say." Joel contradicted his scolding words by beaming with pride at her. "How can you expect a bachelor to know how to decorate a home?"

She laughed softly, a well-modulated, musical sound. "Well, I am sure I'm not the first lady to notice the lack of more delicate touches."

"No, you're not, Miss Sutton." Micah felt the strange need to take control of this conversation. Being a pastor didn't mean he had to let an old friend manipulate him. "Our church organist often drops similar hints."

Miss Sutton's smile dimmed slightly. "Does the lady visit often?"

Micah had to pucker his lips to keep from laughing. He'd been the object of some aggressive marriage-minded women, but he hadn't expected a finishing school graduate to be so obvious in her flirtation, never mind her brother's machinations.

"She visits at least once a week when she brings over some of her excellent cooking to feed this starving bachelor." Only a tiny bit of guilt pinched his conscience, but it was enough to require that he clear up the situation right away. "Dear old Mrs. Foster is like a mother to everyone in the church." He wouldn't mention that she was also a Union war widow. No need to bring up the evils that had divided the country twenty years ago and sent Micah's abolitionist

uncle north to fight for the Union, a stain on the family that many of their Southern neighbors were unwilling to forgive or forget.

"Isn't that just lovely." Miss Sutton's full smile returned. "Every church needs for its older women to set a good example and teach the younger ladies their Christian duty."

"Indeed." Micah waved toward an inner doorway. "Please permit me to show you to your rooms."

They followed him through the narrow hallway to their side-by-side bedchambers. Stepping into hers, Miss Sutton viewed the furnishings Mrs. Foster had so generously provided. "How utterly, delightfully quaint. I just know I shall simply love staying here."

Micah hoped his smile didn't look more like a grimace. "Please make yourselves at home. Tonight we'll have prayer meeting over at the church, so perhaps a restful nap and another meal at the hotel would make for a convenient supper." Micah had debated with himself about where to take them for their noon meal after they arrived. He'd decided the hotel would suit Miss Sutton more than Williams's Café, although he felt disloyal to Miss Pam for thinking that. It had proved to be a wise decision.

"Nonsense." Miss Sutton unpinned her elegant traveling hat and set it on the mahogany dressing table. "I will fix supper for us. You just show me your kitchen."

"Once you taste Elly's cooking, you'll never go back to that hotel." Joel again beamed with pride. "Not to say dinner wasn't satisfactory, but hotel food can never hope to compete with home cooking."

"I'm not sure I have anything on hand—"

"Nonsense," Miss Sutton repeated. "If you're lacking anything I need, we can send that errand boy who brought our luggage."

"Fine, strong boy, that Adam," Joel said.

"He is." Micah had managed to hail Adam as they'd left the train station. On his noon break from classes at the high school, he'd cheerfully agreed to bring the Suttons' two trunks and four suitcases to the parsonage while Micah took his guests to dinner. But the lad would have other responsibilities as soon as school was dismissed for the day. Still, he couldn't refuse Miss Sutton's offer to cook. If need be, he would go to the mercantile himself. "Let's see what I have on hand."

They made their way up the hall to the cozy kitchen. While the lady continued to exclaim over the quaintness of this and that around his home and Joel continued to beam with pride in his sister, Micah worried the edges of the envelope in his frock coat pocket. The letter had been slipped under the front door in his absence, and he'd managed to scoop it up before his guests saw it and became curious. From the ill-formed letters of his name on the envelope front, so at odds with the fine linen stationery upon which they were written, Micah couldn't begin to guess who it came from. Curiosity and a hint of concern prodded his decision not to delay reading it. Did one of his parishioners have an urgent need? Perhaps they'd waylaid Adam and asked him to deliver the missive when he brought the trunks.

"If you'll excuse me for a few minutes, I'd like to check the sanctuary for tonight's meeting and make sure my sermon notes are in order." He headed for

the back door. "As I said before, please make yourselves at home."

"You run along, Reverend Thomas." Miss Sutton continued her search of the kitchen cabinet as though it were her own. "I'll have supper prepared in plenty of time so we can eat before prayer meeting."

"I'll come with you." Joel took a step in Micah's direction.

"You've had a long trip." Micah held up his hand to stop him. "Why not rest so you'll feel like attending the meeting."

"Ah." Joel blinked. "Very well." Disappointment clouded his face.

Micah was beginning to wonder what had happened to this man he'd known all his life. After those few minutes of warmth at the train station, he'd become more like a politician than a cherished old friend. Perhaps the trip had exhausted him and this was merely his way of soldiering through until he could get some rest. A mild suspicion that perhaps Joel's sister was part of his exhaustion slipped into Micah's thoughts. He quickly dismissed it as uncharitable toward the young lady, though he had to confess her lively chatter had worn him out a bit, too.

Leaving the house by the kitchen door, he strode across the wide yard that separated his home from the church. Before he reached the back entrance, Grace hailed him from the road. After a morning with Miss Sutton, he welcomed his good friend's appearance.

"Got a minute, Rev?" She dismounted from her horse and tied it to one of the hitching rails that extended along the front of the property, then strode

toward him across the church's side lawn. Only a hint of snow lay between the blades of brown grass.

"I always have time for you." He beckoned for her to follow him into the church.

In his small office, made even smaller by his large oak desk now moved into it from the extra parsonage bedroom, Micah waved her to the seat across from him. "What can I do for you?"

She took an envelope from her vest pocket. "Just wanted to bring you up to date on our escaped outlaws." She pulled a letter from the envelope and passed it over to him. "After not seeing hide nor hair of them since their escape in early October, seems they're finally getting serious about this revenge business."

The Rev rarely showed shock or surprise, but right now he actually gaped as he read the note. He reached into his coat pocket and produced an envelope identical to hers. Grace bit her lip to keep from showing her alarm. It was one thing for Hardison to seek revenge against her for stopping the robbery. Another thing entirely to threaten this godly man, who'd only tried to help him. Had often visited him in jail. Had sat behind him during his trial, still trying to save his sorry soul, to no avail.

"I haven't had a chance to open this." The Rev did so now and laid the letter beside hers.

Even upside down, Grace could read the message, written in the same chicken scratch as hers.

Prepare your best funeral sermon. You will use it often in the coming days.

The Rev huffed out a humorless laugh. "He didn't sign it, but there's no mistaking who wrote this. Not only did Marybeth injure Hardison's shooting hand, she ruined his writing. These messages are far too intelligent to be from Deke Smith. Deke probably can't even spell *funeral*." This time his laugh was lighter but still without humor.

"At least he's not threatening you." Grace's relief for the Rev was short-lived as she realized that Marybeth Northam had probably received a note as menacing as her own. "I'll ride out to Four Stones Ranch and see if Marybeth got one of these." She gathered her letter and tucked it away in her pocket.

"Surely he wouldn't harm a woman who—" As always when the topic arose, a bit of red appeared on the Rev's tanned cheeks.

"A killer like Hardison won't care about that." A sick feeling stirred in her stomach at the thought. She stood and put on her hat, the Rev also standing politely. She started to settle her gun belt, which had gotten too high on her hips as she sat, but decided to wait until she got outside. Right now, the Rev was watching her with concern, and she didn't want that look to change to disapproval, no matter how uncomfortable the heavy belt was.

"Be careful." Now his gray eyes turned soulful, and his warm, kindly smile sent one of those silly, foolish feelings through her. "Don't let Hardison surprise you with an ambush."

She had to stamp out for good her reactions to his kindness, so she settled her gun belt on her hips after all, hoping he'd stop looking at her with whatever that intense look was. "That's what they pay me for."

Before he could escort her to the back door, she stepped across the tiny room and outside. Over at the parsonage, she could see that Miss Sutton through the kitchen window. So she'd already become the lady of the house. All the more reason for Grace to make herself scarce, especially now that Hardison hadn't threatened the Rev. She wouldn't entirely relax her concern for him, but surely Hardison would only target those who'd directly been responsible for taking him down and ending his gun fighting days.

As she rode south out of town toward Four Stones Ranch, she pondered the maliciousness of the outlaws. For Hardison to send that note to the Rev was nothing short of returning evil for good to someone who'd offered true friendship to the scoundrel. A man couldn't get more rotten than that. Not only did Grace plan to protect her friends and loved ones, she had every intention of making sure the Rev never had to bury anybody but Dathan Hardison and Deke Smith.

At Four Stones Ranch, she rode around to the back door, as everybody did in these parts. A body only went to the front door if he was a stranger, was coming to a party or didn't know the local customs. She was met by three barking sheepdogs with wagging tails. The friendly critters weren't much in the way of watchdogs, but they had proved to be pretty good at herding cattle, the reason Colonel Northam had brought them over from Scotland to begin with.

This being a cold day, smoke streamed from the chimney over the kitchen. Grace looked forward to some hot coffee and maybe a sweet roll, the usual hospitality offered by folks around here. She'd been so busy checking on various people in town regard-

ing the threatening letters that she'd forgotten to eat dinner.

She dismounted and tied Mack's reins to the rail, then strode to the back door. Charlotte Northam saw her through the mudroom glass and beckoned her inside.

"Welcome, Grace." The short, slightly plump lady—a second mother to Grace and her sisters— pulled a chair out from the kitchen table. "Have a seat. Marybeth will be downstairs in a few minutes. She and Rand have decided to move back to their place since everything's been quiet these past two months. Susanna and Nate have already gone back home."

"Thank you, ma'am." Grace took a seat and accepted the steaming cup of coffee her friend offered. A gray cat wound around her legs, and she reached down to scratch it behind its ears, trying to calm herself. "Hello, Fluffy." She took a sip of the hot coffee and let it slide down her throat. "When Susanna and Nate hear my news, they may turn around and move right back."

"What news?" Marybeth waddled into the kitchen, both hands on her round belly. Rather than sitting with her usual poise, she plunked down into a chair across from Grace and expelled a weary sigh. Poor thing. She had maybe a month to go before the baby was due.

With some effort, Grace dismissed the sad reminder that she would never be in that condition. Giving birth might be hard, even dangerous, but in her quiet, most truthful moments, especially after

spending time with her baby nephew, she admitted to herself how much she longed for a child of her own.

Instead of harboring such useless thoughts, she needed to stick to business. She pulled Hardison's letter from her vest pocket and shoved it across the table.

Eyes wide, Marybeth opened and read it, with Charlotte Northam right behind her.

"Lord, help us." The older lady put a hand to her lips, and her eyes reddened. "I have no doubt they mean to make good on their threats."

Marybeth just sat there staring.

"So you didn't get one of these letters?" Grace asked.

"No." Marybeth heaved out a long sigh. "At least not yet. Mother Northam, do you know where Rand is?"

"He and Nate took a load of hay out to the cattle in the near pasture." She took a step toward the door. "I'll get him."

Grace stood. "Let me go. I can do it faster."

"Thank you." Charlotte moved back to her daughter-in-law and hugged her shoulders. "Don't worry. Our menfolk will take care of everything." She glanced up at Grace. "And Grace, of course."

Grace couldn't take offense at being second fiddle to the Northam men in their mother's eyes. They were like brothers to her and her sisters, and she admired them as much as their own womenfolk did. "Where's the Colonel?"

"Oh, that husband of mine!" She sounded a mite peevish. "He took the train to Denver on business, in the middle of winter, of all things, when a snow-

storm could come along and close La Veta Pass for weeks. And after promising the children he wouldn't miss their Christmas play at the church."

"Hmm." Grace let it go. Maybe she'd be peeved with a husband under the circumstances, too. Of course, she'd never have a husband, so it was pointless to speculate. "I'll go see the boys."

"Tell them to watch out."

"Yes, ma'am." Grace touched the brim of her hat and headed out the door.

Before she reached the barnyard, Adam Starling drove up in the wagon he used for deliveries. Mrs. Winsted's fourteen-year-old grandson, Everett, sat on the bench beside him. Upon seeing her, Adam ducked his head.

"Howdy, Adam, Everett." Grace ambled over to the wagon and surveyed the boxes containing flour, sugar and other staples. "You boys delivering groceries?"

"Yessum." Adam didn't look her in the eye but jumped down and reached into the wagon for a box. His hair hung over his collar, and his dark boyish beard and mustache gave him a disreputable look.

Everett Winsted, tidy in every detail, including a fresh haircut, gave her an engaging smile. "Howdy, Deputy." The boy's round face and big blue eyes formed a picture of innocence, and he had a respectful manner to boot. Soon he'd be able to deliver groceries for his grandmother all by himself and wouldn't have to keep company with the likes of Adam Starling.

"Need any help?"

"No, ma'am." Adam still averted his eyes. "We

can manage." He started for the back door, followed by Everett.

She watched them for a few seconds, especially Adam. If that wasn't a guilty boy, she'd hang up her badge and take up knitting. She mounted Mack and headed out to the near pasture.

Rand saw her at a distance and stopped forking hay out of his wagon to meet her at the fence. Nate joined them.

"Howdy, Grace. What are you doing out this way on such a fine day?"

With the cold wind starting to pick up, the day was anything but fine. Grace just handed him her letter.

Reading over his brother's shoulder, Nate emitted a low whistle, but Rand sagged against the fence. "Marybeth." Without another word, he started toward his horse, which grazed on the hay near the wagon.

"She knows. I went to the big house first."

Rand paused, and Grace gave them a brief report, including Adam and Everett's delivery.

"You go on, Rand," Nate said. "I'll take care of the hay." As his brother rode away, he looked at Grace. "Would you mind going back and asking Adam to finish this, if he's still there?" He waved a hand toward the unfinished job of feeding the cattle herd. "I need to get to Susanna and the little ones and move them back up to the big house."

"Sure thing." Grace withheld her opinion of Adam. He was indeed a hard worker. But from the way he avoided her, wouldn't even look her in the eye, she had no doubt he was responsible for the thefts at the mercantile. Which probably meant he was also in cahoots with the outlaws. With his recent sloppy

appearance, maybe he was trying to look like his evil friends.

Riding back to the Northams' ranch house, she considered several motives for Adam's descent into crime. Maybe he was tired of working so hard. Or— she tried thinking charitably as the Rev always did— maybe the boy needed money for his father's illness. The old man would benefit from seeing a specialist in Denver, but the family couldn't afford it. Hardison was rumored to have a stash of money he'd stolen over the years. He could have offered Adam a hefty reward for helping him take revenge. A desperate sixteen-year-old boy who felt the weight of family responsibility on his young shoulders would have a hard time resisting such easy cash.

The question was, how could Grace learn the truth without giving away her suspicions to the boy? And without making the Rev cross with her? His good opinion was precious to her, and she hated the idea of losing his friendship over a boy who appeared to have taken a wrong path in life. Not that she didn't already need to cool that friendship due to Miss Sutton's presence.

Back at the house, she caught the two boys as they were driving away.

"Adam, Everett. Wait up." She cantered over and gave them her best friendly smile. "Can you all give a hand to the Northams by finishing up feeding their cattle?" She hooked a thumb over her shoulder. "Out in the near pasture?"

"Yes, ma'am!" Everett's blue eyes sparkled with excitement. "That'd be fun."

Grace chuckled. He was new to the West. Real soon, he'd get over the idea that ranch work was fun.

"Yessum." Once again refusing to look at her, Adam stared at the reins in his hands.

Yep, he was guilty all right. Now Grace just had to prove it.

Chapter Six

After editing his message for tonight's meeting and spending an hour or so working on his latest novel, Micah set the hymnals on the pews and then headed back to the parsonage. The moment he opened the kitchen door, the aroma of fried chicken set his mouth to watering. Miss Sutton stood at the stove, a frilly white apron covering her blue dress, a change from her traveling suit.

"Come on in, Reverend Thomas." She cast a quick smile over her shoulder. "Supper will be ready in about twenty minutes. Why don't you relax and read your newspaper? Joel fetched it from town when he went to buy the chicken."

For a moment, Micah could only stand and stare. Delicious, mouthwatering smells notwithstanding, why did he feel as if he'd suddenly become a guest in his own home?

Miss Sutton questioned him with another glance and one perfect, arched eyebrow.

"Yes. Yes, of course." He stepped toward the hall-

way door, then remembered his manners. "Supper smells wonderful, Miss Sutton."

"Why, thank you." She sounded as if the compliment came as a surprise, but her smug smile told a different story.

Micah couldn't fault her for being confident. Most ladies in Esperanza had high opinions of their own cooking. Some of them were right.

In the parlor, he greeted Joel and chatted with him for a few minutes before picking up the *Esperanza Journal*. Mindlessly skimming the stories, he wondered what Grace and Sheriff Lawson would think about a front page story exposing Hardison's presence in the area and his threats. He'd have to speak to them this evening at prayer meeting.

After supper, he and his guests walked over to the church. Miss Sutton didn't try too hard to hide her displeasure over using the back doors of both house and church. Micah would make sure to use front entrances when he escorted her in the future.

Supper had been filling but still left a lot to be desired. He couldn't fault the light, fluffy biscuits or the mashed potatoes and gravy. The chicken, on the other hand, couldn't be compared to Mrs. Foster's fried chicken. Maybe the older lady wouldn't mind telling Miss Sutton which spices she used to make hers so tender and tasty. Not exactly something Micah could recommend, but nothing kept him from praying about it. The Lord did say that His children could cast all of their cares on Him. Surely that included the food one ate. Micah chuckled to himself, then quickly dismissed his grin. Tonight's meeting was far too important for any kind of merriment.

People's lives were at stake, and as their pastor, he must set a sober tone to the gathering.

"Where would you like to sit?" Joel spoke to his sister as he gazed around the empty sanctuary.

"Why, what a charming little church." Bible in hand, Miss Sutton also studied the room. "I do believe it would be appropriate for us to sit on the front row with our host." She gave Micah a sidelong look and a smile. "If that's all right with you, Reverend Thomas."

"Certainly." Micah's collar suddenly seemed a bit tight.

To his relief, parishioners began to file into the sanctuary, most coming to the front to greet him. He presented each one to his guests, including newspaper owner and editor Fred Brody. Micah noticed a spark of interest in Fred's brown eyes as the tall, gangly young man bowed over Miss Sutton's gloved hand.

"Miss Sutton, I would be pleased if you and your brother would give me an interview for my newspaper's social column."

Social column? When did that debut? Micah gave Fred a questioning look, but the newsman had eyes only for the young lady.

"Why, we would be delighted, wouldn't we, Joel?" She gave Fred a cool smile, belying her words.

Her expression improved slightly when Micah introduced banker Nolan Means, who came with his sister, Anna. Nolan's eyes, like Fred's, sparked with interest as he kissed her hand.

"How nice to meet you." She sounded a bit more sincere this time. "Joel and I must come to your bank

tomorrow and arrange a transfer of some of our funds from our bank in Virginia."

"It will be my pleasure to serve you, ma'am." Nolan invited her to sit with Anna and him, but she politely declined.

"Perhaps next time? I feel it only appropriate to sit with our host tonight." She gave Micah another one of her simpering smiles, and again, his collar felt as if it had shrunk.

He didn't have time for this. Far more important matters must be attended to rather than flirting young misses. As if to punctuate his thoughts, Sheriff and Mrs. Lawson entered the church, with Grace and Mrs. Foster right behind them. Grace escorted Mrs. Foster to the organ and then joined her parents on the front row. Micah felt a pinch of disappointment when Grace didn't even look his way. He certainly could use her support, but recently she seemed to have taken a step back from their friendship. On the other hand, Sheriff Lawson didn't usually attend church on Wednesday nights, so his presence would reinforce the somber tone of the meeting.

As he went to greet the lawman, he saw in the corner of his eye that Miss Sutton had approached Grace and her parents, George and Mabel Eberly.

"I do believe you have our seats." She spoke in her well-modulated, finishing school tone, but there was an edge to her voice nonetheless.

Micah couldn't see the older Eberlys' expressions, but in profile he saw thunder on Grace's brow.

"Why, honey, there's plenty of room." Mabel Eberly, another one of those motherly women his congregation was blessed to have, stood and gave Miss

Sutton a warm embrace. "Just set yourself down by me, you and your brother. We're so glad to have you here visiting the parson."

One would think the dear lady had assaulted Miss Sutton. The younger woman stiffened, gasped and cast a quick, startled glance at Joel. Joel shrugged—his usual gesture when his sister gave him that look.

George Eberly also stood, shook hands with Joel and offered a welcoming word. Grace appeared to be busy with her Bible. Or maybe she was praying for patience. Micah sure was.

"Evening, Preacher." Sheriff Lawson gripped Micah's hand and gave it a hearty shake. "I know you're surprised to see me tonight. Wouldn't want to interfere with the prayers, but this is the closest thing we have to a community meeting here in Esperanza. When the rest of the folks arrive, do you mind if we talk about those notes everybody's getting? I found one on my desk an hour ago."

Hiding his alarm, Micah once again focused on the truly important issues. "Problems and prayers go hand in hand, Sheriff. Who else has received a note?"

"Andy and Frank, the two cowboys who guarded the outlaws over at the Del Norte jail. Nolan Means, though you wouldn't know it from that phony smile he's wearing. I expect he doesn't want to alarm young Anna. I have to credit him for that. Old Edward MacAndrews, of all people. Rand and Marybeth got theirs, one each, this afternoon out at Four Stones Ranch. Several people came by the place today on business, so no telling who left the notes. They were tucked under the boot scraper by the back door so somebody'd be sure to find them. I expect it's com-

mon knowledge that Rand and Marybeth are staying with his parents. I'm glad to see the whole Northam clan stayed home tonight, as I advised them."

Micah felt sick to his stomach. So the outlaws would even threaten a young expectant mother. Could such evil men be redeemed? Yes, the scriptures were filled with stories of vile sinners who came to Christ. Micah must keep believing, must keep teaching his congregation that redemption was for everyone and that God was fully aware of this danger now facing the community.

"Sheriff, what would you think of plastering this story all over the front page of the *Journal*?" As he spoke, Micah warmed to the subject. "Maybe include the pictures from the outlaws' wanted posters so newcomers to the area could see what they look like. Not only would that alert the community, but it would inform the outlaws that everyone is on the lookout for them. They won't be able to surprise anyone."

"Well..." The sheriff drawled out the word. "I'm not so sure about that." He scratched his jaw, making a rasping sound as his fingers combed over a day's growth of his salt-and-pepper beard. "Let me think on it for a bit."

The sanctuary soon filled to overflowing, with cowboys young and old standing at the rear so ladies and older folks could sit. If nothing else, this unusual burgeoning of midweek attendance, in the winter, no less, gave an indication that most everyone had heard about Hardison's threats. It meant the good people of Esperanza had every intention of joining with their neighbors to protect the community. While Micah would rather they all made a practice of coming on

a regular basis, maybe the Lord would use this occasion to show them the benefits of praying together. To that end, he took his place at the front of the room.

"Welcome, everyone. Shall we begin by standing and singing 'A Mighty Fortress Is our God'?"

Grace could hear Miss Sutton's voice clear down the row. She must be used to singing solos, because she sure did sing loud. But it was pretty, too. Not as pretty as Grace's sister Laurie's voice, but nice enough. A minister's wife should have a nice voice, so that boded well for the young lady's prospects with the Rev, especially if she also played the piano. Grace tried to be glad for him, but it wasn't easy. Maybe not even possible.

When Miss Sutton tried to get Grace's parents to move, Grace came near to telling her off. The Rev had always said nobody could claim a pew as their own in this church. If somebody wanted to sit on the front row, they could. Of course, most folks preferred to sit farther back, like Grace's sister Georgia, who sat in a middle row with some of her friends. But Miss Sutton just arrived in town today. Wasn't even a part of the community, at least not yet, so she had no call to displace anybody.

Of course, Ma had stood up and hugged that stuck-up lady. Grace wanted to laugh at the shock on the girl's face. Cold as a fish, that one. Her brother had just stood there and let his sister do the talking, and now they were all five squeezed into that one pew with no room for the Rev to sit with them. Oh, well. He usually stood at the front, so he wouldn't mind. From the lift of Miss Sutton's chin, she sure did.

Well, Grace minded her minding. Who did she think she was?

The familiar words of the song she'd begun to sing without thinking sifted into Grace's mind.

"Let goods and kindred go,
this mortal life also;
The body they may kill:
God's truth abideth still,
His kingdom is forever."

Grace forced her thoughts to the issue at hand. She could let goods and possessions go, but not her kindred, not her friends. It was her job to make sure no one in this community was killed by those outlaws, and she had every intention of making sure she protected them.

The song ended on a rousing "Amen," and everybody took their seats. The Rev took his place at the lectern and delivered a short sermon about evil not being able to prevail against the power of God. After he finished, he held up a piece of paper.

"Here are the prayer requests for tonight." He read the list, which included everything from financial needs—no names mentioned—to health issues to a child's prayer to have a pet dog. Kindhearted man that he was, the Rev believed in casting all care upon the Lord, no matter how trivial it might seem to others.

Included in the requests for health was one for Mr. Starling. Grace noticed none of the Starling family had attended, but they rarely did. Now if she could just figure out how Adam had managed to deliver all of those threatening letters without being noticed. It

chilled her to the bone that she hadn't caught him in the act at the Northams' ranch. She needed to be more watchful. Must never let herself get careless like that again.

After several folks stood and offered prayers for various requests, the Rev took his place on the platform again. "Before we have our closing prayer, we need to address the matter of Dathan Hardison and Deke Smith."

The room got quiet. Not a rustling paper or shuffling boot, not even a sniff or a cough disturbed the silence. Even Miss Sutton froze in place, which made her look like a porcelain doll—and just as empty-headed. Guilt pinched Grace's conscience. The woman couldn't help being beautiful any more than Grace could help being too tall.

"I'll turn the meeting over to Sheriff Lawson." The Rev sat on the opposite side of the room, his handsome face creased with concern. Not worry. Just concern. Grace admired that about him. She wished she could have as much faith that God would look out for the good people of Esperanza. If He was looking out, Hardison and Smith never would have escaped the Cañon City State Penitentiary in the first place.

The sheriff stood and moved to the front of the room, and everyone else sat up and took notice. Tall and broad-shouldered, Lawson inspired confidence with his no-nonsense, take-charge bearing.

"No need to tell you what this is about," the sheriff said. "You all know Hardison and Smith escaped from prison." He went on to explain about the threatening letters and who had received them, himself included. For some reason, he didn't mention the letters

were written on stationery stolen from Mrs. Winsted's mercantile. Grace would ask him about that later.

"Reverend Thomas had the idea that we should put pictures of these varmints on the front page of the newspaper." He looked at Fred Brody. "That all right with you?"

"Yes, sir. A fine idea. I'll—"

"Good." The sheriff wasn't one to let people ramble on, and Fred could talk the rattles off a rattlesnake. "We'll make sure everybody in Rio Grande and Alamosa Counties has a copy of the paper. With that many people on the lookout, these outlaws won't be able to make a move without somebody seeing them. If you do see 'em, report their location to me or to Deputy Eberly." He narrowed his eyes and surveyed the room, making eye contact with numerous people. "I don't want a single one of you to take on these men. Is that understood?"

A hum of "yessir" and "wouldn't think of it" filled the sanctuary. Grace wanted to add that they could also tell the Rev, but it might sound like she was contradicting her boss. That wasn't the way she operated.

"Now, I want everybody to go about your business just like you would any other time." The sheriff turned to the Rev. "You can proceed with your plans for the young'uns' Christmas pageant." He turned to the banker. "Nolan, I suppose you'll be having your fancy dress Christmas ball up at your house. Go on with that. The Northams planned to have the children out to their place after the pageant as usual, but we'll change that to the church reception hall. On a day-to-day basis, everybody can come to town for shopping, that sort of thing. Just be on the lookout."

After another prayer from the Rev, the folks began to file out of their pews with little conversation. Then Mrs. Foster began a spirited rendition of "Onward Christian Soldiers," and everybody stuck around to sing several verses. Good old Mrs. Foster was sending them off with a fine, encouraging hymn. Too bad encouraging hymns didn't keep people safe.

Two days after the prayer meeting, Micah had just stepped into the sheriff's office when news arrived that the first of the outlaws' threats had become a reality. Andy Ransom, one of the cowboys who'd guarded Hardison and Smith while they'd awaited trial, rode into town to report that his expensive collection of whittling equipment had been destroyed.

"Not only that, but all the dolls and soldiers I'd whittled for the children's Christmas party are broken to bits." Shoulders slumped in dejection, Andy stood in front of the sheriff's desk rolling his hat in his hands. "I've been working on those all year." He straightened as if dismissing his heartbreak. "That's not all. Frank's saddle was slashed so bad he can't use it."

"Is Mrs. Lewis all right?" Micah felt sick to his stomach over this latest development. He would go see her right away.

Andy nodded. "Scared but unhurt. The poor old gal is a mite deaf, so she didn't hear a sound yesterday while Frank and I were out feeding the herd. It was dark when we got back to the bunkhouse, so I waited until this morning to report to you. Frank stayed to clean up the mess. And to be there for poor Mrs. Lewis."

"Cowards." Sheriff Lawson stood and strapped on his gun belt, then pulled out his Colt .45 and spun the chamber to be sure it was fully loaded. "I'll go out there and see what I can see. Grace." He called toward the back room.

"Yessir." She came through the door carrying a broom, no doubt from sweeping out the jail cells. Seeing Micah, she gasped and her eyes widened in surprise. "Something wrong, Rev?"

He was a bit surprised himself at the odd little lift of his heart over seeing her. It had been two days since prayer meeting, but he'd somehow missed her. Maybe it was those two days with Miss Sutton…

Grace brushed the back of her hand across her face, leaving a smudge on one cheek that made her look incredibly winsome.

Micah couldn't help but smile. "Hello, Grace."

"Ahem." The sheriff cleared his throat noisily and nodded toward Andy. "Andy here tells me the outlaws have made good on their threats." He repeated what the cowboy had said. "I'm going out there now."

"I'll go with you." She disappeared briefly and returned without the broom—or the smudge on her cheek.

"Sheriff," Micah said, "do you mind if I go along, too? I'd like to see how Mrs. Lewis is doing." He didn't like the idea of the spunky widow being frightened in her own home.

The sheriff gave him a curt nod. "My horse is saddled, so I'll head out with Andy. You two come when you're ready." He walked toward the door, then turned back. "Have Homer Bean come over from the

mercantile and watch things here in case something else happens."

"I'll talk to Homer," Grace said to Micah as she tugged on her winter jacket. "You head over to the livery stable and get our horses."

"Yes, ma'am." Micah doffed his hat to her, trying to lighten the moment.

She snorted as she walked out the door.

At the livery stable, Adam Starling made quick work of saddling Mack for Grace and Ginger for Micah. Then, oddly, he made himself scarce when Grace arrived. Micah still hadn't convinced her that Adam couldn't be the thief, but surely no one would ever think the youth could destroy someone else's property or frighten an elderly widow.

They rode east into a brisk, icy wind, which made it impossible to talk. Micah's ears stung, and his lungs ached. And yet, just being in Grace's company made the ride bearable for him. If this hardy young woman could tolerate such discomfort in order to do her duty, he could, too.

At the ranch, Sheriff Lawson had already searched the bunkhouse and now circled the house to look for any signs of damage or loss. Andy and Frank followed him, answering questions.

Micah knocked on the back door. "Mrs. Lewis, do you mind if we come in?"

The widow opened the door, and when she saw him, her eyes filled with tears, just as they had when Micah had come out to comfort her in the loss of her husband several years ago. Wearing a black woolen dress and knitted gray shawl, she seemed to have shrunk in those years, and now she trembled. With

Grace right behind him, Micah stepped inside and pulled the old woman into his arms.

"It's all right, Mrs. Lewis." He swallowed his indignation over the senseless acts that had frightened her so badly. It was never easy to hold on to his emotions when one of his flock was suffering, but he needed to stay strong so he could offer comfort. "We're here now. We'll take care of you."

Watching the Rev comforting the old widow, Grace felt something melt inside of her. What a good, good man. How could she not feel such strong affection for him? Hopeless affection, but affection nonetheless. She had to admit it to herself or bust.

She moved closer and patted the lady's shoulder. "Ma'am, I'm so sorry for the scare, but I don't think those outlaws will be back."

Mrs. Lewis lifted her tearstained face from the Rev's shoulder. "You don't?"

"No, ma'am." Grace shoved her hat off and let it hang on its leather strings down her back. "The outlaws are out to get the people who they think caused them trouble. They had it in for Frank and Andy, but you never crossed them, so you're safe."

Mrs. Lewis looked at the Rev as if seeking his agreement. Somehow Grace didn't mind. The important thing was to make sure the lady felt safe, no matter whose words did the job.

"That's right." He squeezed the lady's shoulder. "Now, how about you and I fix some coffee for the sheriff and Grace while they look around for clues."

She gave him a sweet, maternal smile. "That'll

be fine." She headed for the kitchen with the Rev right behind her.

Grace took that as her cue to get busy with her job. She found the sheriff outside with the cowhands.

"With no new snow for the past few days," he said, "it's hard to see anything unusual. Stone and Ransom have ridden or walked all over the place. The sun's a bit warm today, so it'll probably turn to an icy slush pretty soon."

"Do we really need clues?" Grace didn't intend to sound harsh, but her words brought a cross look from the sheriff. "Sorry. It's just that—"

He waved a dismissive hand. "Never mind. I know what you mean." He stared off toward Mount Blanca on the east side of the San Luis Valley. "I'm frustrated, too. Where could these varmints be hiding? More than that, who could be helping them?"

Grace shrugged. "Maybe somebody new to the community?"

He gave her a sidelong look. "Could be. Let's start by investigating anybody who's moved in since the prison break."

"Yessir." Grace would also investigate some slightly older residents. She would start with the Starling family.

The sheriff stuck around for the promised coffee, but as they sat at the kitchen table, Grace could see his boot tapping on the floor, which meant he was impatient to leave. On the other hand, the Rev was his usual relaxed self, a trait Grace admired in him even though she was as anxious as the sheriff to get after the outlaws.

Always insightful, the Rev discerned their moods.

"You two go ahead. I'll stay with Mrs. Lewis for a while longer." He patted the lady's hand across the table.

"Thanks." Sheriff Lawson wasted no time accepting the offer. As he stood and put on his hat, he gave Mrs. Lewis a slight bow. "Thank you for the coffee, ma'am." Then he headed out the door.

"Ma'am?" Like the Rev, Grace had an insight of her own. "How would you like to stay at Mrs. Foster's tonight?"

She brightened up right away. "Oh, do you think she'd mind?"

Grace shook her head. "She's got plenty of room now that the hotel's opened up. I'll help you get ready." As much as she wanted to leave, this was the proper thing to do.

"Oh, now, Grace." The lady spoke with artificial indignation. "I'm not so old that I can't pack a few things for myself."

"And I can stay and drive Mrs. Lewis into town, Grace." The Rev gave her his kindliest smile, the one that always quickened her pulse. "You go on."

"I'll take you up on that, Rev."

Grace hurried out the door after the sheriff, more to get away from her feelings for the Rev than to do her duty. She sure did wish he'd hurry up and marry that Miss Sutton so she could quit feeling so drawn to him. As she mounted Mack, she snorted at her own foolish thoughts. The Rev marrying Miss Sutton was the furthest thing from what she wished. And yet she had no doubt that was exactly what was going to happen.

Chapter Seven

Grace had delayed visiting the Starlings because she couldn't figure out a credible reason to do so. She hadn't mentioned her suspicions about Adam to Sheriff Lawson because he seemed partial to the boy, just like the Rev was. Like many people in town, even Grace before this mess began, the sheriff often paid Adam to saddle his horse or deliver messages for him or run other errands. While Adam needed those jobs to support his family, the way Grace saw it was that they also gave him the perfect opportunity to deliver the threatening messages.

Grace finally decided to grab the bull by the horns. She took a shirt to Mrs. Starling for mending. While she could have quickly repaired the rip in the sleeve herself, this gave her a chance to do something kind for the family. They'd sure need plenty of kindness when Adam was caught helping the outlaws.

When they'd first come to Esperanza less than two years ago, the Starlings lived over the Chinese laundry. Recently, after Widow Beal remarried and took her sewing business to San Francisco, the family of

five moved into her roomier wood frame house near the railroad. While the house had only two bedrooms, it did have a kitchen and dining area, and front and back parlors. Mrs. Beal had used the front parlor to display the dresses she made, but Mavis Starling put it back to its original purpose as a sitting room. Bob Starling occupied the back parlor. He still hadn't healed from the beating he'd suffered at the hands of outlaws down near Santa Fe. About the time he'd seemed to get better, he'd taken a turn for the worse. Still, Mavis remained cheerful and full of faith as she raised and supported her three children, and another one on the way.

Grace felt guilty for thinking ill of the woman's eldest son. But then, it was her job to uphold the law, and she couldn't ignore the way Adam avoided her. Odd that he didn't avoid Sheriff Lawson. Or the Rev, either. Maybe he knew he had them fooled.

"Welcome, Grace." Mavis opened the door wide to let her in, despite the cold breeze blowing in from the northeast. "What brings you here today?"

Feeling very much as if she were lying, Grace held out her second-best plaid flannel shirt. "Caught this on some barbed wire out at my folks' ranch last weekend and wondered if you could mend it for me." That was the truth.

"Of course." Mavis didn't ask why Grace didn't just sew it herself. "Come on in. Will you have some coffee?"

More guilt flooded Grace over the woman's kind hospitality and her own purpose for being here. "No, ma'am." Grace had a feeling that if Adam had stolen one of the blue-and-white coffeepots from the

mercantile, it wouldn't be here but with the outlaws. Still, she needed to check. "On second thought, yes, that would be nice."

The kitchen was warm and cozy and smelled of fresh-baked bread. Four-year-old Jack sat at the table eating a biscuit.

"Hey, there, little man." Grace ruffled his dark brown hair as she sat beside him.

He ducked his head shyly. Just like Adam.

Grace glanced toward the hallway leading to the back parlor. A vague hint of sickroom smell occasionally blended with the more pleasant aromas of the kitchen. "How's Bob?"

As Mavis poured coffee for Grace from a well-used black pot, her eyes turned red. "Oh, as well as can be expected." She bit her lip. "Doc Henshaw thinks his pleurisy was brought on by this hard winter weather. If we could move to a warmer climate…" She cleared her throat. "Will you have some cake?" She gestured toward a freshly made cake on the sideboard that looked just the right size to feed a family of five.

"No, ma'am." Grace patted her belly. "Everybody likes to feed the visiting deputy." Nobody had fed her today, but Mavis didn't need to know that. It was still a fact.

Mavis laughed softly. "And the preacher."

Before she could stop herself, Grace jolted. "Did the Rev stop by?"

"Yes. He came to visit Bob and, like you, brought some mending for me to do." She chuckled softly. "I think he could have managed to tighten those shirt

buttons himself, but he's kind to help us out that way."

Grace felt heat rising up her neck. Here she'd thought herself so clever. She drank her coffee to hide her embarrassment.

"Bob was greatly encouraged by the visit, of course. Reverend Thomas has a way about him that soothes the worried soul."

"That's true." Grace hadn't felt soothed in the Rev's company for some time now, but she sure couldn't say that to Mavis. Instead, she looked around the kitchen, trying not to be obvious in her search for clues. Nothing out of the ordinary here. Too bad she couldn't ask for a tour of the house. Instead she asked after Mavis's two other children.

"Adam and Molly are in school." She gazed out the window and smiled. "Molly's in first grade and loves it. Adam loves school, too. I think he'd like to be a history teacher." Her eyes filled. "I don't know how we'd ever manage his education."

Grace reached over and patted her hand as she'd seen the Rev do for Mrs. Lewis.

Mavis gripped her hand and gave her a grateful smile. "Thank you."

What was she doing here? This wasn't investigating. She had to do something, say something.

"Mavis, have you heard about the threats—"

"Shh!" Mavis eyed her small son. "Jack, run along to your room and play with your blocks."

The boy quickly complied—a testament to Mavis's good parenting. Adam had probably been reared by the same methods. What could have gone wrong with him?

"Yes," Mavis said. "We've heard. You know we didn't move here until after those outlaws were sent to prison. Reverend Thomas said they probably wouldn't waste their time harming people who'd done them no harm." She blew a wayward strand of hair from in front of her eyes. "After the way Bob was beaten half to death even after he gave the robbers the railroad payroll money he was carrying, I'm not sure I agree. Those sorts don't care whom they hurt. So I keep telling Adam to be careful." She bit her lip. "I try to have faith, but if anything ever happened to Adam, I don't know what we'd do."

For the first time since the troubles began, a thread of doubt about his guilt wove through Grace's mind. Why would a young man from such a close, caring family risk all of their futures by throwing in with desperate outlaws?

A rasping, barking cough from the back parlor, followed by a cry of pain, answered her question. What loving son wouldn't look for every chance to help his sickly father? Even if it meant breaking the law.

"I cannot imagine what happened to my cake." Her pretty face a study in misery, Miss Sutton held out the pan to show Micah and Joel the freshly cooked, lopsided, barely risen pastry. "This has never happened to me before."

"Why, no, of course not." Joel walked across the kitchen and put an arm around her waist. "You're an excellent cook, Elly." He looked at Micah with a hint of accusation in his eyes. "Could something be wrong with your stove?"

Micah coughed softly into his hand to keep from laughing. "I won't say it's not the stove. However, at this altitude, most recipes need to be adjusted. At least that's what I've heard Miss Pam say."

The brother and sister looked at each other doubtfully.

"Miss Pam?" Miss Sutton blinked her blue eyes. "Does she cook at the hotel?"

"No. She has her own business, Williams's Café on Main Street, two doors down from the mercantile," Micah said. "Why don't we go there for dinner today? I'm sure she wouldn't mind helping you."

Miss Sutton's face went through a series of expressions, none of which, Micah was certain, she had learned at finishing school. Indignation. Wariness. Defeat. And finally, determination.

"I'll fetch my hat and coat." She set the failed cake back on the stovetop and hurried from the kitchen.

Micah grabbed a hot pad and pulled the pan to safety before the heat further ruined it. "It looks like the cake I once tried to bake. Flat as a pancake, but not bad on the taste buds. Want to try some?"

"Sure thing." Joel laughed. "Can't let it go to waste."

They munched a few bites of the chewy concoction and agreed it was worth saving for later. Maybe they could even add icing or at least molasses.

The two-block walk to the café took less time than usual, even with the blustery wind trying to impede their progress. Miss Sutton marched toward her goal like a soldier determined to scale an enemy's wall. Micah had to admire her resolve. For all of her hau-

hands with each. In the back of his mind, he wondered whether Miss Sutton had planned enough food to feed these extra guests. Before he could hail her across the sanctuary, Grace stepped up beside him.

"You doing all right, Rev?" She eyed the two bodyguards and, after Micah introduced her, along with her title, broadened her smile. "Welcome to Esperanza. It'll be good to have some experienced lawmen to help us out here."

"A lady deputy, eh?" Gareau grunted. "Pinkerton's used women to solve crimes for many years now, so I suppose it's no wonder."

Micah noticed a gleam of approval, perhaps even attraction, in both men's eyes. Oddly, a surge of protectiveness rose up inside of him. "Grace, I'm having Nolan and Anna over for dinner. Will you join us?" Where had those words come from?

Her pretty blue eyes flared briefly in surprise. "Well…"

"By all means, you must come." Miss Sutton joined the group and looped an arm around Grace's. Even though Grace tugged against her grasp, Miss Sutton held firm. "We actually need another lady to balance our party, so do say yes."

The expression on Grace's face could only be called comical, although Micah was probably the only one to notice the combination of shock, horror, puzzlement and—resignation?—that swept across her pretty face. Pretty? Yes, she truly was, especially in her present confusion.

She gave a little shrug and at last pulled away from Miss Sutton. "I need to tell Georgia I won't be going out to the ranch."

Grace's youngest sister stood across the room chatting with Adam Starling. As Grace marched toward them, Adam ducked away.

Micah sighed. If Adam knew Grace suspected him of colluding with the outlaws, would he avoid her that way? When the appropriate time came, Micah would make sure he told him, but only if he could do so without crushing the boy's fragile spirits. He had enough weighing on his young shoulders and didn't need the extra burden of Grace's distrust.

Nothing could have surprised Grace more than being invited to this fancy "do." Not that her own ma hadn't entertained a great deal over the years. But lately the white linen tablecloths hadn't come out quite so often with three of her daughters now living away from home and Grace staying in town. Just a few days ago, Georgia informed her that she, Ma and Pa always ate in the kitchen these days.

Today in the parsonage, Miss Sutton had set out her very own damask table linens and china brought from Virginia. She'd also put together a fine feast, with a large beef roast, mashed potatoes, gravy, winter squash, fresh-baked bread, not to mention apple pie covered in fresh cream for dessert. She'd had to get up mighty early in the morning to prepare this meal.

Now that Grace saw what a fine hostess Miss Sutton was, she surrendered all hope that the Rev wouldn't marry the Southern belle. For her own part, she'd rather be talking with the two lawmen to see if she could learn some new ideas about catching criminals. Instead, Justice and Sean stood outside

guarding the front and back doors, while Grace was stuck in the kitchen helping Miss Sutton, along with fourteen-year-old Anna.

If it had been Grace and her sisters, they would have been laughing loudly and teasing as they worked. Miss Sutton set a different tone in "her" kitchen, with all sorts of gracious ways to instruct her two helpers to do this or that. Part of that graciousness was sending Anna out with sandwiches and coffee to Justice and Sean. Grace appreciated the thoughtfulness. She wouldn't have much appetite thinking of the two men standing outside both cold and hungry.

When they finally sat down in the dining room, Miss Sutton partnered each female with one of the men. Of course as hostess, she sat at one end of the table, and as host, the Rev sat at the other. Grace had to admit they made nice bookends for the table. Miss Sutton instructed Grace to sit beside Nolan and adjacent to the Rev, and Joel and Anna to sit opposite of them. Grace's sister Beryl had attended finishing school and had taught her sisters all about this sort of proper seating, male, then female, and so on. At the Eberly house, though, folks just grabbed a seat wherever they wanted and sat by whomever they chose.

After the Rev said grace and the serving dishes had been passed around, they all fell to eating and talking. Miss Sutton directed the conversation toward pleasant subjects. How soon could one begin to garden here in the San Luis Valley? Would roses grow here? Or tomatoes? Did anyone ever organize a musical gala? Had they invited well-known opera singers to stop here on their tours across the coun-

try? And then she asked the question that almost had Grace setting down her fork and walking out.

"Will all of the children I met this morning be participating in the Christmas play?" Miss Sutton addressed the Rev down the length of the short table. "I want to be sure to write a part for every one of them."

Grace didn't bother to pay attention to his response. So it was settled. After every unattached female had been chasing him for the past seven years, the Rev had finally found his perfect wife. Grace swallowed a bite of surprisingly tasty roast beef, but it lodged in her throat. Which had chosen that moment to close as if to shut down her emotions.

"Why, Miss Sutton." Nolan's appetite was in its usual fine form. With manners appropriate for a banker, he still managed to clean his plate. "How generous of you to take on such a project. Are you certain you can manage such a large group of children?"

She laughed in her musical way. Grace wished her own laugh was as pretty. In her family, she and her four sisters had always been having too much fun to worry about how their laughter sounded. Most of the time, it came out fairly boisterous, although Beryl and Laurie had toned it down after being away at school.

"Why, Mr. Means, a mere seventeen children are nothing compared to the thirty I taught in my Sunday school class back home in Virginia."

Even in profile, Grace could see the admiring expression on Nolan's face. As for the Rev, he still wore his pastoral face. Was he just good at hiding his feelings? Or…

"You will do an excellent job," Nolan said. "I am sure of it." He took a sip of coffee. "Anna could help you, if you like." He looked across the table and gave his sister an encouraging nod.

"Oh, yes, Miss Sutton. Do let me help."

For several moments, the conversation was taken up with Nolan, Anna and Miss Sutton discussing a schedule for practices, with reassurances from Nolan that Sean would be at Anna's side to protect them all.

At the Rev's insistence, Justice and Sean were invited in for dessert. The two grateful lawmen thanked Miss Sutton, as if it had been her idea.

After dinner and dishwashing, Grace excused herself to go on her rounds of the town. At least that was what she told everyone. In truth, she couldn't bear to watch all of those men admiring Miss Sutton's every word and action. Maybe Grace was being petty, but she was also being honest, at least with herself. As she'd known for a long time, she just wasn't the type of woman men were attracted to. Best accept that and get on with life, doing what she could for her community.

Micah knew a budding romance when he saw one, and in his seven years as pastor of this church, he'd never been wrong. The looks passing between Miss Sutton and Nolan Means sparkled like fireworks on Independence Day. Micah couldn't be happier. Poor Nolan had been seeking a suitable wife for a banker since he came to town several years ago, only to lose out to the Northam brothers and Garrick Wakefield. But he'd never looked at Susanna, Marybeth or Rosamond the way he now looked at Miss Sutton. As

for the young lady, she had never smiled at Micah the way she now beamed at Nolan. Nor did she seem the slightest bit concerned over the outlaws' threats against the banker, an indication that she possessed more of that grit he'd noticed the other day.

What a relief. Micah would do everything he could to promote their growing attachment. But where did that leave him, especially since the Lord still seemed to bend his heart toward marriage? How long had Isaac waited for Rebecca? How long had the journey been for Abraham's servant, who traveled to fetch her? Micah could only suppose the Lord wanted him to be patient. He chuckled to himself. *Yes, Lord, I know I need patience, but could I have it right now?*

Yet all the good humor he could muster didn't solve his marriage dilemma.

Chapter Eight

On Monday morning, Grace and the Rev rode behind Sheriff Lawson as they picked their way through the rolling hills west of town, trying to track the outlaws' path away from the MacAndrewses' burned-out house. No new snow had fallen, but just as at Mrs. Lewis's place, too many people had trampled the ground around the property to get a clean boot or hoofprint to connect to anyone outside the community.

Late yesterday, the day after the fire, however, the sheriff had found an unusual hoofprint some distance away leading southwest. It matched the description Grace and the Rev had given him of the one they saw at the broken-down ranch. This morning, when he tried to round up a posse, pickings had been slim. With only Grace and the Rev available, they decided to do a preliminary search and then gather more men if they found a promising trail to follow.

Grace tried to keep her mind on the task at hand, but it was more difficult than she'd expected being out here with the Rev today. Other than his usual

concern about the outlaws, he seemed real happy. Had he and Miss Sutton already come to an understanding? The woman hadn't been in Esperanza for a full week, hardly time for two sensible people to fall in love. Well, one sensible man and a slightly flighty female. But Grace supposed love did crazy things to a person, even a levelheaded minister of the Gospel. *Humph!* What did she know about romantic love anyway?

"Penny for your thoughts." The Rev rode up beside her, pastoral concern on his brow.

Grace started. Had he heard her sound of disgust? Best to head off his insightful probing. "Now, there you go insulting me, Rev. My thoughts are worth considerably more than a penny." She shot him a playful grin like she'd give one of her sisters.

He laughed, that deep, throaty chuckle she liked entirely too much. "Yes, I would think so. What would you say to fifty cents—?"

A rifle shot sounded in the distance. In a split second, Sheriff Lawson tumbled from his saddle without so much as a yip and rolled behind a large boulder. Grace and the Rev sprang from their horses and, crouching low, hastened to his crumpled form. His horse had spooked and now stood shuddering some ten yards away. While Grace watched for the shooter, the Rev cleared small rocks from the ground and turned Lawson onto his back to reveal a bloody hole in his coat on the left side of his chest just above his heart.

"Sheriff. Sheriff." Gently touching his face, Grace kept her voice low, although the shooter had to be at least two hundred feet away.

The sheriff groaned—the best sound she'd heard all day.

"He's alive."

"Yes. Praise the Lord." The Rev opened the sheriff's coat. "It's above the heart, and the blood's not dark red, but that doesn't mean he's not in danger." He coughed and cleared his throat, and Grace guessed he was working to keep his emotions in check. She sure was.

"Lord, save this good man." The Rev tore off his gloves, removed his own jacket and rolled it to make a pillow for Lawson's head. "Grace, we can't get him back to town on horseback or he might bleed to death. Will you be all right here while I go get the doctor and a wagon?"

"Yep. Let me get my rifle first." She whistled for Mack, and the gelding ambled toward her. The Rev's horse followed along. Even the sheriff's mount moved closer.

"Thank the Lord for these boulders." The Rev eyed the cluster of giant rocks giving them cover.

"Yeah." Grace didn't feel very grateful right now, but she wouldn't tell him. Instead, she gripped his arm. "You be careful."

He placed his hand over hers. "I will. You, too."

In spite of their dire circumstances, Grace felt warmth slide up her arm and into her heart. It wasn't her usual giddy reaction to him, but more like a Christian bonding. A feeling that together they would save the sheriff, perhaps even the town. A feeling that together they could accomplish anything.

As the Rev rode away, Grace shook her head. Such foolish musings. Best to stick to what she knew best.

After tying the horses to some dried-out scrub and retrieving canteens and blankets from behind their saddles, she settled down to keeping an eye out for the outlaws and, more important, keeping the sheriff warm and alive.

Micah sat with Grace in the hallway outside Doc Henshaw's surgery. For over an hour, after comforting the sheriff's wife, he'd been praying—pleading actually—for the sheriff's life, just as he had for Grace's sister Beryl three years before. The trip over the rocky terrain on the way back to town had caused more bleeding, and the sheriff still hadn't regained consciousness by the time they reached Doc's house. Perhaps that had been a mercy.

Because the undertaker's hearse was the only conveyance that could accommodate the gravely wounded man in any kind of comfort, its arrival back in Esperanza had caused no little stir. Micah had ridden alongside to reassure everyone on the street that the sheriff hadn't died and to urge them to pray. At present, his own faith dipped with each muted sound coming from beyond the surgery door. After yesterday's brave sermon, he was setting a poor example for his parishioners. But then, he'd always found it better to be authentic and truthful rather than to put on a facade.

When she learned of her husband's injury, Mrs. Lawson wept, of course, but she told Micah that being married to a lawman had toughened her more than her tears suggested. This wasn't Abel's first gunshot wound at the hands of an outlaw. Still, worn out from

crying, Mrs. Lawson now reclined on the settee in the parlor to rest up for whatever came next.

Grace heaved a sigh. "Sometimes God doesn't do things the way we think He should."

Micah's heart warmed over this unexpected expression of faith, and he gave her a sidelong look, questioning her with one lifted eyebrow.

"Well, isn't that true? Don't you always say that?"

"Thanks. Just what I needed to hear." He tried to laugh, but it came out more as a grunt.

She nudged him with her elbow. "Do you mean to tell me you sometimes have doubts?"

He clicked his tongue and shook his head. "Yep. Sure do."

"What happened to 'all things work together for the good'?"

His feelings still close to the surface, he shook his head. "I don't know."

Her expression softened with understanding. "I won't tell anybody."

"It's all right if you do. People shouldn't think I'm above human feelings. I laugh and cry and grieve the same as anyone else. And yes, sometimes I doubt. Then I have to remind myself that God's love isn't defined by life's circumstances but by His own character." The thought briefly warmed him. Then the sheriff's desperate situation came to mind, and he had to reject the unbelief that tried to settle in his heart. "It's not always easy to believe that when bad things happen. As you said, when God doesn't do things the way we think He should."

She gave him a soft, sweet smile. "That's why you're such a good pastor. As it says in Hebrews 4:15,

you're touched with the feelings of our infirmities, just like the Lord."

"Thank you, but please don't assign me too much credit, or I'll fall flat on my face."

"You?" She nudged him again. "No, not you."

The pocket door leading to the surgery slid open, and Doc Henshaw stepped into the hallway wiping bloody hands on a white cloth.

Micah and Grace stood to meet him.

"Where's Mrs. Lawson?" Doc looked through the open door of the parlor and walked toward it.

Grace reached out and touched his arm. "How's the sheriff?"

Before he could respond, Mrs. Lawson appeared in the parlor doorway. "Is he…?"

"He's a tough old hombre." Doc had picked up Western jargon pretty well in the six years he'd been in Esperanza, something Micah had chosen not to do. But then, Doc was married to Grace's older sister, Maisie, and the Eberly girls were known for their interesting word choices. "He'll be laid up for a while, but he'll make it."

Mrs. Lawson sagged against the doctor, not seeming to mind the blood on his white canvas apron. He patted her back. Grace hiccoughed and sniffed. Micah cleared his throat and swallowed hard. *Thank You, Lord.*

"If you're ready, let's go see him." As Doc walked the lady toward the surgery, he eyed Micah and Grace. "Give her a minute, then come on in."

Soon Maisie, who served as her husband's nurse, came out and invited them into the room. Across the way on a low cot, the sheriff lay with his chest

swathed in bandages and his wife seated beside him. Grace approached and scolded him with a few teasing words. By the time his turn came to speak to the lawman, Micah had sufficiently regained his composure so he could appreciate Sheriff Lawson's attempt at humor.

"Forgot to duck," he said with a groan. Once the uneasy chuckles died away, he added, "Pastor, I know you've been praying for me, but could you say a few more words to the Almighty about this broken-down old lawman?"

"Oh, hush." Mrs. Lawson gently patted his shoulder. "You have many good years left to keep the peace. Doesn't he, Doc?" She gave Doc a hopeful, almost-pleading look.

"If he takes it easy and gives himself plenty of time to heal before trying to take on those outlaws again." Doc gave the sheriff a stern look.

"Well, then," Micah said, "I'll pray you'll be willing to rest so you won't interfere with the Lord's healing process."

It was late afternoon when Micah and Grace left Doc's house. Without a word passing between them, they walked to Williams's Café, where they ordered soup, fresh rolls and coffee to ward off the chill of the day.

After a few minutes of thoughtful silence, Grace blew out a long sigh. "I guess you realize it's up to me and you now."

He knew exactly what she meant. "You're right, of course, but I think we ought to have the sheriff deputize a half dozen or so other men." A slight frown crossed Grace's forehead, so he quickly added, "And

women, too. Mrs. Winsted played a big part in keeping Hardison and Smith in check after they tried to rob the bank. She's as handy with a rifle as anyone."

Now Grace blinked, and her jaw slacked briefly. "That's true. She did. And yet she didn't receive a threatening letter."

"Hmm." Micah considered the idea for a moment. "If the person who's stealing her merchandise is in cahoots with the outlaws—" there he went, using Western jargon, after all "—they probably don't want to risk losing their source of survival supplies."

"I ought to just lock up Adam Starling and put an end to it."

Leah arrived with their order, so Micah had to wait to respond. Once he'd given thanks for their food, he took a few bites of the steaming bean and bacon soup. In his own conversations with Adam, he hadn't seen the slightest hint of guilt. In fact, the boy often asked questions about the scriptures that sent Micah to his commentaries for answers. Not many in the congregation did that. "I still think you're wrong about Adam."

"Because you always think the best about everybody." Grace buttered a roll and took a bite with an exaggerated flourish, as if to make it clear she didn't mean to compliment him.

"Not always." He shrugged. "But I do believe in giving people chances to prove themselves."

"Hmm." Grace concentrated on eating her meal for several minutes. "That was good news about Miss Sutton directing the Christmas pageant. I was surprised when Nolan suggested Anna could help. He's usually very protective of his sister."

Micah took the hint. He wouldn't be able to convince Grace that Adam was innocent without solid evidence. "That's true. I'm quite relieved to have the pageant in competent hands."

"Something just occurred to me." She gazed out the window thoughtfully. "It seemed the outlaws were waiting to ambush us."

Another change of subject. "Maybe just one of them, since there was only one shot."

"Huh. Makes no sense." Her eyes narrowed as she looked at him across the table. "This morning when the sheriff was trying to round up a posse, who did he ask?"

Micah could only tell her what she already knew. "He asked Joel, but I insisted that he stay with his sister. No townsfolk were free to leave work, and none of the trusted cowboys happened to be in town. I think he realized most of the ranchers are still busy preparing for a long winter, because he didn't take the time to ride out to Four Stones Ranch to ask Nate and Rand." He had a feeling he knew what her next question would be.

"Did he speak to Adam?"

He was right. "I don't know, but I'm sure you do." He huffed out a cross breath. "You know he spoke to every able-bodied person in town, so he must have spoken to Adam."

"And Adam could have ridden out to warn his friends."

In spite of his long, hard day and delayed dinner, Micah's appetite disappeared. Apparently Grace's did, too, because she laid her napkin beside her plate and hailed Leah to pay the bill. Once the waitress

took her money—she paid for Micah's meal without asking, which didn't sit well with him considering their current conversation—Grace stood and adjusted her gun belt. "I'm gonna find him right now."

Micah stood, too. "Will you let me question him instead?"

"What, and let him get spooked and run away?"

"Grace!" Maybe it was the events of the day finally crashing down on him, but Micah couldn't hold on to his rising anger. To his relief, no other customers were in the café.

As it was, Miss Pam stuck her head out through the kitchen door and questioned him with her eyebrows lifted. "Everything all right, folks?"

"Yes."

"Yes."

They spoke at the same time, which would have been humorous in any other circumstances. Miss Pam gave them a doubtful smile. "Glad to hear it." Then she returned to the kitchen.

Grace marched out the front door, putting on her heavy jacket as she went. Micah had to hurry to catch her by the arm. "Grace, wait."

She spun around, and fire blazed in her bright blue eyes. "What?"

He took a slow, deep breath and nodded toward the livery stable, where Adam usually spent his afternoons caring for the horses that boarded there. "Let's go together."

"This is a matter for the law, Rev."

"Um, did you forget I've been deputized?" He couldn't keep from smirking just a little, something he wouldn't do with just anyone.

She rolled her eyes and huffed out a noisy sigh. "Come on, then. If I say no, you'll just come anyway."

"Ah, you know me so well." Oddly, the thought pleased him, in spite of their current disagreement.

At the livery stable at the end of the street, they found owner Ben Russell in a back stall currying one of the horses. Micah and Grace had brought their own horses here, along with the sheriff's, when they'd returned to town after the shooting.

"Howdy, folks. Be right with you." Ben finished his work and closed the stall door. "What can I do for you?"

"We're looking for Adam." Micah spoke quickly before Grace could show her disdain for the boy. It wouldn't do to give one of his employers cause to distrust him. "Have you seen him today?"

"Sure did." Ben ran a hand through his graying hair, and a shower of dust filled the air. "I sent him over to Del Norte this morning to pick up a couple of my horses. Some tenderfeet on their way to the gold fields rented 'em and never brought 'em back. Sheriff Hobart sent a message to come and get 'em as soon as I could. I don't know when Adam'll be back. Might be tomorrow."

"Uh-huh." Grace took a turn smirking at Micah.

He knew what she was thinking. As they had discussed, if Adam had heard Sheriff Lawson trying to gather a posse this morning before he left Esperanza, he could easily have warned the outlaws on his way to Del Norte.

For the first time since the troubles began, Micah felt a flicker of doubt about Adam. He wasn't ready to write him off yet, but the evidence was mounting.

Sick to his stomach about everything that had happened in this day, he excused himself so he could go home and pray.

Every bit of smugness Grace could have felt over being right about Adam vanished as she watched the Rev walk away toward the parsonage, his shoulders slumped in defeat and his head hanging down. It hurt her to see him dejected that way because he was usually so cheerful, so positive, so full of faith. But it couldn't be helped. If Adam warned his outlaw friends that the sheriff was headed their way, he just as much as pulled the trigger on that rifle.

Without solid evidence, though, Grace still couldn't arrest the boy. What she could do was visit Nelly Winsted and suggest that her son, Everett, shouldn't hang out with Adam. On second thought, she'd have to give Nelly a reason, and word might get back to Adam. Despite loyalty to his family, if he feared getting caught helping the men who gunned down the sheriff, he might hightail it out of town. Besides, Nelly wasn't all that approachable. Like many folks in the area, she thought it was scandalous that Grace wore trousers and carried a gun. If the outlaws threatened Nelly's family, she'd change her ideas real quick, at least about the gun.

Grace would like to ask the sheriff for his advice about Adam, but he didn't need to be bothered while trying to recover. She sure couldn't ask the Rev.

"Grace!" Rosamond Wakefield called to her from across Main Street. "Do you have a minute?"

"Sure thing." Grace strode across the snowy, rutted road toward her lifelong friend. Stepping up on

the boardwalk, she came dangerously close to giving Rosamond a bear hug, mainly because she could use a bit of friendly comforting right now. Instead she maintained her aloof deputy posture. "What can I do for you?"

"Nothing." Rosamond laughed. "I want to do something *with* you." She grasped Grace's hand and grew serious. "Garrick and I heard about the sheriff and are thanking the Lord he's going to be all right. We decided to do what he told us at prayer meeting last week—carry on as usual, just remain vigilant." Her blue eyes sparkled. "So we're continuing with our plans to clear and flood the lot behind the hotel for an ice-skating party. It should be frozen by Saturday. After skating, we'll warm up in the main dining room and have some lovely desserts and cocoa made by Chef Henrique. Henrique has already brewed the cocoa base, so it just needs hot milk. Garrick and I brought a special chocolate pot back from England to serve it in, so do say you'll come."

In spite of the icy breeze and her own cold musings, Grace let the warmth of Rosamond's invitation seep into her heart. She couldn't go after the outlaws until she had a sizable posse, and even then, the weather in the foothills was a constant threat. Also, as the Rev reminded her, this time of year, ranchers needed all of their cowboys so they could finish preparing for the long winter ahead. Here in the San Luis Valley, sometimes that meant clear into early May.

So why not join her childhood friends for an afternoon of fun? A tiny voice in the back of her mind said she might ought to go after the outlaws on Saturday, when all the cowboys would be in town and

the best of the lot could be deputized. She would have to think on that real hard, but for now, she thought a skating party sounded just about right. She could always change her mind later.

"Sure. I'd like that. Is the party open to everyone?" If so, Grace would bring Georgia.

"Oh." Rosamond's pretty face scrunched up like she was thinking. "Well, we planned it for folks around our age, but everyone can use the skating rink. Mrs. Winsted just received a large shipment of skating blades, and Garrick thinks we should purchase some for the use of hotel guests and, of course, friends. I'm on my way over to the parsonage to invite Reverend Thomas and his guests." She leaned close to Grace. "Actually, my original idea was to throw a welcome party for the Suttons." She laughed, which she often did since her marriage to the handsome Englishman. "But the more Garrick and I talked about it, the more quickly it grew beyond that. So, yes, invite whom you will. We can always make more cocoa."

Rosamond had a way about her that inspired others to be as happy as she was. Growing up on the next ranch over from her parents' Four Stones Ranch, Grace had usually fallen into her trap, and now it was impossible to resist.

"I'll be there." She'd have to ride out to her folks' place and get her skates, so she'd invite Georgia to the party at the same time. This was just what Grace needed, a break from the tension of her work. With everybody in town on the lookout for the outlaws, surely it wouldn't do any harm to have a little fun.

What was she thinking? She knew better than that.

She needed to round up a posse right now and head out to surround those killers. Of course it was too late in the day, but maybe tomorrow. And maybe they'd meet Adam Starling on his way back to Esperanza and could force him to lead them to the outlaws' lair.

She headed back to the sheriff's office to write a report of today's happenings before she forgot the details. She set her hand on the doorknob at the same moment that Justice Gareau emerged from the bank next door, followed by Nolan Means.

"Afternoon, Deputy." Nolan nodded in her direction as he locked the door.

Justice tipped his hat and gave her a friendly smile. "Howdy, Miss Grace." A true Southern gentleman, that one. She appreciated being on the receiving end of his respect.

"We heard about the sheriff." Nolan strode—or rather, strutted—toward her. "What are you going to do about that?"

My, he was cross, as though it were all her fault. Hadn't they just shared a friendly Sunday dinner yesterday at the Rev's house? On the other hand, with him being one of the killers' targets, same as Grace, she understood his brusqueness. "Tomorrow I'm going to round up a posse and ride out to where the sheriff got shot." She looked at Justice. "Any suggestions would be welcomed."

The steely-eyed former Texas Ranger nodded. "We should talk. Maybe come up with some strategies."

"Hold on a minute." Nolan's voice took on a hard edge. "You work for me, Gareau. The law in this town hasn't done a thing—"

"Miss Grace." To her surprise, Justice cut off his employer. "Give it a few days. Let the outlaws get complacent, thinking you won't do anything now that the sheriff can't lead a posse. In the meantime, deputize as many trustworthy folks as you can in case the outlaws decide to attack again. By the end of the week, you can call that posse together real fast and ride out to where the sheriff got shot. See what you can see there. They may not even still be in that location."

All the time he talked, Grace could practically see steam coming out of Nolan's ears.

"If I think of anything else, I'll let you know." Justice tipped his hat again. "Ma'am. Mr. Means." He gave Nolan a nod, as if ordering him to proceed toward home. Nolan might be paying Justice's salary, but it was clear the former Ranger was the one in charge, at least in regard to the banker's safety.

Grace had to hide a laugh. It never was wise to offend the town banker, but if he weren't such a starched collar, she wouldn't want to anyway. He'd been mighty grateful when she stopped the robbery three years ago, but now he acted like it was her fault the outlaws had come back. All the more reason to catch the killers and put an end to Esperanza's danger.

Chapter Nine

Micah found Joel and Miss Sutton having tea in the parsonage parlor. Once again, as he entered the house, he felt as if he were a guest rather than a resident. Still, he did enjoy the warmth of the blazing fireplace, a fire he hadn't had to start himself. When—if—he married, how pleasant it would be to return home to such warmth on these bitter winter days and to smell such mouthwatering aromas as now wafted into the parlor from the kitchen.

"Supper will be ready in an hour, Reverend Thomas," Miss Sutton said. "Let me fetch a cup and pour you some tea." She didn't wait for his answer, but went to the kitchen. In a trice, she returned with a set of her china cups and saucers.

Had she already placed her china in his cupboard? Surely not. While he enjoyed using fine china rather than his heavier, mismatched dinnerware, the situation was becoming awkward. Had he been mistaken about the interest he'd seen only yesterday between this lady and Nolan Means? None of the local ladies had been quite so aggressive in their attempts to lay

claim to him. While such thoughts seemed incredibly vain, he couldn't mistake this attention, which made him entirely uncomfortable in his own home.

"Thank you, Miss Sutton." He accepted the tea and took a sip. Even though he'd had soup and coffee at the café not a half hour ago, the steaming liquid warmed away the chill that had cut through his coat on the walk home. A chill made worse because of his disagreement with Grace and even more so because of his doubts and fears about Adam, and now Miss Sutton's unwanted attentions.

"We heard about the sheriff from Mrs. Winsted this afternoon." Joel shook his head in disgust. "I wish you had let me go with you. Another set of eyes might have caught the shooter."

"And get shot yourself, as well?" Miss Sutton sniffed. "This isn't our quarrel, Joel."

"It is if we're going to settle down here." He frowned at his sister, a rare thing.

She returned the look, and then softened her expression. "In truth, I had hoped to settle in a more populated area, perhaps Denver, where there are more stores. After shopping only twice at Mrs. Winsted's mercantile, I have now seen the entire extent of all her wares. And—"

"By the by, Micah." Joel stood abruptly, cutting her off, and strode across the room to the hall tree by the front door. "Mrs. Winsted sent your mail home with us." He brought two letters and a brown paper package over to Micah.

"Thank you." Micah didn't know whether to be pleased or annoyed that his friend had taken care of his personal business. But then, Micah was al-

ready cross about his disagreement with Grace, so he mustn't let his mood affect his attitude toward his old friend, who'd only been trying to help him.

"It's from New York. Isn't that exciting?" Miss Sutton eyed the package as if it were a present for her. "I've been dying for you to get home to open it. Oh, do open it now."

"Elly!" Joel frowned at her again.

She gave him a little pout, which Micah found amusing. Clearly the young lady was already bored with Esperanza, despite her enthusiasm for working with the children's Christmas pageant.

"Well, open it," Miss Sutton repeated.

His heart hammering with sudden excitement that swept away the drama of the day, Micah studied the package. As he'd requested, the return address didn't bear the publisher's name, only his editor's name and a street address. Apparently his editor understood authors who needed to remain anonymous. "Hmm. Maybe later." Could they detect the waver in his voice? See the shaking of his hands?

"Oh, you men." Miss Sutton sniffed again and then blinked. "Oh, dear. My potatoes are burning." She hurried to the kitchen, and the clanging of a pot lid soon reached their ears.

"Whew." Joel chuckled. "Sorry about that, Micah."

"Don't give it a thought." He gathered his mail and stood. "I need to run over to my office for a while. Please excuse me."

"Of course." Joel didn't give voice to the disappointment so apparent in his eyes.

Was Micah a poor host? He'd done very little entertaining since coming out West and had few mem-

ories of his parents' rare guests. Still, he had to open this package or he'd burst. Leaving by the front door to avoid Miss Sutton in the kitchen, he crossed the side yard and entered the rear of the church, locking the door after him. Hands still shaking, he carefully cut the strings and unwrapped the brown paper. Inside was a cardboard box containing three copies of his novel. *His novel!* He lifted out one volume, a beautiful brown tooled leather book with an attractive, colorful dust cover picturing a dramatic showdown between his hero sheriff and a masked gunman. Above the picture, the title read *Rio Grande Sheriff.* Below the picture: A Cowboy Storyteller.

Micah sat back and sighed. How ironic to receive this today of all days. The rising bubble of joy and excitement he'd experienced just moments ago burst like a punctured balloon. He'd been inspired to write the story because of the failed bank robbery three years ago, before Sheriff Lawson even came to Esperanza. He'd wanted to write about the good, courageous people who lived here, to let readers back East know they weren't all country rubes but, rather, the backbone of America. Not only that, but he'd written the book to entertain, to amuse. But now reality slammed into fiction. Real people, real lives. And when a sheriff nearly met his end today at the hands of evil men, Micah could only wonder whether he'd made a big mistake to write such a book. Maybe he should wire his editor and tell him not to send a shipment of books to Esperanza.

He rewrapped the package and hid it at the back of a lower desk drawer. Maybe tomorrow he would feel better about the whole thing, but for now, he felt the

strong need to get on his knees and pray for the very real situations before him. The sheriff's recovery. Adam Starling. And most of all, Micah's disagreement with Grace, which caused him more misery than he could account for.

He returned to the parsonage just as Miss Sutton was putting supper on the dining room table. On his way to his room to freshen up, he stopped in the parlor doorway and gaped. Joel still sat on the settee, his eyes wide as he read a book—*Rio Grande Sheriff.*

"Say, Micah." His friend grinned at him knowingly, and a shard of fear pierced Micah's heart. "Look at what I picked up at Mrs. Winsted's store today."

How on earth had his friend discovered he was the author?

Snow fell that night and continued throughout the next day. Grace saw no point in trying to track the killers, especially after Justice had advised waiting. Even if a posse rode out, they could find more trouble getting trapped if the snowfall turned into a blizzard than if they encountered the outlaws.

As she sat in the sheriff's office pondering possible courses of action—and coming up with nothing—her heart dropped considerably. Maybe she wasn't cut out to be a deputy after all. Maybe she'd be better off just staying out at her parents' ranch and working with them. They were getting on in years, and without a son to take over, they needed all the help they could get. With two sisters married and two more who were likely to do the same, she was the

only one Ma and Pa could count on to remain single and take care of them.

And yet it was her disagreement with the Rev that bothered her now because she cared for him more than made good sense. Even worse, she'd always respected his opinions, so his insistence on Adam's innocence was yet another cause to doubt herself.

One thing was sure. She couldn't quit her job until Hardison and Smith were behind bars or six feet under. Somehow she had to make one of those happen before anybody else was harmed.

Fourteen-year-old Everett Winsted dashed into the office, bringing with him a blast of icy air and flurry of large snowflakes. He quickly closed the door and then pulled off his stocking cap to reveal a thick thatch of brown hair. "Good afternoon, Deputy."

Grace's heart jolted. Had something happened at his grandmother's store? At his mother's ice cream parlor?

"How are you today, ma'am?" The placid look in Everett's eyes indicated he hadn't come about some emergency.

My, she was getting jumpy these days. In the past, she would have gone to the Rev and talked it out, maybe discussed some scripture verses and prayed. But she wasn't about to go back to the parsonage, not as long as that Miss Sutton was there. Rosamond was busy with her high school and her husband's new hotel. Maisie was busy helping Doc and taking care of their new baby.

"You all right, Miss Grace?" Everett stood across the desk from her, an anxious, concerned look coming over his freckled face.

"Sorry." Grace tried to grin at the boy, but her lips were chapped and it hurt too much. "What can I do for you?"

He gave her a shaky smile, probably because the cold weather had frozen his cheeks, and pulled a book from inside his woolen jacket. "Grandmother sent this over. She thought you might enjoy reading it." He set the book on the desk.

"*Rio Grande Sheriff.*" She picked it up and studied the brightly colored dust jacket. The two-man stand-off pictured there didn't appear very realistic. "Huh. Your grandma sent it, you say?"

"Yes, ma'am. A shipment of twenty books arrived yesterday, and she thought you might want to read it while the weather's keeping you indoors." He gave her a sheepish grin. "I think she's hoping you'll like it and tell everybody to come buy a copy."

Grace opened the leather book and thumbed the pages. She wasn't much of a reader, but this would keep her busy while she couldn't do something about the outlaws. The book didn't appear to be one of those ridiculous dime novels that made cowboys and ranchers seem like fools. Maybe this author, this Cowboy Storyteller, would have some solutions for her. That was, if he wasn't some sissy Easterner writing about a place he'd never been and this wasn't an insult to everything she held near and dear.

She gave Everett a nod. "Tell your grandma I said thanks." She wouldn't tell the boy, but of course she'd pay for the book. These things didn't come cheaply. Besides, giving a gift to a deputy might appear to

some folks as a bribe. Grace might not be the cleverest deputy in Colorado, but nobody could claim she wasn't honest.

By Wednesday morning, snow had stopped falling. Micah and Joel spent a good part of the afternoon shoveling snow from in front of the church and along the path to the reception hall. The three-year-old addition to the church was where Miss Sutton would hold her first rehearsal for the Christmas pageant. After being indoors all day Tuesday, Micah enjoyed being outside in the winter sunshine and appreciated the exercise. He also felt better about some of the problems plaguing him.

Monday evening, when Micah had found Joel reading his novel, he'd thought his secret was out. But Joel's sneaky look merely indicated he'd found a way to amuse himself, since his sister wouldn't let him out of her sight. All day Tuesday, he had insisted upon reading the book to Micah and Miss Sutton. After his initial alarm, Micah settled down to listen. Joel and Miss Sutton weren't familiar with the area or the residents, so they probably didn't recognize any of the settings or characters. To his relief, they did seem to enjoy the story.

Sometimes Micah laughed along with them. Other times he cringed, wishing he'd worded this or that passage differently, or made parts of the plot more realistic. What had he been thinking when he wrote some of those scenes? He also noticed some places where the editor had made a change or two, but he had no quarrel with that. Unsure of himself as a writer, he'd given the gentleman permission to cor-

rect any mistakes or inconsistencies as he saw fit. All the while Joel read, however, Micah had to remain detached so his friends wouldn't suspect he was the author.

As he listened, however, one thing he couldn't deny was his renewed enthusiasm for the story. He had nothing to be ashamed of, and he no longer felt the book was in the least bit frivolous. His characters worked hard, trusted in God and cared for their neighbors when adversity struck, just like the people of Esperanza. If readers could learn real-life lessons from the story, then Micah had done his job as surely as if he'd preached a sermon. After all, Jesus Christ had told stories in the form of parables in order to deliver important life lessons. Micah regarded that as permission to do the same.

He was further rewarded in that revelation on Tuesday night when Miss Sutton spoke of how interesting and helpful the book was because it informed her about the West. Now she felt more equipped to endure the hardships of this land, whatever the future brought. Nothing could have encouraged Micah more. He must look for time to finish his second novel, the one about Grace, so he could offer more of the same to interested readers.

"Whew!" Joel stuck his shovel in a snowbank and rested his arms on the handle. "It's been far too long since I did any kind of work." He inhaled a deep breath, then coughed. "Uh-oh. Just froze my lungs." He laughed and coughed again.

"The altitude usually has an effect on newcomers, too." Micah's arms and legs also burned from the exertion. He hadn't been able to exercise for a couple

of weeks, and it was beginning to show, especially with eating the pastries Miss Sutton made every day. He didn't dare turn down her offerings for fear of offending her. Maybe this was why so many pastors he knew had portly physiques.

At the end of their labors, she had a hearty soup and fresh-baked bread waiting for them. After eating the meal, Micah felt invigorated and eager for prayer meeting. Miss Sutton had a sparkle in her eyes, too, and spoke with enthusiasm about this evening's rehearsal.

On the way over to the church after supper, she clutched a stack of papers upon which she had written parts for each child. "I hope I've done this right."

"It will be perfect, I'm sure." Micah never knew what to think of her. One minute, she wanted to move to Denver and go shopping. The next, she couldn't wait to work with small town children and spoke as if their pageant would be as grand as any professional production.

Families began arriving long before the hour set for prayer meeting. They shepherded their eager children into the reception hall, where Micah greeted each one. Adam Starling brought four-year-old Jack and six-year-old Molly, both of whom bounced up and down with excitement as they greeted their friends. The warm smile on Adam's face as he watched them was at odds with the perpetual anxiety in his eyes. He took a minute to chat with his schoolmates Georgia Eberly and Anna Means, then joined Micah by the door.

"How are your folks, Adam?" Micah asked as they walked toward the sanctuary.

He shrugged. "Pa's the same." He sighed, a sound of soul-weariness that made Micah's heart ache for one so young. "Ma's doing the best she can."

They reached the church and entered through the double front doors, then removed their hats and coats and hung them in the cloakroom just inside the entrance.

"I know you're a big help to them," Micah said. "Is there anything the church can do? That I can do?"

Adam looked around and seemed relieved to see the empty sanctuary. "No, sir. The church already does so much for us." He grinned. "Some folks give us jobs to do that they could easily do themselves." He glanced down at Micah's frock coat. "Although I'm sure Ma sews buttons on better than any bachelor."

Micah chuckled. "I'm sure of it, too. Say, would you mind helping me put the hymnbooks out?"

As they worked silently for several minutes, Micah considered how he could turn this conversation toward the issue of the outlaws.

"I understand you had to retrieve some horses from over in Del Norte on Monday. Did you get back before the snow started falling?"

"No, sir." While most people would simply set the hymnals down randomly, Adam carefully lined them up on each pew. Diligent as always in every job. "But I did come back yesterday morning before it got too bad."

"That's good to hear." An uneasy feeling hit Micah's stomach over what he was about to say, but he needed to press on. "Did you think about taking refuge at some ranch on the way, maybe an abandoned

cabin near the river, in case the snowfall turned into a blizzard?"

Adam didn't so much as blink. "No, sir. I'm not familiar with that area, so it probably wouldn't have been wise to get off of the road. Wouldn't want to get lost, especially not at this time of year."

Relief knocked the wind from Micah's lungs. When he could catch his breath, he said, "Good idea." Now if only he could ask why Adam avoided Grace, maybe he could set this whole matter to rest.

As if summoned by his thoughts, she entered the sanctuary. Micah hadn't seen her since Monday, and in spite of their disagreement, his heart lifted in that odd little way it did whenever he saw her. Adam gave her a furtive glance but continued his work, even when she paused by the pew where he was aligning the hymnbooks.

"Evening, Rev. Evening, Adam." She kept her gaze on the boy.

Micah had a strong urge to intervene, but decided to let the situation play itself out. "Good evening, Grace."

"How're your folks, Adam?" Grace's stare didn't waver.

Even in the dim light of the lamp-lit sanctuary, Micah could see color rising up in Adam's cheeks and a shy grin play across his lips as he spared Grace the briefest of glances. "Fine." He swallowed hard. "Thank you." Another swallow. "Ma'am."

This was the same boy who not ten minutes ago had spoken so comfortably with Anna Means and Grace's sister Georgia. A boy who easily chatted with people all over town as he did his many odd

jobs. What had brought about the change in him? Was it Grace's badge, as she insisted, causing him to feel guilty for colluding with the outlaws? Or was it something else?

She scowled at Adam and opened her mouth, but before she could speak, Micah decided he would indeed intervene.

"Grace, I didn't get over to Doc's today to check on the sheriff. Do you know how he's doing?" Instead of looking at her, he kept his eyes focused on Adam. Again, the boy didn't give any hint of guilt, as he surely would if he'd helped the outlaws gun down Sheriff Lawson.

Other people began to fill the sanctuary, so Grace stepped closer to Micah. "He was doing well enough this afternoon for us to move him back over to his house, but it wore him out real bad." Her demeanor turned friendly and relaxed, the way she usually acted around Micah. He was glad she felt at ease with him, as he did with her. Losing her friendship would make him sad. More than sad.

"If he's better tomorrow," Grace continued, "he'd like to deputize several more men to ride out with me when the time comes. After prayer meeting, I'll be speaking to the ones he's asked for."

Micah gave her a sober nod. "If we don't have more snowfall in the next few days, we might be able to put an end to this whole mess."

"Let's pray it works out that way."

"Indeed, we shall." Micah's heart lifted once again. In spite of the threats terrorizing their community, it appeared that Grace's faith was growing. He couldn't be more pleased.

Mrs. Foster came in and took her place at the organ and began to play, so Grace gave Micah a nod and moved across the sanctuary to join her parents in the first row.

Adam sidled up to Micah. "I heard what Miss Grace said." He gazed in her direction, a half smile on his lips. "Do you think Sheriff Lawson would deputize me so I could ride along with the posse?"

Micah took a step back. "I don't know." He could hear the shock in his own voice. "Why would you want to do that?" Did he want to divert the posse away from the killers, or did he want to help catch them? Micah hated to be plagued by these constant doubts, but he wouldn't be doing his duty if he didn't question everything, everybody.

Adam shuffled his feet. "Well, this community has been awful good to me and my family, so I want to do my part." He ran a hand over the back of the nearby pew. "Can I tell you a secret?" He glanced over his shoulder to where Rosamond and Garrick now sat. "I mean, *may* I tell you a secret?" He grinned. "Don't want my English teacher to catch me using bad grammar."

Still in a state of wonder, Micah chuckled. "Indeed you don't. And, yes, you may tell me your secret."

Adam cast another furtive glance in Grace's direction. "I want to be a law officer, just like Deputy Grace."

Hiding his shock, Micah studied the look in Adam's eyes. What he saw there wasn't admiration for the lady's occupation, but for the lady herself. Oddly, it pleased and annoyed him at the same time. What on earth was the matter with him? One thing was certain. Adam Starling

was not the one helping the outlaws. But after promising to keep the boy's secret, how could Micah tell Grace that Adam was sweet on her and that shy boys often avoided the girls they admired for fear of saying something foolish? Even if he could tell her, with her aversion to being complimented, she'd never believe it.

Micah patted Adam on the shoulder. "That's a fine ambition, son." With a prayer meeting to conduct, he moved to the platform and needlessly adjusted his notes on the lectern while he collected himself. This revelation about Adam had complicated matters. The sooner they caught the outlaws, the better.

Chapter Ten

After the Rev's final prayer of the evening, Grace sought out the men Sheriff Lawson had asked for. "If you can come with me now, the sheriff will deputize you. That way we'll be ready to ride out at any time."

With the Rev, who'd already been deputized, and six other men, Grace led the way to the Lawsons' tidy little house on Randolph Street.

"Oh, Grace, I'm so glad to see you." Wringing her hands, the usually calm Mrs. Lawson welcomed the large party into her parlor. "Abel's been so grumpy because Doc won't let him out of bed." She waved toward the chairs and settee. "Gentlemen, please have a seat while I make sure he's ready to see you."

After Mrs. Lawson left the room, Grace looked around at the men, who spoke quietly amongst themselves. All except the Rev, who gazed at her, a half smile on his lips and—was that a twinkle in his eyes?

"What are you thinking, Rev?"

He shrugged. "Nothing much. Just that I have complete confidence in your leadership."

A warm feeling surged through her heart. But

while Nate and Rand Northam stated their agreement, Andy Ransom, whose whittling tools had been destroyed by the outlaws, scowled and stared down at his hands. Frank Stone and Homer Bean appeared indifferent. Rafael Trujillo leaned back in his chair, crossed his arms and narrowed his eyes. Two men unwilling to follow her didn't bode well for a posse's success.

Maybe the Rev had noticed their attitudes toward her and that's why he spoke out. She gave him a smile and a brief nod for declaring his confidence in her. While it should gall her to think she needed his support in order to do her job, with killers on the loose, she didn't have the luxury of pampering her own ego. Besides, it felt good to know they were still friends after all.

"Abel will see you now." Mrs. Lawson spoke from the hall doorway.

Grace and the men filed into the small bedroom and surrounded the four-poster bed where Sheriff Lawson sat propped up on pillows against the mahogany headboard.

"Evening, gentlemen." He coughed and then gripped his chest where the bullet had struck. "Pardon me for not getting up, but Agnes has me so mollycoddled and henpecked, I doubt I'll get out of this bed before spring."

The men chuckled, and two of the married ones voiced their understanding and sympathy.

"Agnes," the sheriff said, "pass out those spare badges I never thought I'd use in this peaceable town." He waved a hand toward the tin stars on the bedside table. When each man had one in hand, he said, "Raise your right hand. Do you solemnly prom-

ise to uphold the laws of the State of Colorado, Rio Grande County and the incorporated town of Esperanza, Colorado?"

A chorus of "I do's" filled the small room.

"Then by the authority vested in me by Rio Grande County and the people of Esperanza, I deputize you for the duration of the pursuit of the outlaws Dathan Hardison, Deke Smith and anybody else in their gang." He ran out of steam on those last words and slumped back against the pillows. "Go get 'em, men."

Grace knew he hadn't meant to exclude her in his charge to the posse. From the first day he'd arrived in town, Sheriff Lawson had shown respect for her abilities. He probably didn't even notice that some men in town dismissed her as a deputy, saying she was a woman out of her proper place. Too bad he'd chosen two of them to be on her posse.

"Nice weather for skating."

On Saturday morning, Micah sat on a wooden bench beside Justice Gareau while thirty or more people skated around the brand-new frozen pond behind the hotel. Around the edges of the rink, hay bales offered soft landings for inexperienced skaters.

"And yet here you sit." The easygoing bodyguard chuckled.

Micah laughed, too. "Well, we didn't have many frozen ponds in Virginia, so I never learned this particular sport."

"Same for me in Texas," Justice said. "Anyway, I have to keep an eye on Mr. Means and Miss Anna." He nodded toward the banker and then over to his

sister, who was taking a turn around the rink with Sean O'Shea, the other bodyguard.

Although Joel and Miss Sutton also came from Virginia, they appeared to have learned to skate. They kept close to Nolan and Anna, laughing as though they'd known each other for years. Across the rink, Nate and Susanna Northam helped five-year-old Lizzie and three-year-old Natty move across the ice.

Grace glided past Micah and Justice, a smile on her pretty face and her glorious red hair streaming behind her like a banner as she skimmed smoothly over the ice. Pleased that she had taken his advice and come to the party rather than leading the posse into the snow-covered hills to chase Hardison, Micah enjoyed watching her nimble movements. Not only could she glide forward, she could also skate backward and perform turning leaps that would make a ballet dancer proud. Some of those leaps coincided with a similar lilting of Micah's heart. At first his feelings confused him, but he attributed them to pastoral happiness for his good friend. A young lady should have this sort of fun more often, but many times Grace seemed determined only to be serious, only to concentrate on her work.

"Miss Grace is one fine-looking woman." Justice gazed at her with much the same admiring expression as Micah had seen on Adam Starling's face three nights ago. "Look at her go."

Suddenly cross, Micah bit back a sharp retort. Although Adam's admiration had annoyed him, Justice's regard put him in an uncharacteristic bad temper, for which he could not account. Why did he

suddenly feel so protective of Grace? Well, because a grown man's admiration was far different from a callow youth's, that was why. He had a responsibility to look out for his friend.

"Maybe I will try this skating business after all." Justice stood. "Looks like good exercise."

Micah didn't need to think twice. "Good idea." He joined Justice at the table where a hotel clerk handed out the skating blades.

The devices came in several lengths and attached to a person's own boots by way of clamps. Micah found a pair that seemed the right fit for his leather shoes and sat on the bench to secure them according to the clerk's instructions. That was the easy part. Standing on the blades on the frozen dirt and walking toward the ice was another matter altogether. Micah's ankles wobbled, one wanting to turn in, the other wanting to turn out. Clearly he would not be able to maintain his pastoral dignity. After this experience, he might not even be able to stand in the pulpit tomorrow morning.

Justice wasn't doing any better. He'd clamped his skates to his cowboy boots, which had a higher heel than Micah's shoes. While making him taller, they didn't help his balance.

In spite of their careful, wobbling steps as they walked the few paces to the rink, the moment they stepped on the ice, their feet slipped out from under them, their arms spun helplessly in the air and they promptly fell onto their backsides. For Micah, the pain wasn't nearly as bad as the indignity of being spread-eagled for all to see. But when some of the

male skaters began to guffaw and Justice joined in, Micah dismissed his foolish pride and laughed, too.

Grace skated toward them and came to an abrupt stop inches from Micah's foot. "Let me help you up." She held out a hand.

"I don't know..." Micah rolled over onto his hands and knees and tried to get one foot under him. The foot shot out like greased lightning, and he landed face and belly down on the frozen pond.

"I'll take your help." Justice still sat where he fell, and he looked up at Grace with a helpless, hopeful grin.

"I believe she offered to help me first." Micah couldn't believe his own words. What was wrong with him? Instead of further self-examination, he reached up to Grace. "Help?" He put a pathetic note in his voice that far outdid Justice's plea, to the amusement of everyone around them.

Grace grasped his hand, gripped his elbow and took a solid stance, allowing him to lean into her as he stood. And he actually did stand. Holding both of his hands, she skated backward, pulling him along in spite of his wobbling ankles and the bend of his torso. Remarkable woman. She was actually holding him up. Her strength no doubt came from working on her parents' ranch. He'd grown up thinking women should be weak and helpless. Grace belied all of that. And he couldn't admire her more.

"Try not to bend forward that way." She breezed along, but not too fast. "Hold your shoulders back."

"I'll try."

Micah straightened and almost fell over backward.

Grace pulled him upright and steadied him without so much as a hitch in her own stability.

Beyond her, he could see Justice with Garrick and Rosamond Wakefield on either side of him holding him upright and giving instructions. Nolan skated over and spoke to them, and the Wakefields led the bodyguard back to the side of the rink.

Micah had his own struggles to deal with at this moment, but in the back of his mind, he found the banker's actions petty. What harm could come to him and his sister with well over thirty people skating around them, not to mention many well-armed local residents not a block away doing their Saturday shopping?

"Having fun?" Grace smiled—the most relaxed look he'd seen on her face in months—as she continued to skate backward and pull him along.

"Yes. Oops!" He jerked back and forth and, once again, she steadied him.

"Uh-oh." Grace brought the two of them to a stop and focused beyond Micah toward Main Street.

Carefully turning his head so as not to throw them both off balance, he followed her gaze. Seamus O'Brien, Rand's brother-in-law and the Northams' ranch foreman, stood at the edge of the rink talking with Nate Northam. The expressions on both men's faces warned of trouble.

Grace tugged Micah over to them. "What's happened?"

Seamus swept off his hat. "Ma'am, somebody just butchered six Northam steers. From the look of it, they hauled away some meat, but most were just killed outright and left to rot."

* * *

Grace knew it was her fault. If she'd been out looking for the outlaws instead of wasting time ice-skating, she could have prevented the loss.

"We'll get them, Nate." She reached out to grip her friend's shoulder, only to hear an "Oof" and a thump beside her. "Oh! Rev, I'm so sorry." Couldn't she do anything right? She'd thoughtlessly let go of him, and now the poor man was backside down on the ice. His sheepish grimace would have been comical if more serious matters didn't need tending. "Here, let me help you."

He waved her away. "Thanks, but I think I'll just take these off before I stand." He unclamped the skates and then accepted her help up. "Nate, can you save any of the meat from those steers?"

Nate shook his head. "Not usually. We can probably save the hides for leather." He beckoned to his wife. "Susanna, why don't you take Lizzie and Natty into the hotel for some cocoa."

A fairly new skater, Susanna nonetheless managed the few yards to the edge of the rink, holding her children by their hands. Grace noticed the double-bladed skates the little ones wore, probably made by Bert, the Northams' blacksmith. Maybe the Rev could use a pair of those until he learned to get his balance on the ice. But this was hardly the time for such a frivolous notion.

"Let's ride out to see what we can see." She included the Rev in her comment. "No use gathering the whole posse until we have some idea of where they went."

"Good idea."

Nate stepped away to speak privately to Susanna.

She nodded solemnly and stood on tiptoe to kiss him before leading the children to the hotel's back entrance. "They're going to take a room here until this mess is over."

"I'll tell the Suttons." The Rev walked around the rink to talk to his guests.

Near enough to hear whatever the Rev said, Nolan Means became agitated. He gripped Joel Sutton's shoulder. "You and Miss Sutton are moving into my house until this is over." He sent an accusing glare in Grace's direction. "With our two bodyguards, you'll be safe from those murderers."

"If you think that's best, you have my blessing." The Rev seemed awfully willing to give up Miss Sutton's company, at least from where Grace stood. While the others got ready to leave, he walked back to Grace. "I can be ready to go with you in less than a half hour. Will that be soon enough?"

"Yep. I'll tell the sheriff. You go to the livery stable and get our horses saddled."

"Will do."

He walked several steps away and passed Dub Gleason and his friends, who'd been lazing around the ice-skating pond but not joining in the fun. Grace had grown up with these fellas, and they were the ones who had begun to torment her once she got taller than they were. They liked to sit around town smoking and jawing and not doing a lick of work. And torment her. Every time she saw them, she cringed. Why couldn't she get past such painful memories?

"Hey, Reverend," Dub, the leader, called out in his lazy, nasally voice. "You takin' orders from that skinny, gawky female deputy?"

The others laughed derisively. Never before had they made such remarks when someone else could hear them. Why, oh, why did their cruelty have to rear its ugly head in front of the Rev?

Her heart aching and her face burning with shame, Grace strode away before she said or did something they would all regret.

Since dedicating his life to the Lord, Micah hadn't often lost his temper, one of the worst of his boy-hood faults. But the tensions of the day—both the challenge of ice-skating and the news of the butch-ered steers—had him on edge. So when Dub insulted Grace, he spun around without thinking and grabbed the front of the young man's shirt and lifted him to his feet.

"Don't you ever, *ever* let me hear you insult Miss Eberly like that again." He shoved Dub back down. "Do you understand?"

All four of the laggards gaped at him.

"We didn't mean no harm, Reverend," one of the others said, and the rest chimed in their agreement.

"No harm?" Micah stood over the man. "Don't you ever think about how your words and actions do plenty of harm to others?" He should walk away right now, but something kept him rooted to the spot. He'd never preached a fire-and-brimstone sermon, but maybe it was about time. "Dub, you are a lazy bum. While your father works his fingers to the bone to run his ranch, you take his money and then sit around town with these other bums. I know you all ride over to Del Norte to drink and gamble. If you want to know where that can lead you, ask Rand

Northam. He ended up in a gunfight and killed Cole Landon, and now Cole's cousin is trying to take revenge on this whole town." Maybe not the whole town, but enough of the most industrious citizens to make big trouble for everyone if all of them were murdered.

The other boys looked at Dub, maybe to see how he was reacting so they could copy him. To his credit, Dub did look somewhat abashed. "I remember when that happened."

"And what are you doing to help? Are you going to sit in your usual spot on the boardwalk outside Mrs. Winsted's mercantile and make jokes about all the people they kill? Where were you when Hardison tried to rob the bank? I'll tell you where Grace Eberly was. She walked into that bank and took Hardison and Smith down and saved everyone from losing their hard-earned money, including all of your parents. Now she's working hard to keep this town safe, including your sorry selves. If any of you had even an ounce of courage, it still wouldn't match the courage that fine woman possesses."

Dub stared down at his feet. "I ain't never said she wasn't brave."

"She's just so...so *tall*," said Earl, who stood about five feet four. "Ain't natural for a woman to be so tall."

"Ain't natural for a man to be as ugly as you." Dub slapped his friend on the shoulder.

The others laughed, and Micah had a hard time not joining in. Seeing Dub's possible repentance had cooled his anger. Now to try to set them on a better course.

"So, answer me. What are you boys going to do to protect your town?"

They shrugged and looked around at each other. So much for the effects of his spontaneous sermon.

"Well, at least stay out of the way while good people try to do it." He took a step toward the livery stable, then turned back. "And the next time you see Miss Eberly, you tip your hat and smile like you mean it."

When a quartet of "yessirs" followed him up Main Street, Micah's heart welled up with an emotion so strong, he couldn't even name it. All he could do was pray that God's grace was at work in the hearts of those young men.

Grace dismounted and joined Rand and Nate Northam in trying to sort out the many cattle and horse hoofprints in the snow around the bloody steer carcasses a half mile from the main Four Stones Ranch house. In the slushy, half-thawed snow and mud, they couldn't tell one print from another or which way the culprits had fled. Too bad the sheriff or Justice Gareau weren't here. Grace hadn't learned all that much about tracking other than looking for the obvious, so she could use the help of more experienced lawmen. But with the sheriff shot just last Monday and Justice under strict orders from Nolan, she'd have to rely on her own instincts.

Several yards away, the Rev squatted close to the ground and searched for clues, too. Grace still felt the sting of her friend being taunted just because he was helping her chase the killers. After they'd met up at the livery stable to ride out here, he'd been his

usual pleasant self, almost jovial in his attempts to cheer her up. Or so it seemed to her. But she had more important things—at least more *immediate* things to worry about than her own hurt feelings.

After a good half hour of studying the area and finding nothing, she gave up. "They must have wrapped that flank of beef they stole real good. There's not even a trail of blood to follow."

Rand heaved out a big sigh. "Let's get back up to the big house and have some coffee. Then maybe we can figure out what to do." He waved to Nate and the two cowboys, Wes and Sam, who'd been searching with them. "Let's go."

"It seems strange that they're all over the place," the Rev said as they rode toward the house. "East of town, north of town, then west and now south. Doesn't give us much in the way of clues as to where they might be hiding."

"I've been thinking the same thing," Grace said. "We also don't know how many of them there are so we can be sure to outnumber them. But then, if the entire posse goes in one direction, they can go another way or even scatter. If we divide up, they might pick us off, just like they did the sheriff."

The others grunted or voiced their agreement, to a man sounding as discouraged as Grace felt.

They rode into the barnyard to an eerie silence. Grace looked at Rand to see if she was imagining things.

His eyes narrowed as he searched the property. "Something's not right."

"There!" Nate jumped from his horse and ran toward the back porch. "Seamus!"

his injury. He grabbed his wounded chest and lay
k down with a groan. When he recovered, he ad-
ssed the group around his bed.

'You won't solve anything by going off half-
ked at night in the middle of winter. You'll just
se more problems by getting lost or frozen to
th." He coughed and groaned again, his weari-
s evident. "Rand, as hard as it is for you, you
d to wait until morning. Then you and Nate take
dy and Frank and search south and west of Four
nes. That's the area you know best. It's also the
st logical place for them to hole up.

'Rafael, you and your vaqueros take the area ex-
ding north from your ranch. Reverend, you go
ad and have services. Then get me ten more men
leputize from the congregation. You and Grace
figure out how to divide them up and how you'll
er the western part of the county. We won't
ry about looking east. There's too many occu-
d ranches between here and Alamosa for them to
id being seen." After giving them a few practical
gestions on what to look for, the sheriff leaned
k against the headboard, clearly exhausted from
long speech. "Be careful, men." He gave Grace
rt nod. "Be careful."

he group dispersed to make further preparations.
h the Suttons moved to Nolan Means's house,
ah now had room for Nate and Rand to stay at
parsonage. Rather than sleep, Rand paced from
n to room until his older brother talked him into
ing some much-needed rest before their coming
al. In the morning, the two brothers and their

Grace and the others followed suit, hurrying across the long-harvested kitchen garden toward Rand's brother-in-law, who lay facedown below the bottom step.

Nate rolled him over, and he groaned. A bloody hole marked the spot on the lower left side of his chest where a bullet had struck him down. His rifle lay several yards away.

"Thank the Lord he's alive." The Rev knelt on Seamus's other side and brushed dirt from his forehead and cheeks. "Let's take him inside."

"Marybeth!" Rand dashed up the back steps.

Grace followed right behind him. Of course the outlaws had to try to kill Seamus. He was Marybeth's brother and would do anything to protect her.

They charged into the kitchen, finding nothing, nobody. Only the wail of a child broke the silence.

"Randy!" Rand and Grace dashed through the hall into the main parlor. "Mother!"

Charlotte Northam sat bound to a ladder-back chair, a cloth tied over her mouth. On her lap sat two-year-old Randy, who wailed as he tried to tug away the cloth. At the sight of his pa, he increased his screams and lunged for Rand, who caught him before he could hit the floor.

Grace released Charlotte's gag and untied her. "What happened?" As if she didn't know.

"They shot Seamus." Charlotte shook violently, but anger, not fear, burned in her eyes. "They took Marybeth. I don't know where they were going." Now she collapsed against Grace and sobbed bitterly. "Oh, Rand, I'm so sorry we couldn't keep her safe. If only your father were here."

Clutching his son, Rand looked lost, hopeless. "I shouldn't have left her here. Seamus said he could protect Marybeth by himself for the short time we'd be gone, but we forgot Hardison had it in for him, too. He was with me when I killed Hardison's kin."

Grace looked down at the tea towel they'd used to gag Charlotte. "Are you hurt, Charlotte? There's blood here." She held up the embroidered linen towel.

"I don't think so." Charlotte sniffed back another sob. "That horrid Deke Smith tried to strangle Fluffy, and she bit him hard. He grabbed the tea towel to stop the bleeding." She wiped a sleeve across her lips and shuddered. "And to think he put it over my mouth."

Grace glanced around the room, looking for the gray cat. The poor critter was probably hiding someplace in this big house after its ordeal.

"We have to find Marybeth." Rand handed Randy back to Charlotte. "Son, you stay with Gramma. Mother, will you be all right? We'll leave Wes and Sam here with you."

She nodded. "I don't think they'll return. They have what they want." She began to cry again. "What kind of beasts would try to harm a young woman in her condition?"

Grace gripped her shoulders. "Charlotte, Randy needs his grandma to be strong. Can you do that?"

"She's going into town." Nate entered the parlor, with the Rev right behind him. "Mother, you and Randy will stay at the hotel with Susanna and the children. I told Wes to get the buggy ready. And we're taking Seamus to Doc."

"Good." Grace felt a surge of str[...]mination well up inside her. "We'll [...] and figure out what to do."

Across the room, she saw the Re[...] smile and nod, and her heart warmed [...] this. They could save Marybeth. *Ple[...] us save Marybeth.*

Seamus stopped bleeding, much to [...] lief. Micah and Sam, a ranch hand, bu[...] man up in blankets and laid him in a[...] drove him to town, and Micah stayed [...] the Northams pack for their move. [...] making sure Mrs. Northam and little R[...] ficient clothes, which Grace helped ther[...] the brothers needed to pack food and [...] camping out in the winter wilderness. [...] noon, they headed toward Esperanza. [...] nightfall would soon be upon them, R[...] perate to begin the search for his wi[...] already sent Wes ahead to warn the ot[...] men to get ready.

Micah couldn't fault Rand for his se[...] He had his own dilemma. Should he [...] services tomorrow morning and go [...] or should he hold services as usual so[...] tion could gather to pray? After Mrs.[...] settled at the hotel, they went to Sh[...] house for his advice.

The news of the shooting and ab[...] brought the dedicated lawman out [...] But swinging his legs over the edge o[...] his feet on the floor brought on a pa[...]

Grace and the others followed suit, hurrying across the long-harvested kitchen garden toward Rand's brother-in-law, who lay facedown below the bottom step.

Nate rolled him over, and he groaned. A bloody hole marked the spot on the lower left side of his chest where a bullet had struck him down. His rifle lay several yards away.

"Thank the Lord he's alive." The Rev knelt on Seamus's other side and brushed dirt from his forehead and cheeks. "Let's take him inside."

"Marybeth!" Rand dashed up the back steps.

Grace followed right behind him. Of course the outlaws had to try to kill Seamus. He was Marybeth's brother and would do anything to protect her.

They charged into the kitchen, finding nothing, nobody. Only the wail of a child broke the silence.

"Randy!" Rand and Grace dashed through the hall into the main parlor. "Mother!"

Charlotte Northam sat bound to a ladder-back chair, a cloth tied over her mouth. On her lap sat two-year-old Randy, who wailed as he tried to tug away the cloth. At the sight of his pa, he increased his screams and lunged for Rand, who caught him before he could hit the floor.

Grace released Charlotte's gag and untied her. "What happened?" As if she didn't know.

"They shot Seamus." Charlotte shook violently, but anger, not fear, burned in her eyes. "They took Marybeth. I don't know where they were going." Now she collapsed against Grace and sobbed bitterly. "Oh, Rand, I'm so sorry we couldn't keep her safe. If only your father were here."

Clutching his son, Rand looked lost, hopeless. "I shouldn't have left her here. Seamus said he could protect Marybeth by himself for the short time we'd be gone, but we forgot Hardison had it in for him, too. He was with me when I killed Hardison's kin."

Grace looked down at the tea towel they'd used to gag Charlotte. "Are you hurt, Charlotte? There's blood here." She held up the embroidered linen towel.

"I don't think so." Charlotte sniffed back another sob. "That horrid Deke Smith tried to strangle Fluffy, and she bit him hard. He grabbed the tea towel to stop the bleeding." She wiped a sleeve across her lips and shuddered. "And to think he put it over my mouth."

Grace glanced around the room, looking for the gray cat. The poor critter was probably hiding someplace in this big house after its ordeal.

"We have to find Marybeth." Rand handed Randy back to Charlotte. "Son, you stay with Gramma. Mother, will you be all right? We'll leave Wes and Sam here with you."

She nodded. "I don't think they'll return. They have what they want." She began to cry again. "What kind of beasts would try to harm a young woman in her condition?"

Grace gripped her shoulders. "Charlotte, Randy needs his grandma to be strong. Can you do that?"

"She's going into town." Nate entered the parlor, with the Rev right behind him. "Mother, you and Randy will stay at the hotel with Susanna and the children. I told Wes to get the buggy ready. And we're taking Seamus to Doc."

"Good." Grace felt a surge of strength and determination well up inside her. "We'll gather the posse and figure out what to do."

Across the room, she saw the Rev's encouraging smile and nod, and her heart warmed. They could do this. They could save Marybeth. *Please, Lord, help us save Marybeth.*

Seamus stopped bleeding, much to everyone's relief. Micah and Sam, a ranch hand, bundled the foreman up in blankets and laid him in a wagon. Sam drove him to town, and Micah stayed behind to help the Northams pack for their move. In addition to making sure Mrs. Northam and little Randy had sufficient clothes, which Grace helped them to assemble, the brothers needed to pack food and blankets for camping out in the winter wilderness. By late afternoon, they headed toward Esperanza. Even though nightfall would soon be upon them, Rand was desperate to begin the search for his wife. Grace had already sent Wes ahead to warn the other deputized men to get ready.

Micah couldn't fault Rand for his sense of urgency. He had his own dilemma. Should he cancel church services tomorrow morning and go with the posse, or should he hold services as usual so the congregation could gather to pray? After Mrs. Northam was settled at the hotel, they went to Sheriff Lawson's house for his advice.

The news of the shooting and abduction almost brought the dedicated lawman out of his sickbed. But swinging his legs over the edge of the bed to put his feet on the floor brought on a painful reminder

of his injury. He grabbed his wounded chest and lay back down with a groan. When he recovered, he addressed the group around his bed.

"You won't solve anything by going off half-cocked at night in the middle of winter. You'll just cause more problems by getting lost or frozen to death." He coughed and groaned again, his weariness evident. "Rand, as hard as it is for you, you need to wait until morning. Then you and Nate take Andy and Frank and search south and west of Four Stones. That's the area you know best. It's also the most logical place for them to hole up.

"Rafael, you and your vaqueros take the area extending north from your ranch. Reverend, you go ahead and have services. Then get me ten more men to deputize from the congregation. You and Grace can figure out how to divide them up and how you'll cover the western part of the county. We won't worry about looking east. There's too many occupied ranches between here and Alamosa for them to avoid being seen." After giving them a few practical suggestions on what to look for, the sheriff leaned back against the headboard, clearly exhausted from his long speech. "Be careful, men." He gave Grace a curt nod. "Be careful."

The group dispersed to make further preparations. With the Suttons moved to Nolan Means's house, Micah now had room for Nate and Rand to stay at the parsonage. Rather than sleep, Rand paced from room to room until his older brother talked him into getting some much-needed rest before their coming ordeal. In the morning, the two brothers and their

men left town before the sun appeared over the Sangre de Cristo Mountains.

In his sermon, Micah charged his congregation to cast every care on the Lord, because God cared for each and every one of them. He forced himself to speak at his customary pace even though he wanted to finish his message quickly and join the search for Marybeth. Seated several rows back with her parents and sister Georgia, Grace nervously tapped her foot and fidgeted. Micah wished he could console her, but he knew she was as desperate as he to rescue the young mother.

After church, she rounded up a dozen men, all eager to help. To his surprise, and Grace's, Dub Gleason insisted on participating.

"I heard what you said yesterday, Reverend." Dub hung his head. "I do want to do something for my town. Might was well start with this."

Grace watched Dub warily and then stared at Micah, one eyebrow raised.

He shrugged. "Let him come. We need every man we can get. That is, unless you have any objections."

"Nope. I know he can ride and shoot. That's what counts."

While Micah gathered his supplies for the search, Grace took the men to be deputized. By noon, they had divided into three groups to cover the western part of the county. With hard freezes every night and cold temperatures during the day, they would first look for threads of smoke in the sky to lead them to the outlaws' lair. Tracking horse or human prints would be more difficult because the sun usu-

ally turned the snow to thin layers of slush, which refroze the next night.

"I guess we're stuck with you, Dub." Grace had tried to get one of the other groups to take him, but none of them would.

Micah could see the rejection cut into Dub like a knife. Maybe now he would understand how his own indolent actions had given him a bad name and would take a step toward growing up, finally.

They searched their designated area for several hours, at one point meeting up with other searchers. Grace took advantage of the encounter to send one of the men to Del Norte to ask for Sheriff Hobart's help. Before nightfall, a harsh snowfall not quite bad enough to be called a blizzard drove them back to town.

Exhausted but determined, Micah, Grace and Dub set out early the next morning. They hadn't ridden a mile from town when a high-pitched voice hailed them from behind.

"Deputy! Reverend!" Everett Winsted waved a gloved hand in the air. As he rode near, Micah noticed his red, swollen face.

"What are you doing out here?" Grace sounded more puzzled than angry. "Go on back to town, boy."

"I—I have to tell you something."

"Did somebody find Marybeth?" Micah kneed his horse over by the boy and put a hand on his shoulder.

"No." Everett swiped at tears freezing on his cheeks. "I don't think so."

"Then what?" Grace asked.

"I—I know where the outlaws are." His words came out on a sob.

"What?" Micah, Grace and Dub said together.

"What are you talking about?" Grace growled out the words. "How do you know that?"

"B-because I'm the one who's been helping them."

Chapter Eleven

Reining in her anger as best she could, Grace studied the baby-faced boy and knew he was telling the truth. She traded a look with the Rev, but saw no smugness in his expression, only sorrow. That helped her to calm down a whole heap. So she'd been wrong about Adam. Well, when the time came, she'd be glad to offer an apology.

"Why would you want to help those killers?"

Everett sniffed and wiped his nose with his wool coat sleeve. "I didn't plan it. They made me."

"How could they *make* you steal from your own grandma?" Grace glared at him with her severest deputy look.

"I-it didn't start out that way. I was exploring in those hills—" he pointed north of the road "—and they asked me to help them. Said they didn't have any money and needed food." He gulped back a sob. "I didn't know who they were, and I thought it'd be charitable, like Reverend Thomas always talks about. So I brought 'em supplies and food. They said they needed guns to shoot game, so I got the guns. Then

they wanted me to deliver the letters. When I found out what they said, I told 'em I didn't want to do it anymore. They said they'd kill Grandma and burn down her store if I didn't." Now he sobbed in earnest. "I couldn't let 'em hurt Grandma, could I?"

"Why did you wait so long to tell us?" Grace asked.

"I was scared." From the way Everett shook in the saddle, he was still badly frightened. "But when they shot the sheriff and took Miss Marybeth, I prayed somebody would stop 'em. When you didn't find them yesterday, I knew I had to…to confess."

Grace huffed out a cross breath. Those wretches had pulled the poor boy in like a man landing a prize trout. What had they planned to do with him after they finished their evil deeds? She didn't even want to know.

Her throat closed, and she swallowed hard and instinctively looked to the Rev for emotional support. In his remarkable gray eyes, she saw only compassion and sorrow.

"Where are they, Everett?" It was Dub who managed to speak first. Grace had never heard the slightest kindness in his voice before, but he almost seemed to understand the boy's dilemma, one foolish boy to another.

"There's an old ranch about three miles from here." He pointed north again. "That's where you'll find them."

Again, Grace traded a look with the Rev.

He nodded. "Probably the same place where we had our target practice. We should have thought of

it before." To the boy he said, "How many men are there, son?"

"There were five, but two left. I never did see them. So just three." Everett seemed to have his emotions under control now and appeared eager to help. "Mr. Hardison, Mr. Smith and Mr. Purvis, but I only ever talked with Hardison and Smith. I heard them say Purvis shot the sheriff for putting him in prison. They've got plenty of ammunition, so you probably need a whole bunch of men to get 'em."

"Well, then." Grace gave him her best big-sister grin. "You go back to town and tell everybody we've found them and need help to take them down."

"Yes, ma'am." Everett beamed a big smile and reined his horse around.

"Everett." The Rev held out a hand to stop him.

"Yessir?"

"You don't have to tell them about your part in this. Just tell them we have the outlaws cornered and need all the help we can get."

Grace nodded her agreement. They could sort out the boy's punishment when this was over. Right now, they had a young mother to save. If it wasn't too late.

Micah had a hard time not berating himself for failing to see Everett was the one helping the outlaws. It should have been obvious. But he'd been fooled by an innocent-looking face, an agreeable attitude and wide-open blue eyes. So much for his ability to discern a person's character and motives. But all of his self-recrimination wouldn't save Marybeth.

"What now, Miss Eberly?" Dub asked. "Do we wait for the others?"

She shot him a wary look, as if she didn't trust him. No wonder. Micah also wondered if it was foolish to trust this young man. If he was part of Hardison's gang, maybe he'd turn on them. Everett had said there'd been five. Could Dub be one of those who supposedly left? As always, Micah traded a look with Grace. In their silent communication, they agreed they couldn't postpone helping Marybeth.

"Let's go." She urged her horse forward.

Micah caught Dub's eye and tilted his head toward Grace. The young man didn't hesitate to follow her, a good sign. If he planned to betray them, he'd want to be behind them both. Still, Micah would watch him.

Yesterday's snowfall covered the landscape with deep, powdery drifts, which posed a constant threat to both man and beast. They moved slowly, taking care with every step not to fall into a hidden gully or ravine. After attempting to take a shortcut over a group of hills, they had to backtrack and go around, breaking new paths through the snow as they traveled. After a short stop to eat sandwiches and drink cold coffee, they reached the outskirts of the abandoned farm by early afternoon.

"They may have a lookout. Come with me." Grace rode behind a mass of boulders and dismounted. Micah and Dub followed her. "We'll leave our horses here." She drew her rifle from the saddle holster and checked its chambers for bullets, then likewise checked her pistol.

The sober, determined look on her face suddenly struck Micah as wrong. This beautiful young woman should be smiling. Enjoying life, ice-skating, going to parties, being courted by beaux. She shouldn't be

the main defense of a town the size of Esperanza. Some upstanding man should be taking care of her, someone like Justice Gareau, who clearly appreciated her finer qualities. But even that thought didn't sit at all well with Micah. Instead, his heart ached over the way some people treated her. If she was injured—or worse—in this terrible situation, he would be as inconsolable as her family. He had to make certain she was safe, no matter what happened to him.

Before they could spread out, Dub whispered, "There." He pointed to a man on a hill above the cabin and not a hundred yards away. He snorted out a laugh. "If that's their watchman, they must want us to find them."

Grace studied the man, who crouched against a rock wall huddled under a blanket while the smoke from his cigarette quickly vanished in the wind. "You may be right. He should have seen us riding in." She looked around. "We need to approach him carefully from different directions, so spread out. See what you can see. I'm going to put that varmint out of his misery." She glanced around, trying to figure out the best way to get behind him.

"Grace, wait." The Rev grasped her arm, not something he'd ever done. The strength of his grip sent an oddly reassuring shiver up her arm. "Shouldn't we wait for the rest of the posse?"

She stared at him briefly, then had to look away. She hadn't seen fear in his eyes, only caution. But this was a time for action, not lollygagging. She shouldn't have brought him. If something happened to him—

"Rev, I can't just stand by while they've got Mary-beth in there."

"Then let me take care of the watchman."

"No, I will."

Dub blew out a loud breath. "Oh, for the love of—" he glanced at Grace "—*grits*." He snatched his rifle from its sheath and the length of rope from the back of his saddle. "I'll go."

"It'll take more than one person." The Rev followed Dub before Grace could stop him.

Bother! Her posse had just rejected her authority. Now she had no choice but to follow after them. While she didn't have time to ponder it now, she wondered why Dub had looked at her and then said *grits* instead of what most men who cursed around her said at the end of that sentence. Probably because he didn't want to curse in front of the Rev. But then, wouldn't he have looked at the Rev?

They maneuvered through the snow and around and up the hill, making sure to stay downwind of the man. It was blowing pretty hard now, enough to cover most sounds up here. After they reached the other side of the rock wall, Grace and the Rev moved one way around it while Dub went the other. At Grace's low whistle, Dub stepped around the rock into the outlaw's view on one side, while Grace came up on his back.

"What the—" The man stood and leveled his rifle on Dub.

Grace slammed her rifle butt into the back of the man's head. His hat flew in one direction and his rifle in the other. While Dub hog-tied him like a steer about to be branded and Grace stuck the man's

handkerchief in his mouth, the Rev snatched up the firearm.

"Now what?" The eager gleam in his gray eyes dispelled Grace's concerns about his suitability for the task ahead.

She also appreciated his looking to her for direction this time. "We get this varmint down the hill and then see what we can do about the rest of 'em."

Among the three of them, they managed to carry the heavy man back to where they'd left their horses.

"Dub, you stay here with this one. Keep an eye out for the posse so you can let them know where we are."

"Yes, ma'am."

Once again, Grace considered this sudden change in her former tormentor. When this was all over, she'd have to confront him to find out what had brought it about.

Moving carefully from the cover of boulders to bushes to an old shed, she and the Rev approached the ramshackle cabin. Other than an occasional whicker or snort from horses in the barn, no sounds emanated from the area, at least none that could be heard over the wind. Above the cabin, which had seen some improvements since Grace and the Rev came here in October, a curl of smoke wafted from the chimney. At least Marybeth wouldn't be freezing. If she was still alive.

Grace motioned to the Rev that she would check the barn. Before she could touch the door, it slammed open, and Dathan Hardison emerged, a pearl-handled Colt .45 pointed straight at her midsection. Grace recognized the weapon. It was the one Everett had stolen from his grandma's store and put into the hands of

this killer. Grace might have to die, but she prayed the boy would truly understand the error of his ways before it was too late for him.

"Well, well, what have we here? A freaky female deputy and a sissy parson." Hardison wore a rough brown woolen coat and the tan Stetson stolen from the mercantile. His untrimmed brown hair and beard stuck out in all directions, a sad look for a man who'd always taken such pride in his appearance.

"Afternoon, Hardison." Grace grinned like they were meeting at a church social. "How's that shooting arm of yours?" Marybeth had badly wounded his right arm, so it was a wonder that he now held the pistol steady in that same hand. If he still had any weakness, maybe she could get a shot off before he did.

"Not as bad as you'd like. It's been healing for three years, and I've been practicing these past two months. Getting pretty good, if I do say so myself. I'll be happy to face any man who wants to draw on me." He leveled his evil eyes on the Rev, and Grace prepared to jump in front of him. "Howdy, parson. In spite of your annoying preaching, I never did repent. But then, if you do-gooders didn't have examples like me, how would you warn the young'uns to avoid a life of crime?"

"Afternoon, Hardison." The Rev tipped his hat with one hand and, still holding the watchman's rifle in his other, shivered and tugged his coat close like he was cold. "I'm sorry to meet up with you again like this."

"Ha! Same to you." Hardison snorted out a laugh. Then his passable features turned ugly and snake-like, revealing his true heart. "All right, girlie, par-

son, drop your guns and get inside, both of you." His eyes wild, he waved the gun.

Grace did as he said, setting down her rifle, unbuckling her belt and letting it slide to the ground. The Rev also set down the outlaw's rifle, held up his hands and moved toward the cabin. Clever man. When he'd tipped his hat, he'd distracted Hardison's attention from the handgun he'd concealed.

Grace tried to think of a way to trip on the steps into the cabin. Such a distraction could throw Hardison off, and maybe the Rev could draw his gun. But where was Deke Smith? And would they shoot the Rev if she failed to subdue either one of them? Right now, she couldn't be sure of anything.

"Get in there," Hardison barked.

Grace opened the door to a rush of warm air, the aroma of beef stew and the welcome sight of Marybeth Northam kneeling beside a man on a cot.

"Grace!" Marybeth painstakingly pulled herself to her feet and fell into Grace's outstretched arms, weeping.

Grace held on to her friend, smoothing her uncombed hair and whispering words of assurance. She sounded so wise, so strong, but Micah could see how her hands shook and her lips quivered. He felt pretty shaky himself.

A low fire burned in the fieldstone fireplace, providing a surprising amount of heat to the room. Or perhaps just coming in from the cold made it seem warm to him.

"What happened?" Grace addressed Marybeth as if Hardison weren't even there, much less that he held

a gun on her. She looked at Deke, who lay sweating and shaking on the cot, his eyes closed, and questioned Marybeth with a look.

"I think he has cat scratch fever." Marybeth cast a sympathetic glance in the small man's direction. "When they came to the house, Fluffy bit his hand, and it's swelled up terribly bad. From the red streaks around it, it looks infected. I think it's blood poisoning." She squeezed her eyes shut and shook her head. "They killed my brother." She buried her face in Grace's shoulder.

"No, they didn't." Grace glared briefly at Hardison. "Seamus is going to be all right."

Marybeth gasped and cried in earnest. "Oh, thank the Lord."

Hardison, who seemed to be enjoying the scene, scowled at the news that his victim hadn't died. "I'll have to finish that job after I take care of you fine folks." He barked out a derisive laugh. "I suppose I should save the little mother until last. She's been taking care of ol' Deke, and I think she's about to convert him. I guess when a man's about to meet his maker, he repents. That's my plan."

Micah felt sick to his stomach. Even the bitterest of his Virginia neighbors hadn't been this cruel, this evil. Not asking permission from their captor, he knelt beside the cot and touched Deke's forehead. The man was burning up with a fever and had thrown off his single wool blanket, one that looked suspiciously like those sold at Mrs. Winsted's store.

"You should take him to a doctor," Micah said.

Hardison sneered. "Oh, yeah? He was the one who tried to strangle that beast. Let him suffer."

"Deke." Micah tamped down his temper and gave the sick man his full attention. "Deke, can you hear me?"

The man's eyes fluttered open and then closed again. "Howdy, Reverend." His voice rough and scratchy, Deke managed a shaky smile. "Miz Northam's been preaching to me. You gonna do that, too?"

"If you want me to, Deke." Compassion filled Micah's heart. If he wasn't mistaken, this was indeed going to be a deathbed conversion. And like the repentant thief hanging on the cross beside Jesus, this man could have salvation if only he would ask. At least he hoped the man would see the Light. "I'm sure Marybeth spoke to you about the Gospel. You know Jesus Christ, the Son of God, died for your sins. No matter how big or small our sins, if we put our trust in Him, He'll forgive us and save us. Don't you want to do that?"

"Don't I have to confess 'em all to you?" A violent shudder went through Deke's body.

Micah tucked the woolen blanket up closer to Deke's chin. "Only if you want to." He gave his full attention to the dying man, but in the back of his mind, he wondered why Hardison hadn't stopped them from talking. "All you need to do is tell the Lord you know you're a sinner and can't save yourself. Ask Him to save you. You can do that now."

"I b'lieve I will." Deke's eyes cleared, and he stared up at the unpainted ceiling. "Lord, You know I'm a sinner. Ain't never done a decent thing in my life." He shuddered again. "Caused heartache for lots of folks who didn't deserve it." He cast a guilty look at Micah. "Even killed a few men. But, Lord, if You

can see fit to forgive me, I'd be much obliged." A soft smile spread across his thin, cracked lips, and he closed his eyes.

For a moment, Micah thought he had died, but his chest still rose and fell erratically. An ominous death rattle accompanied each breath. Maybe the Lord would spare him for a little while longer.

"Well, now, ain't that sweet?" Hardison leaned against the wall, sneering. "What a worthless polecat you turned out to be, Deke, being taken down by a *cat.*" He spat on the floor and then moved closer to the cot. Leaning over his partner in crime, cursing the sick man for a fool and a coward, he seemed to be searching for signs of life.

Micah stood and moved out of his way. If Hardison tried to harm Deke, he'd do his best to stop him, despite the gun in the man's hand. Micah glanced at Grace, who stood in front of Marybeth. Hiding a straw broom close to her side, Grace gave him a brief nod and looked down at his side, silently telling him to be ready to draw his gun. With only one man to manage, maybe they could take him down. But visions of Grace lying on the floor with a bullet wound in her, such as her sister Beryl had suffered three years ago, clouded his mind.

He wanted to do as she suggested, but it was too late. Hardison ceased his rant against Deke and now turned his attention toward Grace. She lunged at him, aiming the sharp broom straws at his gun hand and striking her target. Hardison cursed as the weapon flew across the room. Micah used the opportunity to draw his own gun.

Hardison grabbed the broom, twisted it from

Grace's hand and tossed it aside. In the scuffle, Marybeth fell to the floor with a painful cry. Grace tried to go to her, but Hardison slapped her away, drawing blood on her cheek. Micah saw red, and not only blood. He'd never wanted to kill another man, but this one was pushing him closer to that edge.

"Come on, sissy preacher man," Hardison taunted. "Can't shoot a man?" He snorted derisively. "I didn't think so." He walked across the small room and retrieved his own gun.

Micah tried to pull the trigger. Tried to pray. Everything seemed frozen in time. Could he shoot this evil man? Possibly kill him, knowing he would be eternally lost? *God, help me!* The only answer that came was the certain knowledge that he would have to subdue Hardison and protect the women some other way. Lifting a fervent prayer for mercy and strength, he lowered his gun to the floor and moved in front of Grace and Marybeth, who held each other desperately.

"Micah, no!" Grace cried out behind him.

Micah. Not Rev. Somehow hearing her say his name gave him an odd sort of comfort. No matter what happened, their friendship would be one of the best things that had ever happened to him.

"I may not choose to shoot you, Hardison, but I won't let you hurt these two good women." Maybe he could still jump the man and wrest the gun from him. Despite his boasts, Hardison didn't appear to be in the best of health, and Micah had never felt stronger.

"Have it your way, preacher." Hardison kicked Micah's gun under the cot and took aim at him. "You're a fool, just like all of your kind."

"No!" Grace cried out behind him.

Lord, have mercy. Oddly, Micah felt only peace. He hadn't expected to die this way, but—

Gunfire exploded in the small room. Hardison's face twisted in surprise. He fell forward toward Micah. The gun dropped from his hand. Micah caught him, lowered him to the floor. For endless minutes, silence filled the room.

"Is he dead?" Deke croaked out the words. "I meant to kill him. Is he dead?" he repeated.

Micah stared down at the motionless man and the bloody hole in the back of his coat. "I don't know. I think so."

"Well, I s'pose I ain't goin' to heaven now." A shaky sob emanated from Deke. "Don't deserve it anyway."

Throwing off his stupor, Micah returned to the bedside and knelt down. "None of us deserves salvation, Deke. We've all sinned and come short of the glory of God."

"I couldn't let him kill Miz Northam. She was good to me, even after we brought her here meaning to do her harm, her and her babe." He lifted a wobbling hand and swiped it across his fevered brow.

A sobbing scream split the air, and Micah's heart dropped like a stone. Had the bullet gone through Hardison and struck one of the women? He jumped up from the bedside to see Marybeth writhing in Grace's arms. Grace raised her eyes to meet his.

"The baby's coming."

Chapter Twelve

Grace felt strangely calm. But then, she'd delivered countless calves and colts and kittens, and had been at Doc's side when her sister Maisie gave birth to Johnny. She could handle this as long as Marybeth was strong enough after the ordeal she'd already been through. As always with childbirths, if there were complications, only the Lord could save either mother or baby.

"We need to get her off the floor." She tilted her head toward a second cot in the corner of the room.

"What can I do?" the Rev asked as they moved a whimpering Marybeth to the bed and settled her in.

"Add a log to the fire." Grace tilted her head toward the fireplace, then looked around the shabby shack. Through a doorway, she saw a small kitchen. "Boil some water. Find some clean rags."

To his credit, the Rev didn't hesitate to do what was needed. Nor did he seem put off by Marybeth's impending delivery. Every day that she knew the man, he surprised her with new shows of strength. When he stepped in front of her and Marybeth to

shield them from Hardison's gun, her first reaction was that she should be the one to protect them all. But then, hadn't she always dreamed of having someone to be strong for her? The Rev had been just that, and it had felt good to her, mighty good.

When she'd accidentally called him Micah instead of Rev, she'd realized for certain that she loved him. Had actually known it for weeks, but tried to ignore such useless feelings. After all, when all of this settled down, he would marry the proper Miss Sutton, and that would be the end of it.

Marybeth cried out again, putting an end to her ruminations. When her pain subsided, she gave Grace an apologetic grimace. "I'm such a crybaby."

"Pshaw!" Grace huffed indignantly. "Even a cow bawls when she's giving birth."

"Thanks, Grace." Marybeth giggled and then grimaced. "I've felt like a cow for weeks now."

"That's not what I meant." Couldn't she say anything right? She'd meant to console her friend, but ended up insulting her.

"I'm only jo-oking." Marybeth gritted her teeth and twisted on the cot as if trying to get away from the pain. After a few moments, she exhaled a long sigh and closed her eyes, appearing to rest.

Grace let her be and went to the kitchen. The Rev had found a pan and was dutifully stoking the cast-iron cookstove to boil the water. Or rather, the snow. On the back of the stove sat a cast-iron Dutch oven holding the remnants of beef stew that still smelled good. The scoundrels had probably made Marybeth cook for them.

"No water in here, so I had to scoop up a pan of

snow out back." He looked a bit harried, like maybe he needed approval.

It tickled her innards to see him show his humanity this way. "Good idea."

"It looks like it's from yesterday's snow, so it's probably fairly clean." He glanced up from his work. "Will that be all right?"

"That's why we boil it." At least that's what Doc, Grace's brother-in-law, always said. She leaned against the doorjamb and crossed her arms. "Do you suppose we should toss Hardison's sorry carcass outside? It galls me to think of a sweet little baby being born in a room with a dead killer. I mean, a dead repentant sinner is one thing, but Hardison—"

The Rev stopped in the middle of placing another piece of wood into the stove. "I'm not sure he's dead. Are you?"

"Oh." Shame surged through her chest, and with it, a realization. Marybeth and the Rev had been kind to Deke. The Rev had even faced down Hardison, refusing to shoot him, though the varmint would have killed him if not for Deke's interference. Like Jesus, he was willing to lay down his life not only for his friends but for a wicked sinner like Hardison. Grace would just as soon have shot them both and asked questions later. "No, I'm not sure."

What she was sure of was a brand-new understanding of one of the Rev's favorite sermon topics: God's grace. It was for everyone, not just "good" people. That was important to know, because she didn't feel like a very good person right now. Not her willingness to protect the innocent, but her *eagerness* to kill the killers was all the more proof that she didn't

deserve the love of a man like the Rev. Not only was she too rough in her ways, but her heart was just as deplorable as her actions.

"I'm going to leave this to come to a boil," the Rev said, "and go out to let Dub know what's happened in here."

Marybeth called out to her before she could respond. Which was a good thing, because right now, her throat felt all clogged up with emotions, and she had no idea why.

Micah reached Dub and the now-conscious Purvis just as some twenty riders came up the road. Led by Rand and Nate Northam, the group included Doc Henshaw, a fact that made Micah's knees go weak. God was so good, so amazing.

Eager to let the posse know the lay of the land right away, he waved, called out and smiled. "She's safe, Rand. Everything's going to be all right."

Rand reined his horse to a stop. "Where is she?" Fear and hope collided on his face.

"In the cabin." Micah hooked a thumb over his shoulder. "Doc, there's some work for you in there."

The two men galloped the hundred yards to the cabin while Micah and the rest of the posse approached more slowly and helped to sort out other matters. The outlaws' and Marybeth's horses needed to be saddled and brought from the barn. Dub and several other men took charge of Purvis and headed back to town with a promise to send a buggy or wagon for Marybeth. The rest waited to see where they might be needed.

Micah entered the cabin just as Doc drew the woolen blanket over Deke's face.

"This man wasn't in good health to begin with." Doc shook his head and sighed. Just as Micah wanted to see men's souls saved, Doc longed to save their bodies. "The infection from the cat bite was the final straw."

A deep ache opened up in Micah's chest. At least Deke had turned to God in his last moments. Hardison sat in a half-broken overstuffed chair, his legs sprawled helplessly as if he couldn't move them. His pale face was twisted into a snarl, although he looked near death, too. Across the quiet room, Rand and Grace knelt beside Marybeth, who had yet to bring forth her child.

Doc must have already checked Hardison's wound, because the outlaw's bloody coat lay beside him on the floor.

"Let me have another look." Doc bent over the man, only to be waved away with a gesture too harsh for a badly wounded man.

"Leave me alone." Hardison spat out the words. "Let me die."

"Can't do that." Doc tried again, this time succeeding in pulling Hardison away from the back of the chair. "Hmm. Still bleeding. I need to take out that bullet."

"Why? So you can watch me hang? Just let me die now." He coughed, and Micah could see more blood oozing from his back.

Marybeth cried out again, and a shiver ran down Micah's back. In this moment, he agreed with

Grace. A baby shouldn't be born under these circumstances—or with an audience.

Doc checked Marybeth and then returned to Hardison. "Reverend, would you help me?" With the floor rough and cold, they had no place to lay the outlaw, so Doc would have to lean him against Micah while he worked.

Hardison had lost all ability to fight. He slumped against Micah, only emitting a few curses and cries of pain while Doc removed the bullet and patched up the wound. As Micah supported him, he prayed for the man's soul. He didn't realize he spoke aloud until Hardison whispered roughly, "Don't waste your time."

Grace didn't know who needed her help the most, Doc or Rand. As Marybeth's time drew nearer, Rand paced the room between her pains and rushed to her side when she cried out. The anxiety on his handsome face suggested he was on the edge of panic.

"Hey, settle down, Pa." Grace grinned at him, trying her best to appear relaxed herself. "Babies are born every day, and Doc's the best at bringing them into this world."

"You're right." Running a hand through his dark brown hair, he grinned sheepishly. But his eyes strayed to Deke's covered body on the other cot and the now-unconscious Hardison slumped in the overstuffed chair.

The Rev stood by the door. As always, he seemed to be looking around to see how he could help. Grace smiled at him, and he returned a warm grin that even lit up those remarkable gray eyes. She basked in that

look for as long as she could before Marybeth needed her again.

"I have an idea." The Rev put on his coat and walked to the door. "I'll be right back."

Curious, she grabbed her coat and followed him out. In truth, she just wanted to be near him. Soon enough he'd be married, and she'd have to keep her distance.

"Do you think you can do that?" The Rev spoke to Nate and the three remaining posse members who'd stuck around to help where needed.

"Sure thing. Should have thought of that myself." Nate appeared grateful to have something to do. "Let's go." He beckoned to the others, and they all headed toward the barn.

"What did you tell them?" Grace let herself enjoy the moment.

He shrugged in his humble way. "Just to look for ways to make a travois to carry Deke and Hardison back to town."

"We all should have thought of that." Grace shook her head. The Rev certainly had done more to help put an end to this whole mess than she had. Maybe it was time to hand in her badge.

A new kind of cry came from within the cabin, the lusty cry of a healthy newborn baby, followed by Marybeth's joyous laughter and a hearty whoop from Rand. Grace and the Rev traded one of their special looks and both grinned.

"A new life." Grace's eyes burned, but for once, she let the tears come. "God is good."

"Two new lives." The Rev's eyes were suspiciously

red, too. When she questioned him with a look, he added, "Deke. His new life with the Lord."

"Oh. Yeah." Of course he would think about a man's soul. That was the main business of his life. Grace could only pray for such a tender heart. "Well, let's go see if it's a boy or a girl."

Micah had never been so glad to return home as he was that Monday evening. Deke's body had been delivered to the undertaker, and Micah would give him a Christian burial on Wednesday before prayer meeting. Jud Purvis, the third outlaw, was locked up in jail, where Justice Gareau—no longer needed to guard Nolan Means—watched over him until he could come to trial. Hardison still lingered between life and death at Doc's house, where Sean O'Shea stood guard to be sure the outlaw wasn't faking. Seamus was still at Doc's, too, but on the mend. Marybeth and her sweet baby daughter had traveled back home in a buggy driven by her doting husband. Nate had collected his wife, children, mother and nephew from the hotel and joined his brother in the refuge of Four Stones Ranch.

To Micah's surprise, Joel and Miss Sutton had already moved back into the parsonage once they'd heard the outlaws had been apprehended. The young lady had even prepared an exceptional supper of chicken and dumplings. She seemed particularly happy, but Micah was too tired to ask why. For some reason, he felt a lingering sadness over the day's trials. And he missed Grace. Missed her quiet ways. Something he might not have noticed if Miss Sutton weren't such

a—he searched for a kind way to refer to her—a *lively* talker.

Just as they were about to sit down to supper, Grace arrived. It felt to Micah as if the sun had come out, even though it was long past sunset. "Sorry. I don't mean to intrude. Just wanted to return this." She handed Micah his Colt Peacemaker.

"Thank you, Grace." He chuckled. "I didn't even realize I'd left it there." With all of the dramatic events that happened this day, no wonder he'd forgotten the gun. He must write down those events before he forgot them so he could use them in his next novel. "Will you stay for supper?"

"No, thanks. I need to get over to Mrs. Foster's and be sure she's all right. I know she'll have supper waiting." She glanced around the parlor, her eyes focusing at last on the coffee table. "Huh. I see you have a copy of that book Mrs. Winsted's been selling. What did you think of it?"

Micah's heart did a strange little hop. "It's… interesting. Have you read it?" *Did you like it? Would you read more?* Suddenly her opinion mattered to him more than anything in the world.

"Couldn't get past the first chapter. I took it back to Mrs. Winsted." Grace shrugged. "Georgia would probably like it."

"What—" Micah's voice squeaked a little, and he cleared his throat. "What didn't you like?"

"Well…" she drawled, gazing off thoughtfully. "It's pretty much like most of the dime novels Mrs. Winsted sells. Whoever wrote it didn't know much about what cowboys or sheriffs really do out here." She snorted softly. "Probably some Easterner wrote

it. They all think we're dumb as rocks anyway." She turned to go. "See you at prayer meeting Wednesday."

"Wait." Miss Sutton flounced into the room, a happy smile on her pretty face. "Grace, I'm so glad to see you, but I must disagree with you about the book. *Rio Grande Sheriff* may seem slow at the beginning, but I believe the adventures of the hero are every bit as realistic as what you and Micah have endured these past few days." She snatched up the book. "Why, I would even say this is more in the style of Mark Twain or Charles Dickens. It's certainly easier to read than Nathaniel Hawthorne."

Micah shot a glance at Miss Sutton. She thought the book was slow at the beginning? Hmm. Maybe he needed to start the next book with a bit more excitement.

"You must give it another try." Miss Sutton held the book out to Grace.

"No, thanks." Grace winced and stepped back like she'd just been offered a rattlesnake. Micah's heart plummeted. Even with Miss Sutton's recommendation, she wouldn't read it. "Mrs. Foster has a copy I can read if I get especially bored." She moved toward the door. "Y'all have a nice evening." She pulled her hat up on its strings and placed it over her glorious auburn hair, which looked particularly fetching tonight because it was slightly rumpled. "G'night, Rev. Miss Sutton. Joel." She waved to Joel, who stood behind his sister.

"Now, Grace, you must call me Electra." She chirped her words as happily as a spring robin. "I believe we've been friends long enough, don't you?"

"Yeah. Sure. G'night." Her shoulders slumped as she walked out.

Micah's heart went with her, but he didn't know whether it was because he wanted to help with whatever had depressed her or because he wanted to explain the book. Either way, he couldn't bring himself to go after her when she so clearly wanted to be alone. He could only pray that the Lord would sort things out for her over time. And yet, her rejection of his book, into which he'd poured only the best of intentions and a considerable amount of his heart, wounded him more than he'd thought possible.

Grace couldn't understand why the icy evening wind stung her face so badly until she realized she was crying. She swiped at the foolish tears and increased her stride along the dark street toward Mrs. Foster's house.

Micah. Miss Sutton had used his Christian name as though she'd always known him. Or should Grace say *Electra*? She still thought it was a silly name, but if she could bring herself to be friendly with the woman, she might try Elly, as her brother addressed her. Or she might call her Mrs. Thomas after she and the Rev got hitched.

Grace sniffed back the extra tears that thought caused. *Bother!* What was wrong with her? She'd always known the Rev wasn't for her. Their experiences at the cabin only made it more certain. She didn't have the tender heart a minister's wife needed. She was too rough in all of her ways. Now if she could just convince her foolish, illogical heart of those realities, she'd feel much better. Sure she would.

Early the next morning, she paid a call on Sheriff Lawson, who was still giving his wife fits over having to stay in bed.

"Sure wish I could have been out there with you." The lawman fidgeted where he lay. "I hear you and the reverend managed pretty well, though." He offered a smile, a rarity for him, and settled his steely-eyed gaze on her. "Good job, Deputy."

"Yessir, well, about that." Under that gaze, Grace did her own share of fidgeting. What she was about to do took more courage than facing Hardison. Before she could change her mind, she unhooked her tin badge from her leather vest and set it on the bedside table. "I'm done, sir. Justice Gareau needs a job, and I think he's the man to be your new deputy. Sean O'Shea's another good man. The two of them should be all the backup you need to take care of this town."

Lawson stared at her for a full fifteen seconds, his jaw slack and his eyes wide. "Why, Grace," he finally managed, "you're an excellent deputy. Even Andy Ransom and Rafael Trujillo have said they admire the way you brought down Hardison. They didn't do anywhere near as well as you. Couldn't even catch those two other gang members who are still out there somewhere. You have the respect of the entire town. Why do you want to quit?"

"Maybe—" Mrs. Lawson stood in the doorway, a knowing smile on her lips "—just maybe she'd like to get married."

Grace felt like she'd been smacked. But she could see the lady meant no harm. She shuffled her feet. "No, ma'am. Not me. I just need to help my folks out at the ranch full-time now." She swallowed hard.

Who on earth did Mrs. Lawson think she was going to marry? Who on earth would want to marry the likes of her? The best thing for Grace would be to move back to the ranch and come to town as seldom as possible.

The sheriff reached over to the bedside table and clumsily took the badge in hand. "Do this for me, Grace." He held the shield out with a shaky hand. "Stick around until I'm back on my feet." He gave her another one of his rare grins.

She thought he might be pretending how shaky he was, but wouldn't insult him by suggesting it. Reluctantly, she lifted her hand, accepted the badge and heaved out a long sigh. "If you insist." She looked at Mrs. Lawson, whose gaze seemed almost maternal, something Grace didn't quite understand. What was the woman thinking? "Ma'am, would you please make sure this old codger gets well soon?"

For a moment, she feared she'd crossed a line of respect, but the sheriff's benevolent smile and a chuckle that obviously pained him reassured her. As far as she was concerned, though, she felt as trapped in the job she used to love as if she were the one behind bars over at the jail.

Despite his exhaustion, Micah's troubled thoughts kept him awake. How could he write a novel with a heroine inspired by Grace when she thought so little of his first book? He had no doubt the truth would eventually come out that he was the author. What would she say when she found out? No matter how pure his intentions, if his story about her caused her

pain, he simply could not write it. But then, hadn't the Lord opened the way for him to publish his stories?

Or was he mistaken? Was it his own pride that drove him to create these fictions? It wasn't as if he was seeking fame, only an additional income so he could marry and provide for his wife. Of course, he did love to create the stories and had always felt the Lord approved. But then, if he was mistaken about the Lord wanting him to write, maybe he was mistaken about His direction for Micah to marry. He'd certainly been wrong about the Lord sending Miss Sutton to be his wife.

He laughed to himself. Miss Sutton had ceased her flirtations days ago, much to his relief. He prayed she would find happiness, but she seemed to already have found it. Perhaps it was her involvement in directing the children's pageant or perhaps her hopes of moving to Denver. And with her commendable housekeeping and cooking skills, one day she would make some good man an excellent wife.

And what of Micah's matrimonial call? Would the Lord give him more direction? In truth, he now realized that since sensing God's call to marry, he'd depended more upon his feelings and assumptions than on prayer and seeking God's will. He would rectify that now. Kneeling beside his bed, he asked the Lord to make clear His will, for marriage or singleness, for writing additional books or for informing his publisher that there would be no more stories by the Cowboy Storyteller.

As he climbed back in bed and closed his eyes,

Grace's lovely face flashed before him. If that was the Lord's answer about his writing, Micah still didn't understand what he was supposed to do.

Chapter Thirteen

Micah conducted a brief graveside funeral for Deke Smith in the graveyard north of Esperanza. Grace came but stood back near the fence. Other than Mr. Macy, the undertaker, and Adam Starling, who'd helped carry the coffin and dig the grave with pickax and shovel through the frozen ground, Deke had no mourners. At least Micah could take comfort that heaven now rejoiced over a sinner saved.

For his own part, he thanked the Lord that Deke had kept Hardison from killing Grace and Marybeth. And him, of course. After having a killer point a gun at him and fully intend to shoot, Micah felt extremely grateful to be alive. Nothing like a brush with death to make a man count his blessings.

He wanted to say something to that effect to Grace, but she left the graveyard before he had a chance. She'd avoided him for two days now, and he couldn't imagine why. After their success in saving Marybeth and stopping the outlaws, they should be celebrating. Together.

When he returned home for supper, he found

Nolan Means chatting with Joel in the parlor. From the kitchen came the sound of two female voices, Miss Sutton's and Anna's. Seemed he would be having guests tonight. *Seemed* they needed another lady to balance the party. But Grace had moved back to her parents' ranch, so he couldn't delay supper by going out to invite her. He hoped she would come to prayer meeting so he could ask her if she was all right.

"Good evening, Reverend." Nolan stood to shake his hand. "I hope you don't mind our intrusion."

"Not at all." Micah noticed the banker had relaxed considerably now that the outlaws no longer posed a threat. "You're welcome here anytime."

"Electra said you were a true Southern gentleman in regard to hospitality." Nolan took his seat again.

Electra? He addressed her by her Christian name? Micah glanced at Joel, who returned a sly look. "I'm sure she and Joel appreciated *your* hospitality and the protection of your bodyguards." Micah chuckled. "And I doubt Miss Sutton expected to find the Wild West quite so wild."

"And yet she has adapted admirably." The pride in Nolan's eyes was nothing short of proprietary. "So much so that just today she has consented to be my wife." His chest puffed up like a bantam rooster's.

As overwhelming relief swept through him, Micah dropped into his favorite overstuffed chair. Although Miss Sutton's initial interest in him had quickly cooled, as his had for her, he'd felt a lingering disquiet about the whole situation. Now it was settled, and he didn't have to worry any longer. "Congratulations." He jumped up from his chair and crossed

the room to shake Nolan's hand. "Congratulations! I am very pleased for you."

Joel chuckled. "Sorry you lost out, Micah, but—"

"But—" Micah wouldn't let him finish "—a better man has won your lovely sister." So his earlier suspicions had been right. This courtship had been ongoing from the first time these two had met. And yet with other matters to deal with, he'd failed to comprehend its depth. While he'd noticed Miss Sutton's happiness, he hadn't determined the cause of it. Once again, he became aware of his lack of discernment, something he'd never experienced until these last few months. How could he be so thickheaded? What other issues was he missing among his parishioners? "When will you be announcing the happy news?"

"We'll make the formal announcement at our Christmas ball, but Electra will probably want to show off her engagement ring after prayer meeting tonight." Nolan's face continued to beam with pride. "It was my mother's, made of rubies and diamonds."

At supper, Micah made sure to fuss over the ring, which was indeed quite glorious—just the thing for a lady who hoped to advance as a social leader. After years of searching, at last Nolan had his bride, one who could teach his sister, Anna, the social skills he'd wanted her to learn since coming west. One who could host his annual Christmas party for the more prominent members of the community. Having lovingly accepted all of the children in her care for the Christmas pageant without respect to their social status, maybe Miss Sutton could even put an end to Nolan's snobbishness.

With the outlaws no longer a danger, a new sense

of excitement regarding Christmas came over the congregation. Over the past two days, Mrs. Foster and other church ladies had decorated the sanctuary with pine boughs and red ribbons. The Northams contributed a perfectly shaped pine tree for the reception hall. Mrs. Winsted donated hand-painted, blown glass ornaments and a gold star tree topper, also made of glass, all from Germany, to complete the decorations. Under strict supervision by Miss Sutton and Anna Means, the older children had the privilege of placing the delicate ornaments on the tree, while the younger ones strung popcorn for a garland.

After greeting the children, Micah left them in the good care of Miss Sutton and Anna and proceeded to the sanctuary. In spite of the freezing temperature outside, the room was full to overflowing, as it had been since the troubles began. Micah prayed his congregation would continue to see how prayer could affect the outcome of even the worst of situations.

They sang "While Shepherds Watched Their Flocks by Night" before settling down in their pews to hear Micah speak. As he always did, he gazed around the room to see who had come. He felt a little kick in his chest when he saw Grace seated in the middle of the room with her sisters and her parents. He certainly had missed her.

"Friends, I know you want a report on the outlaws as much as you do a sermon this evening." He smiled. "Maybe in place of a sermon."

As he'd hoped, the congregation laughed. He also heard a few "amens," which brought on more laughter.

"In this case, I believe the story of the outlaws will make a very fine sermon." He briefly told the

story of how he, Grace and Dub had approached the outlaws' hiding place, leaving out the part about Everett Winsted's information. The boy would pay the price for his actions soon enough. "Once Hardison so politely invited us into the cabin…" He paused while more laughter filled the room and then grew solemn to set the tone for his next words. "We found Marybeth alive and well, just as we'd prayed for her. She was tending Deke Smith, who lay near death."

Several folks made comments about his getting what he deserved.

"I understand why you hold that opinion. But let us consider the two thieves who were crucified with Jesus. Many onlookers must have rejoiced to see those two die for the evil they had done. And yet Jesus saw the hearts of the men, and when one thief repented, our Lord forgave him and offered to him the grace of God. That is what happened in that cabin two days ago. Dathan Hardison refused God's grace, but Deke Smith saw his need for Christ's salvation and repented."

A hum of wonder and understanding swept through the congregation.

"These outlaws, these killers each had a list of sins so long none of us could count them. But lest we think ourselves better than they, remember what Paul says in Romans 3:23: '*All* have sinned and come short of the glory of God.' And yet, by grace are ye saved, and that not of yourselves, it is a gift of God." He paused, praying these dear people would understand his words. "What would we do without grace? We would all be lost without it."

As Micah spoke, his gaze connected with Grace's.

Lantern light reflected in her bright blue eyes, making her lovely face radiant. Her sweet, peaceful expression reached into his very heart and set it aglow. Grace. What would he do without Grace? He would be lost without her.

His knees grew weak as realization swept over him. Oh, how he loved her—more than words could say. To him, she was far more than a member of his church. Far more than a mere friend. She was the one he'd been looking for, and she'd been here all the time, right in front of his undiscerning eyes. How had he failed to comprehend that he'd loved her for weeks, for months? She was the woman he yearned to spend the rest of his life with...

Someone coughed, and he realized he hadn't spoken for some time. How long, he couldn't guess. Grace rolled her eyes, wrinkled her nose and gave him their private grin. Heat surged up his neck and into his cheeks. He could only hope no one noticed in the dimly lit sanctuary. But then, the way he felt right now, he wanted to shout the news to the entire world. He loved Grace Eberly!

Grace wrinkled her nose at the Rev. He got lost someplace in the middle of his sermon, and since he was looking at her, she rolled her eyes, too, hoping to help him out. When he finally blinked his eyes and went on with his sermon, she was relieved for him. Poor man. He'd been through so much these past few days. Maybe after prayer meeting, she could encourage him. She'd tell him that his telling the story about the two thieves crucified with Jesus finally helped her to understand God's grace, even though she'd had

the same thought herself at the cabin. Still, the Lord knew it was exactly what she needed to hear and to know after the way she'd judged poor Adam Starling. She had yet to make it up to the boy.

Sitting on either side of her, Maisie and Georgia nudged her with their elbows and then peered around her at each other, both smothering grins with their hands. What on earth were they up to?

The Rev finished his sermon and then read out the prayer requests. Grace committed his words to memory so she could pray for the folks all week. Down the row, Ma wrote the requests out because her memory didn't serve her as well as it used to. It wasn't Ma's only failing recently. All the more reason for Grace to take off her badge and help her folks at the ranch full-time.

Several members offered prayers until the whole list had been brought before the Lord. Then the Rev said the final prayer, and Mrs. Foster struck up "Joy to the World" to end the meeting on a happy note. Children came through the side door and ran to their parents, with Miss Sutton and Anna following behind. Miss Sutton made a beeline to Susanna Northam, but Grace couldn't hear what she said. Anyway, she wanted to speak to the Rev, so she moved in that direction.

"It was his mother's ring." Miss Sutton held up her dainty left hand to display a big, pretty gewgaw that caught the light and sparkled like a red star. She smiled toward the Rev, who was talking with Nolan Means.

Grace's heart dropped like a rock. So the Rev had proposed to Miss Sutton. It was about time. It was

also time for Grace to go home. And stay there. She stepped out of the pew and headed up the aisle. Since admitting to herself that she loved the Rev, she'd tried her best to change her heart, but it just wasn't working. Seeing Miss Sutton with his mother's ring was just too much. Besides, that fancy gewgaw would look silly on Grace's rough hands. She'd lose it in the hay while feeding the horses or doing some other ranch work, that's for sure.

The outside air smacked her in the face, and she felt tears freezing on her cheeks. She'd never been a crybaby, but look at her now. She had to get away before somebody saw her.

"Grace, wait for us." Georgia followed her out of the church, with Maisie right behind her. "What's your hurry?" They caught her and held on like nobody but family would dare.

"Oh, sweetie." Maisie brushed a gloved hand over Grace's cheek. "What's the matter?"

"Nothing." Grace tried to pull away, but they wouldn't let her.

"Didn't you see the way Reverend Thomas was looking at you? Didn't you notice how he lost his place in the sermon?" Her sisters giggled.

"Don't be mean, Maisie." Grace continued to tug against her sister's hold. "Just because you caught Doc's eye…"

"Don't *you* be silly, Grace." Her older sister touched Grace's chin and forced her to look into her eyes. "It's because I know what a man in love looks like that I know Reverend—"

"Hush!" Grace gasped, waving a hand toward the crowd of people emerging from the church. To her

relief, her sisters stopped their teasing. "I'm going home. Tell Ma and Pa."

Georgia eyed Maisie. Maisie nodded.

"On Saturday," Maisie said, "I'll come out to the ranch to help you get ready for Nolan Means's Christmas party."

"Don't bother. I'm not going."

"Not going?" Her sisters spoke at the same time.

"Wasn't invited." Saying the words almost made Grace cry full out, but after a struggle, she managed to hold back her tears.

"The very idea," Maisie huffed, sending a plume of frozen breath into the air. "Well, if you're not invited, Doc and I won't go either."

"That's not right." Grace couldn't allow her sister's sacrifice, no matter how good the sentiment made her feel. "We don't have enough fancy goings-on in this town for you to miss out on the biggest one. Besides, Doc will need an evening out after all he's been through." He'd stayed home tonight to watch baby Johnny and to tend his patients.

"What about what you've been through?" Georgia's loving concern shone in her eyes.

Grace shrugged. "All part of the job." A job she couldn't wait to be done with.

More people emerged from the church, some stopping to offer Grace their thanks for saving the town again. She tried to smile, but the wind had picked up, freezing her lips. Finally freeing herself from her sisters and friends, she mounted up and headed back to the ranch. With every thump of Mack's hoofbeats on the snow-covered road, her heart pounded painfully.

How long did it take to get over a broken heart? Grace prayed it would be soon, or she would surely die.

Micah stood beside Sheriff Lawson's bed, one hand on Everett Winsted's shoulder to keep the frightened boy from bolting. His mother, Nelly, held his other shoulder. She and his grandmother, Mrs. Winsted, had brought Everett to see Micah first thing this morning. Although he'd planned to ride out to the Eberly ranch to see Grace, he couldn't miss this opportunity to help the boy.

"Everett, I want you to tell Sheriff Lawson what you told Deputy Grace and me on Monday." Micah wished Grace could be here to help out, but Justice Gareau said she'd asked him to take care of the jail for a while.

The boy stuttered through the explanation he'd given Micah and Grace about how the outlaws had lured him into their gang, saying they needed help, making him feel important, charitable, *grown-up*—until it was too late. Everett stopped from time to time to sob or blow his nose. To his credit, he didn't make excuses for his actions. All the while, Sheriff Lawson glowered in his menacing way, as though Everett were a hardened outlaw. When the boy finished, he tried to lean against his mother, but she set him upright.

"You wanted to be in cahoots with evil men." Nelly's face was remarkably placid. "Now face your punishment like a man. Sheriff, don't hold back."

The fatherless boy had already repented, and Micah wanted to plead for mercy, but couldn't bring himself to interfere. Justice would have to prevail.

But perhaps if someone had required mercy for Deke and Hardison when they were young, how different their lives might have been.

"Well," the sheriff drawled, "I could put him in jail with that Purvis fella, the one who shot me for putting him in prison years ago. Would you like that, boy? To be with your friend?"

Everett's eyes widened in fear. "No, sir. He's not my friend. I never want to see him again."

The sheriff nodded. "Then I suppose you don't want to join him and Hardison in Cañon City Penitentiary either."

"No, sir." Everett's voice squeaked. "I'll do anything not to go to prison. Let me stay in jail here." He bit his lip. "Just not in the same cell as Mr. Purvis. Please?"

"Hmm." The sheriff scratched his chin thoughtfully and stared off across the room. "Maybe we can come up with a better plan. How about you do some work for the folks in town, the ones those outlaws meant to harm?" He listed several unpleasant tasks, such as keeping the streets clean after horses had left their calling cards—a never-ending task—and shoveling snow from the boardwalks. They settled on six months of unpaid labor to be done after school every day, with a plan to revisit the matter if Everett slacked off. "You can add to that list anything Reverend Thomas needs help with." He nodded to Micah.

"Sounds good to me." Micah grinned as several chores around the church came to mind.

Mercy had indeed prevailed. Now if he could find Grace and tell her everything that was in his heart, all would be right in his world. That was, if she felt

the same way. She still didn't take compliments well, so courting her might turn out to be a problem. His heart light at the prospect of the challenge, he made his way down to the livery stable to fetch his horse. No time like the present to ride out to the Eberly ranch to begin courting the lady he loved.

"Reverend Thomas!" His face creased with worry, Adam Starling hailed him from across the street.

"What is it, Adam?" An uneasy feeling swept aside Micah's happiness.

Adam ran toward him, almost falling on the rutted street. "My pa. I'm going to get Doc. Please—"

"I'll get Doc. You go help your mother."

"No, sir. Please." Adam panted, hardly able to talk. "Pa needs you."

"I'll go to him." He patted Adam's arm and then broke out in a run toward the boy's house. Poor Bob Starling still hadn't recovered from his beating almost two years ago. If he died... Micah wouldn't let himself think about it. Now was the time to bring the Lord's comfort to the family, and it was the Lord Who would take care of their future.

Grace hadn't been cross with her mother since she couldn't remember when. Even now, she held her tongue after Ma insisted she needed baking soda right now and couldn't wait until Georgia got out of school. But the last place Grace wanted to be was in town, where she might run into the Rev or Miss Sutton or, worse, the two of them together.

Unlike last night when she'd ridden Mack fairly hard to get home with only a sliver of a moon for light, Grace listlessly nudged her gelding to a walk.

Which wasn't fair to him. In the cold air, he liked to canter, at least. Care for her horse finally forced her to give him his head, and they arrived at the mercantile all too soon. To her further discomfort, she saw Dub Gleason and his friends seated inside around the cracker barrel. To her *surprise*, they all stood when she entered the store.

"Howdy, Miss Grace," Dub said, with the others offering similar greetings. To a man, she couldn't see the slightest bit of derision in their faces.

"Howdy." Unsettled, she marched past them as she let her hat slide off and hang down her back on its strings.

After Homer Bean took her payment for the baking soda, plus a pretty little figurine she'd chosen for Georgia's Christmas present, she gritted her teeth to walk past the wastrels again. *Again* they stood.

She spun around and fisted her free hand at her waist. "What's this all about?" She refused to stand for it another day, another minute. It was time to have it out with them. "You mocking me?"

They all stared at her wide-eyed.

"No, ma'am, Miss Grace." Dub shuffled his feet. "In fact, I want to apologize for acting like a—" he gulped and cleared his throat "—well, acting rude to you all these years. We all come to see you're a mighty fine-looking woman, not to mention a mighty fine deputy."

She narrowed her eyes and glared at them, one at a time. "What brought on this unlikely repentance?" Unbelievable would have been a better word.

"Oh, nothing," Dub said. "We just saw the error of our ways."

"The reverend lit into us the other day. That's what did it," Earl Aldrich said.

Dub punched his friend's shoulder. "That's not what did it. Not for me. It was seeing what a brave woman you were catching those outlaws. You put all the men to shame."

Grace had grown tired of hearing how brave she was. She'd only done her duty, the same as she'd done all her life. "But the Rev did say something?"

"Yessum." Earl stepped away from Dub, who shot him an angry look. "He just about preached us a sermon right there on the street. Told us we're lazy bums. Said you're a fine, brave woman."

"That's the truth." Shep spoke up for the first time. "He give us what-for."

"Huh." Grace would ponder this information later. For now, she wasn't about to let these "lazy bums" off. "Sounds like you all benefited from the Rev's sermon. Why don't you start coming to church on Sundays so he can improve you a whole heap more?"

She marched out of the store to a chorus of "yes-sums."

On the way home, she felt an odd lump form in her chest. The Rev had protected her with his words, just like he'd protected her with his own life. It only made her love him more. It only made the hopelessness of that love hurt even worse.

She'd known she'd never marry because of the way men saw her. Gawky, too tall, plain. But now, the one man who'd always treated her just right, who'd even changed her mind about romance, was marrying somebody else.

* * *

While Doc did what he could for Bob Starling, Micah took Mavis into the kitchen and served her coffee. Adam, Molly and Jack sat at the table, their eyes on their mother.

"He's still with us." Her voice broke. "At least for a little while."

"Does this mean he can come to our Christmas play?" The hopeful look in six-year-old Molly's blue eyes almost broke Micah's heart.

Mavis gave her a watery smile. "Wouldn't that be nice? But I don't think so, my darling."

"He's sleeping now." Doc entered the kitchen, his shoulders slumped as though the weight of the world rested on them.

"If you need to see to other patients," Micah said, "I can stay here."

Doc nodded wearily. "If it's all right with Mavis, I'll take you up on that. I had a long night with Seamus last night." He held up a hand. "Don't worry. He's fine now."

But Doc wasn't. The young man, close to Micah in age, had dark circles under his eyes and worry lines etched beside them.

"Go ahead." Micah reached across the table and patted Mavis's hand. "We'll be fine, won't we?"

He walked Doc to the door and received instructions on how much laudanum to give the patient if he woke up in pain. Otherwise, all they could do was keep him comfortable.

Micah settled in to stay as long as he was needed. For some reason, the Lord didn't want him to see Grace right now, but he wouldn't complain. He would

see her at Nolan's Christmas ball on Saturday evening. They would dance together. He would ask if he could court her. Or maybe he should ask Mr. Eberly first. Yes, that was it. When the family arrived at Nolan's, Micah would speak to her father, as was proper, and then dance with her, hopefully for the rest of their lives.

But Grace didn't come to the ball. Nor did her parents. Even Doc and Maisie were absent because they wanted to sit with Bob Starling, whose condition remained unchanged. In one of those odd little moments where faith and a hard life seemed to collide, Doc and Maisie said what Micah had been thinking. If Bob could just hold on until after the Christmas pageant and Christmas Day, it would sure be easier on his children.

Despite impressive decorations, excellent refreshments and music provided by a string quartet from Denver, Micah's heart wasn't in the festivities. Like the church, the interior of the banker's elegant brick house was festooned with pine boughs and red ribbons. Sparkling blown glass ornaments decorated the tree, along with a genuine silver filigree garland in place of a string of popcorn. Miss Sutton was in her element, already the beautiful, brilliant hostess any banker needed. And yet nothing in Nolan's party pointed to the purpose of the Christmas season, a celebration of Christ's birth. After Nolan and Miss Sutton announced their engagement, Micah danced with a few single ladies who lacked partners, making sure to give preference to none of them, then made his excuses and returned home.

He couldn't understand why the Lord kept pre-

venting him from seeing Grace, especially since she'd seemed depressed. Surely now that Micah knew he loved her, knew she was the Lord's chosen wife for him, he should tell her as soon as possible.

Or was he mistaken? Did her depression mean she no longer cared for his company?

Or did her belief that she was unfit for marriage go deeper than he thought?

Or was he just a conceited, muddleheaded chump to think she loved him as he loved her?

Chapter Fourteen

After milking the two milk cows and feeding the horses and chickens, Grace returned to the kitchen to help Ma fix breakfast. She'd worn her usual trousers and boots for the chores and planned to stay in them all day so she could work around the ranch. In spite of her charge to Dub and his friends that they needed to go to church, she had no intention of attending this morning. Someday, once the pain lessened and she was able to accept that the Rev had married the right woman to be a minister's wife, she would go back.

"You wearing that to church?" Georgia, already dressed in her Sunday best, set plates and utensils on the breakfast table.

Grace scowled at her youngest sister. "I'm not going," she said under her breath.

Pa chose that moment to enter the kitchen. "What's this?" He gave her a long look, the one that had always made his five daughters fidget. "Grace, you know the rules. As long as you're living in my house, you'll go to church."

Standing by the stove, Ma gave Grace a sympa-

thetic smile. "George, don't you think she deserves some time to rest up from last week?" Somehow she didn't quite sound like she meant it.

"Humph." He settled in his chair and took up his freshly filled coffee cup. "She's had a week. The rest of the posse's been back to their work, and my girls are as strong as any man." He stared at Grace over the steaming cup. "You'll go to church this morning."

As old as she was, Grace knew better than to argue—or to hesitate in answering. "Yessir."

After breakfast and helping Ma and Georgia start dinner to cooking, she went upstairs to freshen up. How lonely these three bedrooms seemed to her. Growing up, she and Maisie had shared a room and the younger three sisters had shared another. Now Grace and Georgia each had their own rooms. With no one to chat with as she fell asleep or when she woke up, her life had become so solitary. Maybe that was why she'd latched onto the Rev's friendship. He was easy to talk to and—

"Hey, sis." Georgia flounced into the room, her green woolen skirt swirling about her legs in a feminine way. How had all of Grace's sisters managed to become so ladylike, while she had remained a tomboy? "I'm going to help you get dressed."

"You are? You're mighty bossy for a sixteen-year-old."

Georgia laughed. "If it'll help, Maisie told me to do it. So you have to cooperate or I'll be in trouble with our big sister."

Big sister, ha! Maisie might be the oldest, but she wasn't any taller than Georgia.

"Please?" Georgia batted her blue eyes at Grace.

"Save that for the boys." Grace huffed out a sigh of defeat. "All right. What did Maisie say I should wear?"

Georgia clapped her hands in delight and began to dig in Grace's wardrobe. When she'd finished gussying Grace up, including an upswept hairdo that made her neck look terribly long, Grace felt like a scarecrow. But what did it matter? Nobody cared how she looked other than her sisters. She'd always been comfortable in her trousers. Even preferred to have a slightly worn look to her clothes and boots so nobody could say she was uppity just because her pa had a large cattle ranch.

Gathering coats, hats and mittens—and Georgia grabbing her new fur muff—they descended the back stairs to meet Ma and Pa by the door. Her parents stared at her for a full ten seconds. Oh, my, she must look awful.

Then Ma smiled. "You look lovely, girls." Of course she couldn't say only Georgia looked nice, so she'd included Grace in her kind words. Ma was like that, never wanting anyone to have hurt feelings or to feel left out.

As for Pa, his eyes got all big around, and his jaw dropped. "Well, Grace… I never…"

"Let's go." Might as well get to town and get this over with.

Maisie met them in the cloakroom at the front door of the church. After greeting their parents, she said, "Good job, Georgia. Grace, quit slumping." She dug a knuckle into Grace's back, forcing her to lift her shoulders.

"Hey, quit that," Grace whispered sharply.

"Shh." Ma lifted her eyebrows in a scolding look.

"I saved seats for you all." Maisie grabbed Grace's arm and led her to Doc and baby Johnny, who were seated halfway back in the sanctuary. Right in back of Miss Sutton. Grace balked, but her family was on her heels, so she couldn't stop now.

"Look." Maisie nodded toward Miss Sutton, who was sitting arm in arm with Nolan Means.

Offended on behalf of the Rev, Grace started to speak, just as Nolan turned around to greet her family. The snobbish banker wore a grin like the cat that got the cream. Miss Sutton also turned and lifted her left hand to give them a little wave. On the third finger, a bright ruby and diamond ring glittered in the morning sun coming through a side window.

"They're engaged," Maisie whispered. "See. I told you—"

"Hush." Pa scolded them with a look that had always wilted Grace like a weed flower in the sun.

Today, she didn't know how to feel. So it was Nolan and not the Rev who'd proposed to Miss Sutton. Was the Rev brokenhearted? He hadn't seemed upset last Wednesday after prayer meeting when he was chatting to Nolan and Miss Sutton was showing off that ring. Maybe Grace would stick around after church and see if he needed to talk. If her good friend needed her, she would be there for him. But was it terrible of her to be just a little bit happy that he wouldn't be getting married after all?

From the moment Grace and her family walked into the church, Micah knew he would have trouble concentrating on his sermon. If he didn't already

love Grace, he would be falling for her now. From her fancy hairdo to her long, graceful neck to her pretty blue gingham dress to the sparkling gold ear-bobs hanging next to her smooth, tanned cheeks, he'd never seen a more beautiful, more elegant lady in all his twenty-nine years.

Good thing he'd written out his sermon notes. Good thing they would be singing a song before he began to preach. Good thing he was sitting down right now or he'd fall over.

Despite his own reaction to her, he could see from the way she fidgeted and cast self-conscious looks around the room that Grace wasn't comfortable. Poor darling girl, she was still suffering from the taunts Dub and his friends had hurled her way for years. Micah understood because he'd had similar experiences in his youth and saw it every day among the young people in the church. While some teasing was to be expected and even welcomed, how well he knew that cruel taunts could nearly destroy a young person.

At just the wrong moment, when he'd turned thirteen or fourteen, was skinny as a reed and had started noticing girls, an attractive, slightly older girl at church took a dislike to him. She remarked that he would never amount to anything because not only was he ugly, but his Yankee-loving uncle was a traitor, and Micah probably was, too. Because the girl's family was prominent, her friends all agreed and began to call him disparaging names. It took him years to get over those taunts and to realize God's love and direction were all that mattered in his life. In truth, though, it had eased the pain somewhat in his early twenties when some of the nicer young ladies began to notice

him. Clearly Grace had never experienced such admiration. Well, he had every intention of making up for it, beginning today.

At seminary one of his fellow students told the other often-starving friends a few tricks for getting invitations to Sunday dinner. Ask the father for a word of advice and linger at his side waiting for an answer. Compliment the mother on her cooking or, if one hadn't dined with the family, compliment her attire and the behavior of her children. Micah had always felt these ploys were a little dishonest, unless he could honestly deliver such compliments. However, today he was tempted to give it a try. Fortunately, he didn't have to.

At the end of the service when he took his place at the door to shake hands with his departing flock, Mrs. Eberly made a beeline for him, parting the crowd with her reticule like Moses with his rod at the Red Sea. The dear, plump lady arrived at his side just a little breathless.

"Reverend, you're coming to our house for dinner, so if someone else has invited you, you just tell 'em we have priority." After her long speech, she inhaled a deep breath.

Micah could hardly keep from grinning from ear to ear. Now he knew where Grace got her commanding presence. Sometimes it came in handy. "Thank you, Mrs. Eberly, I would be delighted."

Grace couldn't wait to get out of her fancy duds. She'd made this dress to wear to Marybeth's wedding three and a half years ago, but hadn't worn it since. Had actually forgotten about it until Georgia

dragged it out of her wardrobe. Now the underpinnings necessary to wear with such a getup had begun to squeeze Grace's middle, especially after a filling roast beef dinner. And her dressy high-top shoes, borrowed from Georgia, pinched her toes.

"Grace, why don't you and Reverend Thomas go visit in the parlor." Ma stood and began to gather the dishes from the dining room table.

"I should help you clean up." Grace had no idea what she'd say to the Rev. His sermon hadn't been the best this morning, probably because he'd read it instead of speaking from his heart as he usually did.

"Nonsense," Ma said.

"I'll help Ma." Georgia began to gather dishes, too. She gave Grace a "what's the matter with you" look the sisters had often given each other when things didn't sit right with them but they couldn't say anything about it at the moment.

Grace sighed. "Rev, let's go to the parlor, or I'll never hear the end of it." She couldn't imagine why they wanted her to be alone with him, but she did want to find some polite way to ask if he was brokenhearted over Electra's engagement to Nolan Means.

"Sounds good." The Rev held Grace's chair as she stood, and her shoe caught on one leg. Fortunately, he grasped her arm so she didn't fall flat on her face. His touch and warm chuckle sent a pleasant sensation up her arm and down her neck. *Bother!*

"Now we're even. You caught me at the skating pond." His gray eyes twinkled kindly.

Oh, how she wished he wouldn't look at her that way.

Only problem with going to the parlor was that Pa had settled in his favorite chair and was now read-

ing a cattlemen's journal. The Rev waited for Grace
to sit. After looking at the settee, she chose a chair.
He chose the settee, which put him closer to her
than to Pa. That was nice. She smiled. He smiled.
Pa coughed.

That silly cowboy book sat on the coffee table.
Grace wished she'd hidden it. Too late. The Rev saw
it, too.

"Changed your mind about *Rio Grande Sheriff*?" His voice sounded a little strained, although
she couldn't imagine why. The Rev was usually the
calmest person in the room.

"Nope. Haven't tried it again. I think Ma's reading it."

"Grace." Pa cleared his throat. "Would you fetch
us some coffee?"

Glad for the distraction, Grace left the room to
obey. When she returned with the coffee service, Pa
was grinning. He set aside his journal and excused
himself. "Gotta check on that heifer." He walked
out of the room and closed the double pocket doors
behind him. Only thing was, the doors didn't quite
meet in the middle, and she could hear him climbing the stairs.

"But—" No heifers up there, she wanted to holler
at him. Instead, she set the tray on the coffee table
and sat on the edge of her chair. "Coffee, Rev?"

"Um. Sure." He tugged at his collar. "I—I just
spoke with your father..."

"You all right, Rev? What did Pa say?" She held
out his coffee, and the cup clattered against the saucer. Why couldn't she calm her nerves?

"He...he gave me permission to c-court you."

He reached for the cup. Just not far enough. The cup fell and struck the edge of the table, shattering and sending hot coffee and china shards in a thousand directions. One pocket door slid open with a loud thump.

"I'll clean it up." Georgia dashed into the room. "You two take a walk."

As they walked across the barnyard, Micah wanted to take Grace's hand. But she still hadn't responded to his announcement that Mr. Eberly had given him permission to court her. In fact, she hadn't said a word after the two of them dropped the coffee cup. Recalling the scene, Micah burst into laughter.

"What are you laughing about?" Grace tried to sound cross, but her grin and bright eyes gave her away.

"Do you suppose Georgia will tell her friends what happened?" That he'd stammered when he told Grace about getting her father's approval for a courtship. That he'd clumsily dropped a fine china cup and saucer. "Do you think I'll lose all credibility with the youth in the church?"

"Aw, I wouldn't worry about it." Grace scuffed her toe into the snow-peppered dirt, kicking a rock an impressive few yards away. "They like you."

And I like you. Love you. But the words wouldn't come.

They stopped beside a corral where several horses pranced about, snorting out clouds of icy air, enjoying the sunny but cold December day. Not too cold for a bracing walk, though. Instead of a walk, Grace lingered near the fence to study the horses, so Micah

leaned against the wooden rails. The smells of the barnyard weren't as sharp as they were in the summer. After seven years in cattle country, he'd grown used to the odors, even appreciated them because of what they stood for. Hard work, honesty, maybe even a tasty steak at the end of a hard day. But mostly he'd come to value the people who worked the harsh land against daunting circumstances. That's why he wanted to write stories about the heroics of people like Grace.

"To answer your question—"

"Why would you want to—?"

They spoke at the same time, and both stopped.

"You go ahead, Grace." He smiled, his heart welling up with love.

"Why would you want to court me?"

"Because I love you and want you to be my wife." Wow. Had he just said that?

"You do?" She blinked those big beautiful blue eyes. "Why?"

Her question was so startlingly honest, so utterly quizzical, that it struck down any confidence Micah had that she shared his feelings. As eloquent as he was in the pulpit—or so folks told him he was, though he hadn't done too well this morning—right now he couldn't think of how to explain himself. Had he been wrong? Did she want only to be a friend?

She stood there looking at him expectantly.

He should have quoted Elizabeth Barrett Browning: "How do I love thee? Let me count the ways." But this was Grace, and she might turn up her nose at poetry. Besides, she'd asked *why*, not *how*. He laughed nervously. "Do you mean why do I love you?

Or why do I want you to be my wife?" Oh, no. That sounded terrible.

To his relief, she laughed softly. "Either. Both."

He prayed for the right response, but her confidence seemed so fragile, he feared he wouldn't understand the Lord's answer. "All I know, dear Grace, is that there isn't another person in the world I'd rather be with than you…for the rest of my life."

Instead of being encouraged, she stood there staring out over the corral as though she was looking to buy a horse. Then she shrugged. "Let's go in and have some of Ma's pie." She turned away from him and walked toward the house.

And with her went his broken heart.

Grace had never known the Rev to lie and didn't think he'd lied just now. He probably did feel some fondness for her or else he wouldn't spend so much time with her. But that didn't equal love; it equaled friendship. The dear man just didn't know the difference. Love should cause a stronger emotion, and yet he'd spoken almost matter-of-factly. Or at worst, he'd sounded friendly, like he was talking to any one of his church members. Love should want to climb up on the barn roof and shout to the sky. Anyway, that's what she'd felt like doing. She wouldn't accept anything less from someone claiming to love her.

She also wouldn't accept him. In spite of all her longings, she knew she wouldn't be a good wife for him. Sure, she could cook and sew and keep house. But a pastor's wife should be—what Grace wasn't. Gentle, not rough. Understanding, not judgmental. Patient, not easily irked. Could she change for him?

Not likely. She could pretend to have all of those fine qualities for a short while, like when she and her sisters had acted out Bible stories when they were children. But when things got hard, Grace would go back to being her old tomboy self.

After eating pie with her in the kitchen, the Rev told everyone goodbye and went home. Grace cleaned up their dishes before going to her room to hide from Ma and Georgia. That worked for about five minutes.

"Didn't he propose?" Ma sat on Grace's four-poster double bed, two handkerchiefs in her hands. She offered one to Grace.

Grace waved it away, then crossed her arms and leaned back in her chair. "I didn't give him a chance."

"Why not?" Georgia, all starry-eyed with youthful romantic ideas, sat on the vanity stool Grace rarely used. "I heard him ask Pa if he could court you, and Pa said yes."

"Well, aren't you just the clever little eavesdropper?"

"I suppose I am." Georgia didn't look the slightest bit repentant. "But Maisie and Ma and I can see you love Reverend Thomas and he loves you. Why wouldn't you at least let him court you?"

"He may like me, but he doesn't love me. He feels sorry for me just like he did at that box social three years ago when he bought my box because nobody else would." There. She'd said it. "He was supposed to marry Miss Sutton, but Nolan won her hand because he's rich. Now the Rev is settling for me because he thinks it's time for him to get married." He hadn't said as much, but she'd guessed it.

"Why, Grace, why on earth would you say such

a thing?" Ma's eyes watered, and she dabbed them with her handkerchief. "You're a beautiful girl, and everyone admires you."

Grace rolled her eyes. "Mothers are supposed to say that."

Ma stood abruptly and marched across the room. Standing over Grace, all five feet of her, Ma grabbed her shoulders and scowled like she used to do when one of her daughters misbehaved. "Why, you silly, silly girl. Haven't you seen the admiring looks most of the unmarried men in Esperanza cast your way?"

"You mean the ones who've taunted me since eighth grade? Nope. Haven't seen any admiration there."

Ma clicked her tongue. "Well, of course they'd hide it. Not many men are man enough to approach such a statuesque beauty as you, especially when you're wearing your gun. Being so tall, you scare 'em half to death."

That thought didn't bring the comfort Ma probably intended.

"The reverend isn't scared of you." Georgia grinned. "He's also taller." She stood, walked to the bed, grabbed one of the posts and twirled herself down on the blue-and-brown cotton quilt. "Oh, Grace, I long for the day when a perfectly wonderful, handsome man looks at me the way Reverend Thomas looks at you. It's so, so dreamy."

Again, Grace rolled her eyes. And yet they seemed so sure. Could they be right? Did the Rev love her?

"But a minister's wife should be prim and proper. I can't be that way." Grace's voice broke on those last words. "I can't change."

"And you shouldn't have to." Ma bent down and kissed Grace's cheek. "Besides, I don't recall you saying the reverend wants you to change. Did he say that?"

Grace blinked "No, ma'am." For the first time since realizing she loved him, hope began to blossom in her heart. "He just said he loves me and wants to marry me."

"Well, then, daughter, you ride into town right now and tell him you accept his courtship."

Grace chewed her lip for a minute. "He said he had to keep vigil with Bob Starling's family tonight. Maybe I'll go first thing tomorrow."

Ma and Georgia traded a look of annoyance.

"All right," Ma said. "But you have to promise not to get cold feet, or I'll send Georgia with you to make sure you do it. And she'll pick up Maisie on the way to help out."

"Yes, ma'am. I promise." And with those words, Grace felt a joy such as she'd never known. Just think. The Rev... *Micah* loved her. It was just about more than she could comprehend.

As he rode back to town, Micah prayed for understanding about what went wrong with Grace. Her eyes betrayed a heart filled with love for him. In spite of his doubts an hour ago, he just knew it. He'd seen the look in every couple he'd ever joined in marriage. Maybe he'd underestimated the depth of her pain. Or maybe she thought she needed to change for him. That was the last thing he would ask of her. Perhaps his love could help her overcome those hurtful ways of thinking.

When he first felt the Lord's call to marry, he'd made a list of qualities his wife should have. First, she must trust the Lord. Then she must care about other people and enjoy ministering to them. On the practical side, she must be hospitable and be able to keep house and cook. And he wouldn't complain if she was pretty. Grace was all of that and more.

And yet, he recalled another asset he'd listed. His wife must be ladylike and modestly dressed to set an example for the girls in his congregation. He laughed at himself. Grace might not possess the elegant manners Miss Sutton displayed. She might not like to wear frilly dresses. But he would gladly surrender his desire for those qualities. Grace more than made up for them by setting a different kind of example. She could tame the Wild West as well as any man, something no fragile flower of a lady could ever do.

But what about him? Was he what Grace needed? How many times had he counseled young couples that a happy marriage wasn't built on finding the right person, but on being the right person? What did he need to change to be the right person for Grace? Perhaps she didn't want to be a minister's wife. Since the Lord had clearly called Micah to the ministry, that was the only thing he couldn't change.

His ruminations came to an end when he arrived at the livery stable and found Adam brushing one of Ben Russell's horses, his forehead furrowed as he concentrated on his work. Had something happened to his father?

"Adam." Micah tried to keep the worry out of his voice. "How are you?"

"Well, sir." He glanced over his shoulder. "Pa's still with us."

Thankful that he'd offered the news, Micah asked, "Don't you want to be with him?"

"Yessir." Adam cleaned horsehair from his brush and let it fall to the dirt floor before resuming the task. "But I need to work, too."

Micah would volunteer to take his place, but the boy had his manly pride and didn't take charity well. "All right. I told your mother I'd stay with him tonight so she could get some rest."

"We're much obliged." At least Adam didn't reject help for his mother. "Tell Ma I'll be home soon."

Micah walked the three blocks to the Starling house and found the mayor's wife, Addie Jones, had brought supper for the family.

"There's enough for you, Reverend." The brown-haired, middle-aged woman bustled about the kitchen making sure Molly and Jack were fed. "I brought biscuits and eggs for breakfast, too."

With food taken care of, Micah had only to entertain the children until their bedtime. He gathered them on the shabby settee in the parlor and took the large family Bible from a nearby table. In the front of the hand-tooled leather holy book, a family history was recorded, going back four generations. Micah was carried back to his childhood when his grandfather used to read to him from a similar Bible, the one that now sat on a stand in his office at the church.

"Look, Molly, Jack. This is your family." He read several names.

The children's eyes sparkled with interest. They

asked about the various relatives, but he had no answers for them.

"Now read about David," four-year-old Jack said. Six-year-old Molly voiced her agreement.

And so Micah read, theatrically embellishing the story with bits of history he'd learned in seminary, sometimes causing the children to giggle with his antics. All the while, he imagined reading the beloved story to his own little ones. Would Grace want to have children? He hoped she did. Micah could imagine sweet little girls and boys with her bright blue eyes and glorious red hair who loved adventure as much as he and Grace did. Tomorrow morning, he would begin his campaign to overcome her resistance to his courtship.

He couldn't wait to get started.

Chapter Fifteen

Grace gave Mack his head and let him gallop most of the way to town. As exhilarating as such runs were, they always winded her as much as her horse, so she slowed him as they neared the church. It wouldn't do to arrive all breathless.

She'd started to wear her blue dress but decided on her usual trousers. At Georgia's insistence, she wore a frilly white shirtwaist Rosamond Northam had made for Maisie's eighteenth birthday. Funny how the starched white cotton, lace trimmings and pearly buttons made her feel more ladylike. Maybe she could get used to this. Sort of used to it. Maybe.

No one answered the door at the parsonage, so she walked over to the church. Empty, too. Disappointed and a bit frustrated, she made her way to Micah's office. Micah? Yes, since yesterday's talk with Ma and Georgia, she had begun to think of him by his Christian name. If he truly did love her, he wouldn't mind. Or so she hoped.

He wasn't in his office. Rather than track him down all over town, she'd leave him a note. She sat at

his desk and gazed around. Books lined his shelves, mostly Bible commentaries. A large leather Bible rested on a library stand, and a globe stood beside it. Did Micah want to travel? As long as she'd known him, she'd never asked him about things like that.

A fancy fountain pen was stuck in a holder on the desk, but she saw no paper. She opened the wide center drawer and rummaged through the clutter. How funny that such a neat and tidy man would have such a jumbled drawer.

Her hand touched a lined tablet, the perfect paper for her note, if it had an empty page. She pulled it out and flipped over the top page. All the pages below seemed to be covered with Micah's neat handwriting. Before Grace knew what she was doing, she was reading his words. The more she read, the more her hair stood on end. This was about her. He was writing a story about her job as a deputy. The ridiculous name of his heroine, Willa Ketchum, wasn't in the least bit funny. She also recognized several other townspeople. Grace bit her lip. How could Micah betray his congregation this way?

No longer caring that she was snooping, she looked in all of the desk drawers. In the bottom right drawer, she found three copies of that horrid, foolish *Rio Grande Sheriff.* An open letter on top of the books was addressed to Micah. It was from his publisher. Stunned to the core of her being, she couldn't even pick up one of the books. So he was the Cowboy Storyteller!

"Grace, what are you doing?" Micah stood in the doorway, his handsome face wrinkled into a frown. "Are you going through my desk?"

She stared back at him for several seconds, trying to contain her anger. "I was looking for some paper to leave you a note."

His jaw clenched and unclenched several times. "Upper left drawer."

She stood. "Never mind. I don't have anything to say to you."

"Fine. The feeling is mutual."

My, my. Didn't he sound highbrow? What had she been thinking to believe he loved her? She strode past him and out the door.

"Grace, wait."

But she wouldn't wait. Wouldn't listen. No reason or excuse for his betrayal would ever change her mind. Or soothe her heart.

Micah couldn't believe what he'd just seen. Grace's intrusion was far worse than Miss Sutton's taking over his kitchen and parlor. Now he could see it was best that Grace had refused his courtship. She was definitely not the wife for him.

Weary beyond words from his night of sitting with Bob Starling, he dropped into his desk chair and began straightening the papers she'd rummaged through. The bottom drawer was open and the copies of his novel exposed, along with the letter from his editor. The tablet upon which he was writing the sequel lay on the desk with several pages flipped over. So she'd read it. And obviously been offended. No surprise there. She'd hated his first book and no doubt hated this one. Well, she didn't have anything to complain about. He was the offended party. The

idea that she would invade his privacy this way hurt and angered him more than he thought possible.

Beneath the tablet, he found a separate page titled, "Qualities of a Proper Wife for a Minister." Had Grace read it, too? In fact, had he actually written down his preferences? Good. Now he had another quality to add. A proper wife must not be a meddlesome snoop.

Too exhausted to think more about it, he shoved the tablet and list into the top drawer and shut the bottom one. He made his way across the back of the church property and into the kitchen. To his vast relief, the house was empty. He fell into bed and let the world melt away.

This time, Grace locked her bedroom door so Ma and Georgia couldn't come in. She took off the frilly blouse and put on her favorite flannel shirt, then lay on her bed and cried her eyes out. In all her born days, she never expected Reverend Thomas to be two-faced or sneaky. He was making money from selling out his congregation. He was betraying their trust. He was making fun of and profit from *her*. A thousand knife cuts couldn't hurt as badly as his betrayal did.

Her tears spent, she poured icy water from her pitcher into her bowl and washed her face. She sat at her vanity and stared at herself in the mirror for a while, counting every line and scar as she brushed her waist-length hair. Ladies like Miss Sutton had lily-white complexions, but Grace's was tanned from a lifetime of working the ranch in the sun. In the winter, her red hair turned darker, but in the summer, that

same sun bleached blond streaks through it. Like her four sisters, she had an oval face. In pictures taken with them, she could see she most closely resembled Beryl. When they were children, people thought they were twins, until Grace grew taller even than Maisie. Always when Grace had looked at Beryl, she'd seen a beauty, one worthy of a rich Englishman's love. Yet when she looked into the mirror, she saw nothing of the sort. Who could account for such a difference?

School was out until January, so Georgia was in town to help Miss Sutton and Anna Means finish plans for the Christmas pageant, to take place on Wednesday, Christmas Eve. That gave Grace some peace for now, but sooner or later she'd have to face Ma. Sooner came far too soon.

"Grace." Ma pounded on her door. "I need your help with supper."

Grace set down her brush. "Yes, ma'am." Her throat still choked with tears, she sounded like she was gargling salt water. Helping Ma would be good for her. Getting back to normal life—normal before she became a deputy—she could work off her sorrows by digging into ranch work. Pa had three men working for him through the winter, but he could always use another hand.

In the kitchen, she sat at the table and peeled potatoes and carrots for tonight's stew while Ma made Christmas cookies for Wednesday's celebration. After countless quiet minutes, Ma plopped herself down beside Grace and set a hand on her wrist.

"Are you going to tell me what happened this morning?"

Might as well get it over with. Grace explained her

reason for being in Reverend Thomas's office, including digging through his desk and, worse, finding the horrible novel hidden in a lower drawer. Her voice broke as she told of the minister's shock and anger at finding her there and her own anger back at him.

"How could he betray his church that way?" Grace looked at Ma, hoping she could make some sense of it. To her surprise, Ma's blue eyes twinkled merrily.

"From where I sit, it's not a betrayal. It's a compliment. An honor, even." She laughed in her warm-hearted way. "You keep avoiding the book, but it's downright fun to read. Only the outlaws do bad or foolish things, and even they…well, I don't want to ruin it for you." Ma laughed again. "So our very own preacher is the Cowboy Storyteller, and his small western town is our own Esperanza.

"My, oh my. Now I can try to figure out who's who. Won't that be fun? I wonder how many Western towns have a mayor who's also the barber. Or three sisters and a female storekeeper who helped wrangle some wicked bank robbers." Ma sat back and shook her head.

"Though I'm sorta sorry I know who wrote it, because it spoils the fun. But it tickles my innards that it's my very own parson." She slapped her hand against her knee and laughed yet again. "Now, I don't think we should tell anybody about this, do you? I mean, what harm does it do if a preacher wants to make a little honest money outside his church wages? The Apostle Paul was a tentmaker so he didn't have to burden the churches with his support."

"But—"

"No buts." Ma got up and set a hand on Grace's

shoulder. "We've always had a lot of fun in our family. Remember how we used to laugh all the time when your sisters were home?" She gripped Grace's chin and bent down to stare into her eyes. "You stopped laughing when Beryl got shot." Sorrow flickered briefly in her eyes. "But by the grace of God, she recovered, and now she's doing fine. More than fine." She hugged Grace. "You need to revive your sense of humor, daughter. You need to laugh like you mean it."

Grace felt a pout form on her lips. She had a sense of humor. She *did*. It was just that…

Willa Ketchum? Without meaning to, she burst out laughing. How had the Rev—Micah—ever come up with such a silly name?

Ma stared at her, one eyebrow lifted.

"Just laughing at something in the Rev's next book."

"Well, good." Ma hurried to the stove and removed a tray of cookies from the oven just in time before they burned. "Now I think you should ride into town first thing tomorrow and apologize to the reverend. He's been your friend for a long time, and I believe he's a forgiving man, just like he preaches."

Ma was right. As innocent as her search of his desk had been, she did owe him an apology. She should have gone looking for him instead of trying to leave a note. If it weren't so late, she'd ride into town tonight to ask his forgiveness.

The last week finally caught up with Micah, and he slept through till the next morning. Rested at last, he woke up knowing he owed Grace a huge apology.

Not for his book, although he knew he could give it up for her without regret. But for his anger. He'd had long nights before, but sometimes it was harder to recover than others. No one wanted Bob Starling to die. Yet the way he barely held on to life brought continuing pain to his whole family. It affected their faith and wore poor Adam down to the bone. If all things truly did work together for good, how could Micah explain all of this to the family? The death of a husband, father and provider was nothing less than a horrible tragedy. How could it ever be considered "good"?

This morning he still needed to finish his Christmas message for tomorrow night, but this afternoon, he'd ride out to the Eberly ranch and ask Grace's forgiveness for his cross words. Then, if she would listen to him, he would explain why she needed to respect other people's privacy. She'd grown up in a family of close sisters. He'd lived a solitary life for most of the last fifteen years. A man needed to set boundaries. She could set some, too, if she liked.

Somehow the words he wanted to say to Grace sounded all wrong, but he couldn't think of another way to say them. By dinnertime, he still hadn't completed his sermon.

Miss Sutton prepared sandwiches for Micah and Joel and then walked over to the reception hall to hold a final practice with the children. Micah longed to unburden himself to his friend, but Joel had already made plans to spend the afternoon with Nolan Means. Perhaps he hoped for a job in the bank. In their few conversations about Joel's future, he seemed a bit aimless, so Micah wouldn't do anything to hold him

back. Besides, since Miss Sutton's engagement, Joel had become more his old self, as if a burden had been lifted from his shoulders.

Micah once again sat at his desk pondering his Christmas message. All he could see was Grace's face on the page.

A knock sounded on his door. What now? He really needed this time to work. Still, he managed a cheerful, "Come in."

Nate Northam opened it and stuck in his head. "Howdy, Reverend. Mind if I sit a spell? I just brought Lizzie to pageant practice, so I'm looking to fill my time until it's over."

"Come on in," Micah repeated as he stood to shake his friend's hand. His message would have to wait until tomorrow, although he didn't like presenting last-minute sermons. Maybe he'd have to pull out last year's message and repeat it. "Have a seat."

"Have you recovered from last week?" Nate sat and placed his Stetson on the chair beside him.

"Pretty much." He chuckled. "Finally."

Nate laughed, too. "Yeah, I knew you needed some more rest during your sermon day before yesterday."

"Ouch." Micah grimaced. "Thanks, pal."

A twinkle in Nate's green eyes reminded Micah of all they'd been through together, both good and bad. "What are friends for?"

What, indeed? "Nate, I'm glad you stopped by. I need a friend's perspective on something." Before he knew what he was doing, Micah had told Nate about everything: writing the book, God's call for him to marry, the proper wife list he'd written, realizing he loved Grace, her refusal to let him court her, how

he'd found her snooping through his desk. If his heart weren't so bruised, he would laugh at the changing expressions on Nate's face, everything from comical to horrified. When Micah finished, he leaned back in his chair. "Any idea of what I should do?"

"I'll have to think on that for a minute." Nate stared off toward the window then returned his gaze to Micah. "One of the first things I learned when Susanna and I married...man, has it been seven years already? Anyway, I learned that nothing is really mine anymore." He chuckled. "So if you really feel God's call to marry, you need to give up thinking this is your desk." He slapped his hand against the finely grained oak. "As you said when you took us through our wedding vows, husband and wife are one flesh."

"But—"

"Reverend, I know Grace. She doesn't have a sneaky thought in her head. From what you said, she truly was just looking for paper to write you a note. Aren't you the slightest bit curious to know what she wanted to write? I mean, didn't you ask to court her? Maybe she changed her mind and planned to say yes."

His words hit Micah hard in the chest, creating a physical ache. He hadn't even thought about that. He'd only thought to scold Grace—*again*, which would surely destroy any chance he had to win her heart. Where was the grace he so often preached about?

"Now, I must say," Nate went on, "I am surprised about that book, but impressed, too. I enjoyed reading it quite a bit. Got more than one laugh out of it. "Most of all, I'm pleased to learn that you love Grace. She's as dear to me as my sister. All the Eberly girls

are. I want her to be happy and won't take it kindly if any man hurts her." He scowled briefly, not a warning, exactly, just a stern suggestion. "Do you think she saw your *proper wife list*?" Sarcasm laced his last three words.

Micah shook his head. "I don't know. It was under the tablet after she left." But he certainly did understand Nate's warning. He hadn't taken it kindly when Dub and his friends had hurt Grace's feelings.

"So, in answer to your question about what you should do, I'll say this—if you love her and still want to marry her, go out and see her. Do whatever it takes to make amends, even if that means giving up writing your books, at least the one about her." Nate leaned forward and rested his crossed arms on the desk. "Susanna and I have had our rough times, but we never let the sun go down on our wrath, as the scriptures say. We talk things out until they're settled." He gave a brief nod. "You think about that."

Used to being the one who gave advice to his friends and church members, Micah now had a dose of his own medicine, and it came from a source tried, true and trusted.

"I will, Nate. Thank you." Micah stood and grabbed his hat from the hat rack. "Now, if you'll excuse me, I have a young lady to court…if she'll have me."

"You want me to put in a good word for you with her?"

Micah chuckled. "Thanks, but no. I need to face my punishment alone."

Nate stood and touched Micah's arm before he could leave. "One more thing."

Micah raised one eyebrow.

"Burn that list. Now, before Grace or anybody else sees it."

As Grace rode toward town, she had no idea what she would say to Micah. Probably best just to start by saying she was sorry for searching his desk. Then tell him he could go ahead and write his silly book. No, best not to say *silly*.

Another rider came into view up the road, and her deputy senses went on alert. She hadn't worn her sidearm, but if that person meant no good, she did have her rifle. As the rider drew nearer, her heart began to pound. *Micah!* She spurred Mack to a gallop and quickly closed the distance between them. Without thinking, she pulled on the reins and jumped from the saddle before Mack even stopped. Micah also quickly dismounted. They stood there in the middle of the road just staring at each other.

"I'm so sorry—" she began.

"Please forgive me." Micah's handsome face had never worn such a sorrowful, pleading expression.

Before she could answer, they were in each other's arms, each clinging tightly to the other as if neither would ever let go. After a few minutes, Micah took a small step back and brushed a hand over Grace's tearstained cheek. The gentle look in his wonderful gray eyes sent a funny feeling through her middle. And then he kissed her full on the lips, her very first kiss ever. Her knees turned to jelly, and her heart felt ready to burst. My, oh my—

"Grace, dear Grace, I love you more than words can say. If you feel the same way toward me, will you

marry me?" The hope beaming from those amazing, probing eyes dispelled the last of her doubts. He truly did love her, just as Ma, Maisie and Georgia had said.

"I do, and I will."

He laughed like she'd never heard him laugh before, a hearty, carefree, joyful belly laugh. "Oh, my darling Grace," he shouted. "You've made me the happiest man in the world."

"Me, too." Heat rushed to her cheeks. "I mean, I'm the happiest woman in the world."

He clasped her hands and pulled them up to kiss them. "It isn't easy to be a minister's wife." Worry clouded his handsome face, as if his comment should somehow discourage her.

Instead, she shrugged. "It isn't easy to be a female deputy. A lady just has to get used to being criticized without letting it get her down."

He caressed her cheek. "You're wonderful. And brave. And strong. And I love you."

Feeling a bit sassy, she gave him a peck on the lips. "I sort of like you, too."

Micah pulled her into a deeper kiss with more enthusiasm than she'd ever expected, putting to rest at last her concerns that he wouldn't proclaim their love from the rooftops, given the chance. After several blissful minutes, he moved back and tilted his head toward Esperanza. "Let's go back to town for coffee."

"All right." They walked quietly for several minutes, their horses clopping along placidly behind them. Grace didn't want to break this sweet silence, but she knew they had to clear the air. Remembering Ma's comment about reviving her sense of humor, one thought came to mind.

"Willa Ketchum? Really, Micah, is that the best you can do?" She struggled to maintain a straight face.

Alarm spread over his face, and he eyed her nervously. "Um, well, I—"

Grace burst out laughing, trying real hard to make it sound more ladylike than her usual guffaw. He blinked. Then he laughed, too, another one of those carefree belly laughs. They took a moment to share another embrace, another kiss. Grace decided she could get used to this.

"I love to hear you say my name," Micah said as they resumed walking.

"You mean instead of Rev?" Suddenly that name sounded too tough coming from a female. Grace felt another bit of warmth fill her cheeks. She never wanted Micah to think of her as unladylike. She didn't want to *be* unladylike. Maisie had softened considerably when she fell in love with Doc. It wasn't that Doc had asked her to, Maisie always said. It was just that he made her feel fully female, in spite of all the men's work she'd done on the ranch. Now Grace understood her sister's sentiments. While she knew this wasn't the primary meaning of Micah's favorite verse, in this case all things truly were working together for good.

"Yes." Micah squeezed her hand. "I never minded Rev. But you and the Suttons are the only ones who use my Christian name. Even my good friend Nate calls me Reverend. It seems to put a distance between us. I don't want anything like that between you and me." He stopped and kissed her cheek. "Grace, I'm not going to finish writing the book." He gazed away

toward the Sangre de Cristo Mountains to the east, then back at her, his eyes filled with tenderness. "I never meant to hurt you."

"I know. Ma helped me to see that."

He chuckled. "I like your mother. And not just because of that."

Grace tugged on his hand, and they walked again. "I want you to write the book."

He stopped. "You do?"

"Yep. Only thing is you have to let me read it before you send it off to be printed so I can tell you what you got wrong."

Happiness shone on his dear face. "I can do that."

They took up their walk again. "Well, one more thing."

He gave her a sidelong look. "All right."

"You *gotta* change that female deputy's name."

Chapter Sixteen

Micah lost count of the blessings the Lord had showered on the people of Esperanza, especially for this Christmas season.

The weather remained cold but clear so everyone could gather at the church on Christmas Eve. The children's pageant turned out to be the best one yet, with the usual delightful mistakes made by the tiny shepherds, wise men, innkeeper and Joseph. Mary, portrayed by Molly Starling, didn't miss a single line and looked properly adoring when she smiled at "Baby Jesus," a porcelain baby doll provided by Miss Sutton. City founder Colonel Northam, who'd been stuck in Denver during the recent drama, arrived in time to see his eldest grandchild, Lizzie, portray the angel who watched over the Nativity scene. The precious sounds of "Silent Night" sung in their sweet young voices—especially the first-verse solo sung by Molly in clear soprano tones—brought tears to many an eye.

After the performance, joy filled the sanctuary. Micah found he didn't need to deliver a sermon after

all. He said only a few words to remind people to focus their thoughts on the Lord and how He had humbled Himself to become a man to save the whole world. The congregation sang "Joy to the World" and then adjourned to the reception hall for a party and distribution of gifts.

Adam Starling stationed himself beside the Christmas tree to make sure the candles didn't catch the tree on fire. Everett Winsted stood close by, emulating the older boy in his helpfulness.

Hanging from the candlelit chandelier in the center of the room was a fresh bouquet of mistletoe. On the long refreshment table, an array of cookies and a large cut-glass punch bowl filled with strawberry punch whetted everyone's appetite. Beside them, a large pile of small, wrapped presents awaited distribution.

Even though Andy Ransom's beautifully carved toy soldiers and dolls had been destroyed by the outlaws, folks had pitched in to provide him with carving and whittling tools and wood from their own supplies. Working day and night and helped by Rand Northam and Frank Stone, Andy had managed to make more toys, enough for every child to receive one.

After the ladies passed out refreshments to all, Micah stood and called out, "May I have your attention, please?"

An expectant hush fell over the room, and knowing gazes shot from one person to the next. Micah felt warmth rising up his neck. He was used to addressing his congregation about spiritual subjects, but speaking of personal matters was harder than he'd thought.

"I am truly blessed to be your pastor. One duty that particularly blesses me is joining couples in marriage. Since coming to Esperanza almost eight years ago, I have conducted countless weddings, and soon I'll have another. As you know, our good banker, Nolan Means, has somehow managed to persuade the charming Miss Electra Sutton to be his bride." Micah lifted his punch cup in a salute to the banker and his fiancée.

As polite applause filled the room, Miss Sutton returned a smile. Nolan's chest puffed up with pride.

"And now I have another wedding to tell you about, one I will not be conducting but, rather, participating in." He reached out to Grace, who shyly moved to his side. Dressed in her blue gingham, she was gloriously beautiful, and Micah felt his own chest puff up proudly.

"Miss Grace Eberly, previously known as Deputy Grace…or Deputy Eberly, depending upon whether you kept the law or not…"

Laughter erupted, and Micah waited until it died down.

"Grace has consented to be my wife." There. He'd managed to get through it. Gathering even more courage, he set aside his punch and tugged on Grace's hand to lead her to the center of the room beneath the mistletoe. With a glance around to be sure no one would be scandalized—Mrs. Foster gave him a firm nod and a maternal smile—he pulled Grace into his arms and kissed her sweet lips like he meant it.

Applause and congratulations seemed to lift the rafters. Micah noticed over Grace's shoulder that several mothers of unattached daughters of mar-

riageable age, who obviously hadn't heard the news, huffed with annoyance or perhaps disappointment, if he wasn't being too prideful to think such a thing. Maybe Micah needed to become a matchmaker, because there were plenty of good men in town for all of their daughters.

"We all have so much to be thankful for." Micah managed to regain his pastoral dignity once he'd recovered from the kiss. "Welcome back, Colonel Northam." The former Union officer acknowledged him with a nod. "Sheriff Lawson and Seamus O'Brien are well on their way to recovery. Although Bob Starling couldn't be here tonight to watch Miss Molly perform so well, he has rallied and can now move around his house with help. He sends his gratitude to everyone who has helped his family." Micah whispered to Grace, "Am I forgetting anything?"

A woman of few words, a trait Nate Northam had told Micah he would one day appreciate, Grace whispered back. "Save the news about Hardison until later."

"Good idea." Micah didn't want anything to spoil this joyful celebration, this joyous season. Tomorrow he would be spending Christmas Day with Grace and her family, all of whom had already welcomed him as a beloved son or brother. On New Year's Eve, those honorary relationships would become official. Micah could hardly wait.

"Grace Eberly, just the person I wanted to see." Electra Sutton accosted Grace at the punch table and grabbed her in a hug like they were old friends.

"Me?" Grace managed not to jerk away from Elec-

tra. Since accepting Micah's proposal, she'd decided that being his wife was a more important and *happier* job than being a deputy. From the moment she'd handed her badge over to Justice Gareau, she'd been trying to act more ladylike. But Electra's bear hug surprised her.

"Yes, you." Electra got a wily look in her eyes. "What would you think of a double wedding?"

"What? You mean yours and mine?"

"Of course, silly." Electra giggled. "Yours and Micah's, mine and Nolan's."

Grace eased away from her several inches. "I expected you to plan some big society doings back East." Then she remembered Micah said he would conduct Electra and Nolan's wedding.

A hint of sorrow crossed Electra's pretty face. "No. Joel and I don't have anyone in Virginia, and Nolan has no one left in New York." She brightened real quick. "What do you say? I don't want to wait until spring or take the time to prepare something extra fancy. If the minister from Alamosa is coming over to conduct your wedding, he may as well do double duty." A sudden frown took over her features. My, this gal was mercurial, a word Grace had learned from Micah. "Do you mind? I mean, I know we didn't exactly start off well, but—"

"Sounds fine with me." Grace couldn't do cozy female stuff with this one like she could with her sisters. But then, maybe she should give it a try. She'd longed for a friend, and now Electra was offering her a very special kind of friendship. And maybe, just maybe, Grace could learn some of Electra's feminine ways. The honest ones, that was. Not that phony fe-

male simpering and flirting and all. "I suppose we ought to ask our fellas—"

"Nolan is over there asking Micah right this very minute." Pointing across the room, Electra chirped like a spring robin, one girlie behavior Grace would never try to emulate.

And so it was that Grace and Micah joined a growing tradition at the Esperanza Community Church. Why have a single wedding when a double one would be much more efficient—and fun? Dressed in Maisie's ivory satin gown, which had needed only an eight-inch flounce added around the bottom to make it long enough, Grace walked down the aisle on Pa's arm. Behind her, dressed in a white satin gown she'd brought from Virginia, Electra held on to Joel's arm. The lady had come west intending to find a husband, and she'd done just that. Their handsome grooms awaited them at the podium with Reverend Casey. Nate Northam and Justice Gareau served as best men, while Georgia and Anna did the bridesmaid honors.

Grace had never noticed how fast a wedding ceremony happened. Before she knew it, she had become Mrs. Micah Thomas and was standing next to her husband and the brand-new Mr. and Mrs. Nolan Means in the reception line in the church hall. Everybody had been invited. Everybody came. Which attested to the popularity of the newlyweds—all of them. Ma had been right. Everybody loved Grace, and more than a few told her they regretted that she would no longer be their deputy.

She would have preferred to economize by only making use of the Christmas decorations that re-

mained in the reception hall, but Electra insisted upon bringing white roses from Nolan's hothouse. The room was filled with their heady fragrance, overpowering the smell of the pine boughs, whose woodsy scent had already worn out. Grace had a feeling Electra would be insisting upon a lot of things in her marriage, if the way she'd been ordering the banker around lately was any indication.

As for Grace, she had a few orders for Micah, too. Some were about the book he was writing. Then that bowler hat had to go. Or maybe she'd just hide it. The thought made her giggle, and her handsome husband questioned her with a look.

"Nothing. Just looking forward to eating some of that cake."

The hotel chef, Henrique, had prepared a lavish, five-tiered pastry with white icing and pretty little pink flowers made of sugar all over it. It sat on the long, white damask-covered table with the punch and cookies.

His teasing smirk showed he didn't believe her. "Yes, I am, too. Looks almost as sweet as you."

Grace rolled her eyes, only to find Micah scowling at her. "None of that rejecting compliments, wife. When I tell you you're sweet, I mean it."

Her eyes stung with happy tears. "Yessir." Seemed she'd be taking a few orders, too.

Across the room, Adam Starling gazed at her for a moment before turning away, his eyes filled with sadness as he began to chat comfortably with Anna and Georgia. At last Grace understood why he'd been avoiding her. Georgia said the boy was sweet on her. She'd resisted the idea until the other day when she'd

tried to talk to Adam. He'd grinned and stared down at his boots, stammering a few incoherent words. Everybody felt at least one hopeless affection in life. Only sixteen, Adam would get over it.

Tonight he sported a new haircut and shave, along with a clean white shirt and pressed trousers, such a different look from his usual rumpled ways. Grace could see a handsome man emerging from the hardworking boy. A startling truth struck her. She'd judged Adam by his appearance, just as Dub and his friends had judged her. It was a lesson she would try to learn. After all, Dathan Hardison had always cleaned up good, but he was the embodiment of evil. Grace prayed for the ability to look beyond a person's outside appearance and into their hearts.

She noticed Maisie and Georgia conferring with Nate and Rand, their heads bent together in a conspiratorial way. A shivaree was in the making for sure.

She leaned close to Micah. "Is there any way we can just…disappear?"

He thought for a minute before shaking his head. "I don't know where we'd go. We live next door."

While his comment sent a nice shiver through her middle, she still tried to think of a way to escape the shivaree.

"Tell you what." Micah whispered in her ear, and another shiver coursed down her neck. "When all of the families leave, we'll invite those pranksters in for coffee. That's what Rand and Marybeth did. It put an end to their foolishness."

Grace laughed softly. "Yes, it did. And since I was one of those pranksters, I guess I just need to endure the revenge." A revenge decidedly different

from what Hardison had had in mind for them. The outlaw still languished in a precarious state at Doc's. Even if he recovered, he would never walk again. But this wasn't the time to dwell on such disagreeable thoughts.

The reception seemed to last forever. At some point, Electra and Nolan had managed to escape unnoticed. Finally, the last family offered their parting congratulations and went home. While some of the older ladies cleaned up the reception hall, Grace and Micah walked through the light snowfall to the parsonage. For a full hour, they sat in the parlor sipping tea and waiting for their friends to arrive with their noisy merrymaking. No one came. That was just fine with Grace.

And from the warm, special smile on Micah's handsome face as he gazed into her eyes, she could tell it was just fine with him, too.

* * * * *

If you liked this story, pick up these other
FOUR STONES RANCH *books*
by Louise M. Gouge:

COWBOY TO THE RESCUE
COWBOY SEEKS A BRIDE
COWGIRL FOR KEEPS

Available now from Love Inspired!

Find more great reads at www.LoveInspired.com

Dear Reader,

Thank you for choosing *Cowgirl Under the Mistletoe*, the fourth book in my Four Stones Ranch series. I always love to read a Christmas story during the holiday season, so I'm pleased that this one is coming out this month. I hope you enjoyed the adventures of my heroine, Grace Eberly, and my hero, Reverend Micah Thomas. When I began writing this series, I had no idea that Micah, the wise, steady young minister who advised my three previous heroes in matters of the heart, would find an unlikely love match of his own with one of the feisty Eberly girls. My heroine also grew naturally from the previous stories. After Grace courageously saved the town of Esperanza in *Cowboy Seeks a Bride*, I knew I wanted to reward her with her own story.

My setting for this series is the beautiful San Luis Valley of Colorado, where I lived as a teenager, graduated from Alamosa High School, and attended Adams State College. Later my husband, David, and I settled in Monte Vista, where my parents owned and operated a photography business, Stanger Studios. Three of our children were born in Monte Vista, and one was born in Alamosa. Even though we moved to Florida in 1980, my heart remained attached to my former home in Colorado. Writing this series has been a sweet, nostalgic trip for me.

Those familiar with the history of this area of Colorado may recognize a little bit of Monte Vista in my fictional town, Esperanza. I could have used the real town, but then I would have shortchanged

the true pioneers of Monte Vista, who deserve accolades for their courage and foresight in building such a fine community. In addition, I wanted the freedom of artistic license necessary to create an interesting story without offending the residents of my former home. Any resemblance between my characters and those who actually settled in this area is strictly coincidental.

If you enjoyed Grace and Micah's story, be on the lookout for more stories set in my fictional town of Esperanza.

I love to hear from my readers, so if you have a comment, please contact me through my website: blog.louisemgouge.com.

Blessings,
Louise M. Gouge

MONTANA COWBOY FAMILY
Big Sky Country • by Linda Ford

When cowboy Logan Marshall and schoolteacher Sadie Young discover three abandoned children, they are determined to help them. But working together to care for the children while searching for their missing father might just leave Logan and Sadie yearning to make their temporary family permanent.

HIS SUBSTITUTE WIFE
Stand-In Brides • by Dorothy Clark

Blake Latherop must marry if he wants to keep his store, so when his fiancée weds another and her sister arrives in town offering her hand instead, he has no choice but to accept. But will their marriage of convenience lead to true love?

FOR THE SAKE OF THE CHILDREN
by Danica Favorite

Silas Jones needs a mother for his daughter, and marriage could help his former sweetheart, Rose Stone, repair her tattered reputation. The single mother, wary of trusting Silas with her heart again, refuses his proposal. But she *is* willing to be his child's nanny...

RESCUING THE RUNAWAY BRIDE
by Bonnie Navarro

On the run to escape a forced engagement, Vicky Ruiz is injured while rescuing a rancher from harm. Now can she find her way past language barriers and convince Christopher Samuels to return the favor by not taking her home?

LIHCNM1216

REQUEST YOUR FREE BOOKS!

2 FREE INSPIRATIONAL NOVELS
PLUS 2 FREE MYSTERY GIFTS

Love Inspired® HISTORICAL

SPECIAL EXCERPT FROM

Love Inspired HISTORICAL

*When cowboy Logan Marshall and schoolteacher
Sadie Young discover three abandoned children, they
are determined to help them. But working together to
care for the children while searching for their parents
might just leave Logan and Sadie yearning to make
their temporary family permanent.*

*Read on for a sneak preview of
MONTANA COWBOY FAMILY by Linda Ford,
available January 2017 from Love Inspired Historical!*

"Are you going to be okay with the children?" Logan
asked.

Sadie bristled. "Of course I am."

"I expect the first night will be the worst."

"To be honest, I'm more concerned about tomorrow
when I have to leave the girls to teach." She looked back
at her living quarters. "They are all so afraid."

"I'll be back before you have to leave so the girls
won't be alone and defenseless." He didn't know why
he'd added the final word and wished he hadn't when
Sadie spun about to face him. He'd only been thinking of
Sammy's concerns—be they real or the fears of children
who had experienced too many losses.

"You think they might have need of protection?"

"Don't all children?"

Her lips trembled and then she pressed them together
and wrapped her arms across her chest in a move so self-
protective that he instinctively reached for her, but at the
look on her face, he lowered his arms instead.

LIHEXP1216

She shuddered.

From the thought of him touching her or because of something she remembered? He couldn't say but neither could he leave her without knowing she was okay. Ignoring the idea that she might object to his forwardness, wanting only to make sure she knew he was concerned about her and the children, he cupped one hand to her shoulder. He knew he'd done the right thing when she leaned into his palm. "Sadie, I'll stay if you need me to. I can sleep in the schoolroom, or over at Uncle George's. Or even under the stars."

She glanced past him to the pile of lumber at the back of the yard. For the space of a heartbeat, he thought she'd ask him to stay, then she drew in a long breath.

"We'll be fine, though I would feel better leaving them in the morning if I knew you were here."

He squeezed her shoulder. "I'll be here." He hesitated, still not wanting to leave.

She stepped away from him, forcing him to lower his arm to his side. "Goodbye, then. And thank you for your help."

"Don't forget we're partners in this." He waited for her to acknowledge his statement.

"Very well."

"Goodbye for now. I'll see you in the morning." He forced himself to climb into the wagon and flick the reins. He turned for one last look before he was out of sight.

Don't miss
MONTANA COWBOY FAMILY by Linda Ford,
available January 2017 wherever
Love Inspired® Historical books and ebooks are sold.

www.LoveInspired.com

LIHEXP1216

SPECIAL EXCERPT FROM

Love Inspired®

A promise to watch out for his late army buddy's little brother might have this single rancher in over his head. But he's not the only one who wants to care for the boy…

Read on for a sneak preview of the fourth book in the **LONE STAR COWBOY LEAGUE: BOYS RANCH** miniseries, *THE COWBOY'S TEXAS FAMILY* by **Margaret Daley**.

As Nick settled behind the steering wheel and started his truck, he slanted a look at Darcy. "So what do you think about the boys ranch?"

"Corey is much better off here than with his dad. He's not happy right now, but then he wasn't happy at home."

"He's scared." That was why Bea had brought him to the barn first to see Nick. "He'll feel better after he meets some of the other boys his age."

"What if he doesn't?" Darcy asked.

"He's confused. He wants to be with his dad, and yet not if he's always being left alone. He doesn't know what to expect from day to day and certainly doesn't feel safe." Those same feelings used to plague Nick while he was growing up.

"I've dealt with kids like that."

"In a perfect world, Ned wouldn't drink and would love Corey unconditionally. But that isn't going to hap-

pen. Ned isn't going to change." He knew firsthand the mind-set of an alcoholic and remembered the times his dad promised to stop drinking and reform. He never did; in fact he got worse.

"How do you know that for sure?"

"I just do." He didn't share his past with anyone. It was a part of his life he wanted to wipe from his mind, but it was always there in the background. He never wanted to see a child grow up the way he had.

"Then I'll pray for the best for Corey," Darcy said.

"The best scenario would be the state taking Corey away from Ned and a good family adopting him. I wish I was in a position to do it." The second he said that last sentence he wanted to snatch it back. He had no business being anyone's father.

"Because you're single? That might not matter in certain cases."

"I'm not dad material." How could he explain that he was struggling to erase the debt that his father had accumulated? If he lost the ranch, he would lose his home and job. But, more important, what if he wasn't a good father to Corey? It was one thing to be there to help when needed, but it was very different to be totally responsible for raising a child.

Don't miss
THE COWBOY'S TEXAS FAMILY
*by Margaret Daley, available January 2017 wherever
Love Inspired® books and ebooks are sold.*

www.LoveInspired.com

Love the Love Inspired book you just read?

Your opinion matters.

Review this book on your favorite book site, review site, blog or your own social media properties and share your opinion with other readers!